SISTER GIN

SISTER GIN

A Novel by JUNE ARNOLD

Afterword by JANE MARCUS

THE FEMINIST PRESS
at The City University of New York
New York

© 1975 by June Arnold
Afterword © 1989 by Jane Marcus
Published by The Feminist Press at The City University of New York, 311 East 94 Street, New York, NY 10128

Distributed by The Talman Company, Inc., 150 Fifth Avenue, New York, NY 10011

Sister Gin was originally published in 1975 by Daughters, Inc. Chapter 12 of this book originally appeared in *Amazons Quarterly*.

Printed in the United States of America
91 90 89 6 5 4 3 2 1

Library of Congress Cataloging-in-Publication Data

Arnold, June, 1926–
    Sister Gin / June Arnold; afterword by Jane Marcus.
        p. cm.
    Bibliography: p.
    ISBN 1-55861-010-3: $8.95
    I. Title.
PS3551.R53S5   1989
813'.54—dc20   89-7926
                                                        CIP

This publication is made possible, in part, by public funds from the New York State Council on the Arts.

Cover art: *Mary Shoemaker* by Alice Neel. Reproduced by permission of the Robert Miller Gallery, New York.

Text design by Loretta Li

Printed in the United States on acid-free paper by McNaughton & Gunn, Inc.

For Parke

*Special thanks to Roberta Arnold and "Miss May"
for their loving assistance with the last chapter.*

SISTER GIN

part one

1

THE FIRST ache was in her sigh. It was deep, heaving her huge chest and pulling out all the pains between her ribs. The second was in her head conventionally splitting. The third was against her dry allergic skin—her weight against her back skin, the sheet against her top skin, her pajamas against her hidden skin. But the other pains came together; like early woman she counted only one, two, many. Many were focused as one spreading sear inside her life.

"Cardboard is the ugliest color in the world!"

An hour passed. Breathing shallowly, one lessened. Inert on wrinkles, many worsened. It was two o'clock. Two pillows against her left side turned into Su, cushioning from there; one beneath her head, Su's hand; one hugged over her chest, Su's softness. Su was back, surrounding Bettina with miniature gusts of love which eased her skin, replaced her sigh, spread kisses over the terrible sear of ignorance. Bettina lapsed back into sleep.

It was five when she woke up smiling. Su would be home soon, would hold her more, would tell her what her raw mind had to know—that the day was fine, that they two were safe now from work, from money, from traffic and jostles of the street; that they two needed only a couch and a tiny space to rock each other in.

Su was her queen of scarves. She had a high delicate neck and a laugh that showed she knew everything. Her neck bent down now and her laugh was about to explode in Bettina's face, bringing her to life. She steeled her cheeks, waiting. She heard a *whshwsh* just off her right ear. It tickled and she turned into the pillow, meeting Su's laugh unexpectedly in the mouth.

"Suzybins!" she said with a giggle in the empty dusk. Other people did not expect dusk at five o'clock in August North Carolina. In Bettina's room it was always as dusk as she could make it. But not empty: Su's smell of herbal handlotion and brazen aftersex pricked her nostrils; her mouth was gluey. She lay her hand just below the downswing of her belly. She moved one finger down and touched and grabbed her whole hand back. "You wait for your Bins," she told the hand, sending it for a cigarette instead. "You just grow up and wait."

Suppose she doesn't come back?

Her hand went back to her belly, puffed up high like a whale. There was nothing in it but herself. It was her Venus mound, her toy—she carried it everywhere, that soft

pillow of what others call fat, what she called her knapsack on front, holding all her belongings for hugging.

Of course she'll come back. Bettina got up and walked
unsteadily through the cardboard boxes to the bathroom
and took all her medicines. She lay back down under her
grandmother's comforter. As soon as the vitamins and alka
seltzer took effect, she would get up and do something
nice for Su—get out ice, start dinner, straighten the house,
vacuum the living room, bring in flowers, meet Su in clean
clothes . . . suppose she never came back?

Her finger snuck down to the depression below her
knapsack to a very low unnoticeable mound. It slipped inside to her button. "All right. But don't wiggle." Her finger and she were still. I'd never get up. Never move again.
I'd die right here of stillness.

The house had the accumulated stillness of a whole day
of nothing moving at all, the air a twenty-four-hour settled-
ness to it—every sound had made its escape. Her finger
moved a millimeter to test if she were still alive. She was.
If Su would come home and get straight in bed with her—
dirty her, dirty bed, cardboardboxes room. She would take
a bath right now. She inhaled the deep just-before-snub-
bing-out drag off her Kool, prelude to taking a bath. It hit
her angry bronchial phlegm and she coughed. She coughed
until she thought her chest would crack at the breastbone,
ribs flying. She coughed deep and rackingly and spit into a
kleenex, examining the yellow for flecks of brown. There
was much brown but no green.

"Soon as I get my strength back." She sunk far down
into the pillows, listening to Su's tires crunch the shell of
the driveway, her step finally start upon the stairs.

"Hi!" she called at the topstep step. "Hi! How are you?"
Su came in dressed like the outside world. "Glad you're

5

home!" She reached for Su's arm and pulled her down for a kiss; too greedy, she got all of Su sprawled off-balance over her hip onto the bed, her face buried in the sheets which smelled like bad bed.

"Just where I want you," Bettina grinned. Su's mouth was precritical. "I was just trying to decide whether to take a nap." Bettina's face quivered mournfully. "There's an awful pain in my chest." Beautiful Su, how can you look so elegant when I'm so sick? "I keep waking up but there's this pain . . ." She held her side pitifully.

"Then you should sleep. I'm going to get a drink." Su wheeled at the door. "To sleep, perchance to wake . . ." She wheeled again in the hall and called back, "Ah, there's the rib."

She was gone. In a minute their very fat butterscotch-colored cocker spaniel sounded clumsily on the stairs, turned her rheumy eyes to Bettina, no longer able to jump up on the bed. "Hi, Nefertiti." Bettina pulled her into the covers. "Su's gone, Nefertiti. She came and she went. Just like that. One lousy pun was all I got. You hear, Nef?"

Bettina collected omens against the day their love would end, predated shards that would tell the hindlooker where the cracks had begun, when the irreparable fissures started their downslant, why the inevitable rift was to be fatal. Nefertiti was one of the first. She had run away when Su was looking after her, slipped unnoticed out the door and disappeared for three days—a two-month-old puppy in a wet winter, a Christmas present from Bettina to Su. Bettina had been sure Su would treat their love the same, let it slip out an open door and perish in a world without shelter. Su's misery over the imagined fate of the lost puppy was effectively doubled by Bettina's ontological grief. The fact that the puppy was found did not diminish the significance of its escape in the least: "It is a portent of the future, mark my words," Bettina said stubbornly.

Now it was future, Su thought, walking back down the stairs she had designed, double flights leading into a larger single flight like stepped fallopian tubes. The air smelled like nothing—air conditioner turned so low to save its preposterous fee that the air was neither hot nor cold, merely dead.

"I don't love you any more." The whispered statement shocked her heart into missing a thump.

"All *right*. I'll come down," Bettina shouted from upstairs. "I'm coming. Just wait a minute. You can be fixing me a drink if you want."

Su was surprised that her heart's missing thump was noticeable since she was only living out the past until her book was complete. She had long ago surrendered to the loneliness of being right. She was right in her health, her weight, her hairstyle. Her writing was right. Everything in her life had been corrected and she had felt, at the beginning of summer, that if something didn't change soon she would hand in her days and quit.

Her biology had. The change was the change, although at first she had not been sure it had come at all—in the terrible heat of downtown June a hot flash could easily pass.

June was the beginning of a summer of recycled ink. Smells of typewriter ribbon and hot presses recirculated through the air-conditioning ducts until by August of each year all the writers at the Wilmington *Commercial-Appeal* expressed hope in terms of a fresh breeze, the favorite negative was musty, and there was hardly an issue which would not benefit from being ventilated. This year, June had brought the last most vigorous wave of Bettina's opposition, coinciding with Union Publishers' offer to collect her book reviews on women's books into a volume to be published a year from this fall—thus giving her time to concentrate on women's books which she had not even thought of doing before.

"How's that terrible book coming?" Bettina stood warm and sloppy in her blue quilted robe which was identical to the one all girls in her class got for Christmas the years around fourteen. Su looked quickly away. Bettina was the kind of fat person people wanted to save. Gray eyes like crystal, lashes and hair black and curly, she looked like one of the Dionne quintuplets which every magazine of the thirties showed surrounding in five a cake of Palmolive soap. The famous little girls had been born on her seventh birthday: May 28, 1934. In her mind they never grew older than five nor herself beyond twelve.

"I'm so glad you're not mad at me," Bettina said from the hallway made into a bar, pondering the bottle of rum (hers) and its soothingly high level. Her level. No parent came over to her bottle and made secret pencil marks. No need to replace the rum drunk with colored water. She poured herself a measure, mixed it with ice and Tang and carried it like a fullblown grin over to the couch where Su sat.

"I am."

"I'm the only one you know who can pick a fight with someone who's sleeping?" Her grin disappeared within the abrasive field surrounding Su. "For godsake." Bettina gulped her orange liquid and wiped her mouth. "If you were mad why didn't you just say so?"

"Do you know what you said to me last night?"

"Nobody pays any attention to things drunks say. Do

they, Nefertiti?"

The word *pays* stuck like an isotype just inside Su's ear. *Pays attention* neatly reversed itself: attention pays. The drunk and forgetful get in gratis. "You said I was pretentious and wholly dishonest, a pretend newspaperwoman who kept my job because I am a token, challenging nothing, bowing and licking . . . you called me a cunt."

"A compliment. Right, Nefertiti?"

"That terrible book, as you put it, is very important to me. You wouldn't understand that. Your ambition never reached beyond the nearest bottle." Su walked with sober coordination to the kitchen door and looked inside. It was Bettina's job to fix dinner, Su's to clean up after. The kitchen was very clean. "Would it be impolite to ask about dinner?" She sighted Bettina down the length of a perfectly-beamed living room, twenty feet. Although Su ate a regular breakfast and lunch in a restaurant (almost never a sandwich), she wanted dinner too. Her energy depended upon meals.

"Why won't you review *Patience and Sarah?*"

"We don't review paperbacks."

"If it were just now coming out in hard cover would you review it?"

"Why should I? There are plenty of other women's books. I'm not a crusader for christsake." Su gritted her teeth, feeling their frailty. I'm only going to live with you until this book is finished and then so help me god I'm . . .

"Why are you so mean?" Bettina said angrily. "Don't you know I feel sick?"

Su, feeling her own stomach suddenly queasy from the sound of *mean*, not its meaning but its mean *mean* noise in her ear, turned back to the kitchen. In a few minutes she returned, a roastbeef sandwich (lettuce, tomato, mayonnaise, mustard, salt and pepper, pickle) on toast on a plate, plate on a tray with a napkin and glass of milk and second martini. Su set down the tray beside her chair and left it to wait until the martini prepared her stomach.

Bettina sat as before, but Su knew the half-finished rum and Tang was a second, lowered to the same level the first had been when Su left the room. Bettina's facial puffs showed the fixedness produced by alcohol on alcohol, more apparent (to the less than expert) as glaze over the eyes. Su was expert. Bettina was her second sodden lover.

"I am angry at you and also not angry at you because I love you," Su said, feeling the strangeness of the words.

Bettina, with a huge grin, half-rose and pulled Su over to the couch onto her lap—only backward, expecting Su to bend into her h-shape bellyfirst.

"You know I love you more than anything else in the whole world," Bettina said.

Su held Bettina's achingly-familiar headbones into her own neck and awkwardly sipped her martini.

"I must stink," Bettina said, righting herself. "I must positively reek of sweaty alcohol, rummy b.o., and un-washed nightmares."

"Which one of us is going to kill the other first?"

"Don't say that! Don't ever say that."

"You think it'll be you and you defend me against it by getting drunk. I know it'll be me and am afraid of getting drunk." Su reached for her sandwich, offering Bettina a bite. Bettina, shaking her head happily, padded across the twenty-foot floor and constructed another rum and Tang. "Mark my words," Su, following behind her, announced as if on stage. "One day, it is inevitable, one of us will . . ."

"*Hush!*" Bettina lunged for her and clapped a hand over her mouth. "I won't hear another peep out of you, not another peep, you hear?"

"Hush yourself," Su said, prying the hand an inch away from her mouth. "It's Mamie Carter."

Mamie Carter Wilkerson, college roommate of Bettina's mother in an era when to graduate from Radcliffe was, for a Southern woman, a brand like a brainmark, illuminating the woman's features with a blue light, emphasizing harshness, determination, will, strength by many names, at the expense of the soft and the delicate which, along with family, were the main qualities which earned the title, beauty— Mamie Carter Wilkerson had been called handsome in her youth and early middle age; she had a stage presence vigorous enough to earn her a reputation as the "other woman" in many Little Theater productions. She had aged suddenly at forty: her punishment for scorning cold cream, Bettina's mother said ("Look at my skin compared to hers," Luz said, "and take heed, Bettina. After thirty, you can't be too careful with your skin."). The sentence did not mean that one really could not be too careful; obviously it would be too careful to sit all day every day in cream—any cream.

Mamie Carter never let Luz's exaggerations escape unpunished. "A degree in Latin couldn't teach you precision," she said often. "You know the vocabulary but not the case. Next time you should study chemistry. Measurement and memorization, that's what your kind of mind needs. Measurement and memorization."

Mamie Carter looked forty at forty. Among women of her class in America, she seemed old while everyone else looked even younger by comparison. But as if age took its full measure at once and then, satisfied, slunk away, Mamie Carter looked forty at fifty and at sixty, growing in effect younger each year while her companions inevitably aged. Now, at seventy-seven, she looked an *old* forty—hair still harshly gray, coarse, wavy, and fairly thick, eyes quilted below and above but darting unhindered in between, seeming to see much too much.

She saw Bettina in her rumpled blue bathrobe, her eyes painful, herself obviously in last night's pajamas.

"How about a drink, Mamie Carter?" Bettina said. "I'm having one from necessity but you can have one for pleasure."

"Did you ever think of all the people who never drink enough?" Mamie Carter leaned toward Bettina like a conspirator, eyes agleam. "Not that they don't have the opportunity, either. They just never take it. Year after year, they go on drinking too little. Year by year. Never enough."

"Can't say that I ever thought of it that way, M. Carter," Bettina said with a chuckle.

"You're barking up the wrong dog, Mamie Carter. That's like the pot telling the kettle it isn't even black." Su cringed as Mamie Carter's silence told her she was too old to be trying so hard.

"Now, Bettina, I certainly thought your mother would have taught you *that*." She ignored Su to punish her because Su was across the room, by the pantry fixing Mamie Carter a martini on the rocks. Mamie Carter couldn't hear across the coffee table and she thought everyone should know this by now. Bettina, who shouted when she whispered (part of her normal excess; she did everything in excess, even nothing), was one of Mamie Carter's favorite conversationalists.

"It's a fact," Mamie Carter said. "Some people never do understand how important drinking is. There's the brain,

12

crowded with thousands of unused cells and no space between. Every logician knows that growth is greatest when there is greatest space, that each incident which destroys cells creates a proportionate increase in the growth rate of those adjoining. Now suppose a group of brain cells are about to enlarge or multiply with a brilliant idea, and they do that—areas of the brain actually do grow when a chimpanzee learns a new skill. The cells are ready to grow in the brain we're discussing but there is no room because the brain is already full of so many cells that aren't being used. It is the martini, the lowly much-maligned martini itself that kills the idle bystanders so the idea-cells can have room to grow."

"How does the martini know just which cells to kill?" Bettina asked.

"Now there is a reason that the brain was full of too many cells: it had to be full of something. No place in the body is there just a vacuum, you know. You might think of those excess brain cells as plastic bubbles for packing, useful for holding everything in place, for holding open the place of future growth. They are scattered everywhere throughout the brain because no one ever knows where a new idea will occur. Easiest thing in the world then, when the cells which are excited by something send down the signal to the elbow, to pick up the martini and, within thirty minutes, kill off the cells that are crowding back that section. I don't know, Bettina," she said with a sip of her own martini. "Probably electrochemical polarization."

"That's the most interesting application of geopolitics I've heard yet," Su said with a hopeful smile. "I bet that's the way tyrants view the people to the east—as bubbles of plastic holding open the land."

"Now, Mamie Carter, you know you don't believe that."

13

"Of course I believe it. Furthermore, dead brain cells are the most efficient conductor of brain messages there are—better than a vacuum even; forming, in fact, an optimum kind of vacuum wherein they hold back space itself." Mamie Carter's eyes flashed with a black giggle and her face turned bright pink in spots as she herself held back a surging gale of laughter.

"One more martini, M.C., and you're going to apply for the Nobel Prize." Su cupped the glasses on her way to the pantry-bar.

"What'd she say?" Mamie Carter asked Bettina.

Bettina's voice, generous and untrained, could be heard and understood across any room; Bettina therefore usually spoke at meetings of all kinds, however far to the rear of the auditorium a too-tempting rum caused her to sit (or stand). Su, dramatist and actress by ambition in college, now swallowed her words or lowered her voice to a faint hum whenever she was even slightly tired or discouraged. Mamie Carter, actress and nearly deaf, hated that quality in Su so much that she never bothered to look beyond it to see how much she and Su might really be the same person; Su, ignorant of Mamie Carter's antipathy, adored her and often wished she were she.

Never more than five feet five and now, at seventy-seven, an inch or two less, Mamie Carter had nevertheless been reduced to flat-heeled shoes many a time to avoid overtowering her romantic opposite—Southern actors being, among many other things, too short for sports. She wore now, on this particular August day of halfwind and occasional steaming rain, with and without sun, indecisive as Su for one felt about her age, sex, life, and chosen home state—Mamie Carter wore an exact duplicate of what Su wore: navy blue suitdress with white collar and cuffs,

14

white (not pearl) earrings, the stocking shade that was sold
for such a costume, and navy blue kid pumps. But their
lipsticks were different. Su, though she had not exactly
left off lipstick during the years when youth and women's
liberation had caused réd, at least, to disappear from almost every woman's face elsewhere, had compromised red
to the extent that only a faint tinge of it remained among
the mostly beige of what went on Su's lips. Mamie Carter,
older and therefore more set in her brain, was just now
toning down the red she had worn for years, the exact
same red of fifteen years at least—the red that was now returning to the pages of *Vogue* and even *Ms.*, now that
Mamie Carter was thinking beige.

But the very slightest beige. Mamie Carter knew her face
and did very little to please opinion.

Su's face was harder to know. In a small rectangle, it appeared in Wilmington's only daily newspaper every day,
just to the left of her name and title: Book Review Editor.
The rectangle had not changed in the twenty years Su had
been working for the *Commercial-Appeal*, but the picture
inside was retaken and rechosen every five or so years in
great agony. Su's profile was sharp, large-nosed, austere,
and extremely interesting: the profile of a keen intellect,
she was sure; the person reading words beneath such a face
would read respectfully and learn. Su's front face was
round and surprisingly childlike even at her present age,
particularly in photographs; its picture had inspired a large
number of mash notes and gained her attention at every
autograph or cocktail party. Su could never choose. She
wanted both kinds of attention: men could have it, why
not she? Kennedy with his boyish face and falling lock had
nevertheless spoken words the country heeded. Or did
they? Not often in Wilmington, to be sure.

15

The present picture, reflecting a certain discouragement on Su's part with her age, sex, life, and chosen home state, was profilic.

"We certainly are delighted that you paid us this visit," Su said, returning the glass freshly frosting and full.

The words were spoken directly at her face; Mamie Carter smiled a glistening thankyou.

Halfway to Huggins's Bookstore, Su realized that she was deadly depressed. The lights of the highway and the slightly misted shapes of cars in the moist air created an unreality, disembodiment, which had caused her to view the depression at first as unreal also; now, halfway there, she sank into its factness with a thud.

She had put on a red suede jerkin with her pale gray full-sleeved blouse and the necklace from Taos which Kip had given her; three beautiful things covering the most visible part of her, surrounding her face. No one, her mother had said often, feels depressed when she looks beautiful. Her mother was wrong.

"Mamie Carter," she said aloud to no one. "Suppose the martinis kill off brain cells around a depressed idea. Or around no idea. Or suppose . . ." No idea it was. Her chain of thought was up against a dead vacuum rather than a bubble creatively holding back space.

The autograph party which Su was dutifully attending was for Maya Pines, author of *The Brain Changers*—a book which Mamie Carter had reviewed for this Sunday's book page. Mamie Carter reviewed two books a year for Su, never fiction, poetry, or children's books. Her reviews were written in the bold, balanced style of the linear decades of the century's first half and were cherished by those who had a taste for them like a family recipe. People subscribed to the *Commercial-Appeal*'s Sunday edition from as far away as Australia just to read Mamie Carter's biannual reviews.

Su found her style stiff, crochetty, trimmed and pared as if it were going into a doll house, and brilliant. But nothing could persuade Mamie Carter to do one extra review—her quota of service to the community had been agreed upon jointly by her total self and her part which handled human obligations.

Mamie Carter had refused to come to the autograph party for Maya Pines for the same reason. And she had added, "The woman wrote a good book, but all the work she was writing about was being done by men. The only women in the book were the chimpanzees, chosen because the females learn faster."

The shopping arcade which contained the bookstore was brightly lit. Su sat in the car with her hands over her eyes. In the dark there are colors—beige, orange, rust, even green. No blue. In the quiet there are noises: pointillism in crickets, high white whine, a faintest underhum—presumably the sounds of your cells going about their business. But sometimes in the dark the colors drop and there is complete blackness, and sometimes in the quiet there is no noise and you hear only the awful absence, hollow, hollow, all bunched up around your ears.

2

NEXT MORNING the depression flipped into anger when Su saw another sassy "book review" lying on her desk, signed "Sister Gin." As usual, it was a page of irresponsible adolescent spewings, embarrassing to read in daylight. Completely unprintable: even the few readers who were themselves complicated or who liked multilevel reading would find "Sister Gin's" "reviews" so deliberately contrary that it was impossible to know what was meant seriously and what sarcastically.

For example, here at last was a highly readable and very human book by a woman on sex—Ingrid Bengis's *Combat in the Erogenous Zone*. But Sister Gin had to attack everyone, her bitterness stemming no doubt from the fact that she was never listened to. And never will be if it's up to me to print her, Su swore.

"Isn't Benghis spelled like Genghis?" Sister Gin had scribbled across the bottom of page one.

She began with a declaratory sentence atypically comprehensible: "Benghis focuses on war with a vengeance not unlike America's own: enemies to do battle with she uncovers however skillfully they hide and, in the rare cases where she meets a noncombatant (conscientious objector, mother, child, or mystic) she creates her own; like our prestidigitating government she can turn a field of rabbits into a hostile camp. For example, on page 139 Benghis meets a woman who has lived for forty years free from any suspicion of crimes of assault; she has no weapons or disguises, she is not even wearing trick glasses. Bare-eyed she faces Benghis; Benghis takes one look at her face and sees 'greedy erotic eyes' . . . the better to eat you with, my dear?"

"What is she talking about?" Su asked out loud although no one was nearby. "What are you talking about" —Su's voice was shallow with irritation. She turned to page 139 of *Combat*. The phrase appeared hidden in a sentence halfway downpage.

"Greedy is the word to watch here," Sister Gin's review continued. "Greedy implies excess and also something you as greedy one are not entitled to, have not earned by legitimate hunger. Greedy means you've already had your share. Because you're middle-aged now, you're going to have to masturbate."

Su put the "review" face down in the drawer in disgust. She re-read her own review of last year: respectful, a careful summary, praise balanced with a tiny fault or two:

19

Women across the country owe a tremendous debt to Ingrid Bengis for her candid look at the "liberated" sexlife of a modern young woman. Ms. Bengis makes clear that women's so-called sexual revolution was won by the men; as a young woman wanting to explore the world, Ms. Bengis discovers that she exists as a person only after she has been approached as a sex object. That this is the nature of the beast is hardly worth writing a book about; Ms. Bengis's contribution is the analysis of a young woman's responses— her own sexual needs on the one hand, which receive the attention from the men as merely her due, and her needs of personhood, created by a liberal upbringing and education, wherein family and school conspired to have her believe she was a person just like her brother. Ms. Bengis is stepping out of the model of the past and insisting she has the right to travel before settling down to marriage. If she were traveling with a man to whom she said she was married, she would have unhindered access to the big world. It is her voiced demand of her right that is new . . .

Su made a tiny correction, added a paragraph at the end for the book and placed the review in the folder marked "Collected Reviews of Su McCulvey" in black. The flat chest and square shoulders of Jerry appeared in her mind like the stiff cover of a finally-published book which, if peeled back to pages, would flap and ruffle, tear in the wind. Su depended upon Jerry to stave off the feeling that she could be killed at any minute. She had dinner with him at least once a week. Walking into a public restaurant with him powerfully behind her dissipated the terror she felt almost constantly—of being discovered, unmasked, labelled.

She called him and made a dinner date for tomorrow night.

Bettina said, "Tomorrow is a first Tuesday. Mummy'll be expecting us for dinner."

Su said, "I promised Jerry I'd have dinner with him."

Bettina snorted. "Promises to him don't count."

"Why don't you go this time without me?"

Bettina's face set rigidly around the mouth. Her thin lips, with their lipstick perpetually washed down or blotted onto cigarette filters, were pale in a pale face. Very little lip was noticeable from a distance. Her round eyes were a clouded unfriendly gray.

"All right, I'll call him." Memories of dinner with Mummy formed a tight left-sided knot in Su's chest. In the beginning of their love affair, no one had been more cherished, more closely watched, more lovingly stared at for each wayward strand of hair or glance, anything which might be a possible source of Bettina, than her mother; now, when every gesture of face, voice, or mind of the woman she had once loved made Su question whether she even loved her at all any more, to see their origins in Bettina's Mummy's ante-grave gestures made Su want to shout die! die! like a flitgun to them both.

Dinner. The meal was starch and steak. Even the vegetable was starch: peas, a limp green starch. Wine was never served at dinner. Iced tea in summer, ice water in winter, milk on request.

Bettina's mother (they were both named Elizabeth) was called Luz. She was telling the two younger women about Columbia University versus Chapel Hill. Su sipped water and thought that the trouble was she no longer listened to people, although she had thought yesterday that the trouble was that she listened too much to other people.

"Grayson Kirk is the most fascinating man! A gentle-

man and scholar. He is exactly what we had in mind years
ago when we said we wanted a college man. But he has
such a brilliant mind too. He's a cross between Robert E.
Lee and Gertrude Stein."

"A cross?" Bettina said.

"Yes, a cross. Like you cross a peach and an apricot and
get a nectarine. Not a cross that you bear, Bettina."

"Maybe we should say, a blend," Su said. "Because—
would those two like each other well enough to let you
cross them?" She felt a flash beginning. "Would Alice like
it at all? And what about Mrs. Lee—would she mind that
Gertrude was a Jew and the child, I mean the cross . . . the
nectarine . . ." The flash rose on schedule and Su felt her
face bead like the silver goblet of ice water. Her white
jersey blouse clung to her flesh beneath the lightweight
jacket, the lower level of her hair to her scalp, and her
thighs to each other.

Luz pretended not to notice. She began eating her
mashed potatoes as if it were necessary to get them off her
plate quickly. Each forkful included within its white hump
a few graygreen peas. Steak would be left until last, not
because it was being saved as the best but because the
teeth Luz had once had to chew steak with were now replaced by a dental plate of porcelain which were teeth in
a very limited sense of the word. She often wondered if
the very old seem childlike because their preferred food is
that of infants or if the very old become as children because they spend so much time sucking.

Luz had finished the potatoes before Su's flash subsided. "Well, how about more potatoes, Su? Bettina?"
Bettina passed the silver dish, barely warm, to her mother.
"No? You're sure, Su? Well then, I believe I will have a
few more."

22

"Now it's really interesting that we say that," Su said. Luz looked up, hands poised above the potatoes, eyebrows high above round black eyes. " 'A few more potatoes,' " Su explained. "One serving contains a potato or at most a potato and a half. A second helping is probably less than one potato. Why do we speak as if we were eating them by the bushel just because they're mashed?"

"I'll bite," Bettina said.

"Don't brag," Su said. Her own teeth could barely be trusted to sever a celery stalk.

"That's very interesting, Su. Why do we do that? Now I know we confuse plurals on words that come from Latin but I don't think 'potato' . . . is it because we want to believe we have many things to eat, not just one which we'll have to divide up?" Luz surveyed the table, analyzing its bountifulness or lack of it; with her foot she pressed the bump in the rug which rang, audibly in this recently-built house, in the kitchen. May was almost as old as Luz; the two women had been coupled by such long association that they had grown to look alike.

"Miss May, we'll have some more biscuits. And anything else you've got out there . . . tomatoes? I don't think there is enough *to* dinner tonight somehow. Could you slice some tomatoes with a little French . . ."

"Mummy, not for us."

"There's really plenty, Luz. More than we can eat."

"Bring the tomatoes, Miss May. After you pass the biscuits." Luz punctuated her request with a full stop by firmly repositioning her napkin on her perpendicular lap.

"It is true," Su said, "that *I* at least wouldn't say, 'could I have some more rolls.' I would of course ask for 'another roll.' "

"And I would ask *you* if you wanted *a* roll," Luz agreed.

"But Luz—how would 'could I have another mashed potato' sound? Would a hostess feel obliged to measure out a quantity equal to one potato . . ."

"What about 'some more potato'—like 'some more rice?' Could I have some more mashed potato, please?" Luz's fork was frozen two inches off her plate while she leaned into the search for a phrase they could all accept.

" 'Could I have some more mashed potato,' " Su repeated. "Now I like the sound of that. I think you have the answer there, Luz. The collective noun is what we need." Su drank the rest of her water to replace what the hot flash had lost. "Do you think I could have some more water too?"

Luz's foot on the buzzer was no firmer than the satisfaction on her face. After requesting water from May, she pursed her lips inward to make them smaller—although to begin with they were of minimum width and thickness, exactly like Bettina's. She needed them small before the next question (which involved sex) could be asked; she did not want to appear to be taking pleasure in what was merely a request for information.

"Bettina, I've been wanting to ask you a question about Phoebe's book." Luz looked directly into her daughter's suddenly veiled gray eyes. "What does *f-u-c-k me* mean?"

"Now, Mummy. You've seen that word before . . ."

"Oh, I know what *fuck* means. Of course." Luz was indignant. "I've seen *fuck you* written in books, heard *fuck it* in movies—it means what we used to mean by *damn it* and really isn't a transitive verb. *Damn it* is actually *dammit*, like *hell*. But Phoebe's book . . . there it sounds like she is using it as the verb transitive."

"Fuck *me*," Bettina agreed.

"She doesn't mean, *damn me*," Luz said.

24

"I think she wants him to sleep with her," Su said.
"The she in the book."

"You don't mean sleep," Luz said.

"No," Su said. "Not sleep. *Sleep.*"

"Well, I've never seen the word used like that." Luz
smiled at Su first, then Bettina. "As the verb transitive.
How is your own book coming, Su? We're very proud to
have our own book review editor collected by New York."

"Ever since Harry Golden they've been scouring the
newspapers of North Carolina looking for another tar to
heel them," Su said.

Bettina burst out laughing.

"How did you get it so fast?" Su said. "It's a back borrowing—there's no such word. Not as a verb transitive."

"Check with Mummy," Bettina said.

"Is everyone finished?" Luz asked. "Are we ready for
dessert? I think we're through, Miss May."

May, moving very slowly, began clearing the plates. She
picked up Bettina's, then Luz's, then Su's, stacking them
one on top of the other; proper clearing of the table had
been abandoned seven or eight years ago. If there had been
one more guest tonight, she would have refused to serve
the table. "Miss Bettina and Miss Su, that's all!" she said.
Her arthritis was too bad. If Miss Luz wanted to have another guest, she'd have to get someone else to serve the
table. May didn't mind cooking for four, but she wasn't
going to serve for anybody but Miss Bettina and Miss Su.

"It certainly was delicious, Miss May. As usual," Bettina
said with a grinning emphasis on the last word.

"You usually likes to eat, I know that," May said.

"You think so," Bettina said. "Just because I've been
known to put away a delectable thing or two that you
cook, doesn't mean I eat everything any old June puts in

25

front of me. Why, I've been known to turn down . . ."

"Your bed when you want to sleep in it." May balanced the vegetable dishes on her pile of plates. "Don't look to me like you've fallen off any."

"I lost three pounds last week."

"You was sick?"

"I was making room for your lemon pie."

"We has chocolate for Miss Su."

"Thank you, Miss May. The flesh is willing but the spirits have weakened the liver," Su said.

"I reckon you'll eat some," May said.

Bettina drained the last melted ice from her drink glass. "Mummy, I'll just make one more light rum and Tang to help make room for dessert." She got up and opened the kitchen door for May, who was in position to back through. May had to turn around and manoeuver beneath Bettina's arm which was awkwardly holding the swinging door inward.

"I sure am obliged," May said. "I sure don't know how I been getting through this door for fifty years without you holding it for me."

"Speaking of liver," Luz said. "I don't think all that Tang is good for you, Bettina." Bettina disappeared into the kitchen. "Would you like to sweeten your drink, Su? I'm sure Scotch and water is better for you than all that Tang."

"Can I get yours too?" Su's left hand stopped just before encircling the old-fashioned glass, drained to the sogginess of its fruit. "Just a little to make us hungry for dessert."

"Just a touch, then."

The first mouthful of chocolate pie sent Su's taste buds reeling back to Scotch. Scotch was succoring her a lot late-

ly. A drink was an increasing necessity to ease the terrible
swelling inside her brain that made her want to rip open
a sluice hole in her skull every afternoon at five (or four-
thirty or four and yesterday three-thirty). Hot flashes were
a mere summer shower compared to the water-head she
created more days a month than not, which Scotch re-
lieved before half a drink was drunk. It's other effect was to
make her feel instantly intoxicated; she could not be, from
half a drink, but still she felt suddenly garrulous, uncon-
centrated, with a failed memory and a tendency to giggle.
Half a drink. This dessert-Scotch was the fourth or fifth in
today's two hours.

Pine needles had fallen on the lawn outside the low
windows blanketing the sparse grass with brown. Nothing
bloomed in Luz's yard in August. She was not interested
in growing flowers anyway; years ago she had planted a
few oleander, spirea, and forsythia to satisfy the criticism
she felt she would receive if she had no flowers at all.
Fortunately she liked the colors of oleander, spirea, and
forsythia; if her yard's respectability had depended upon
her planting hydrangea—if hydrangea were the only available flowering shrub, hydrangea with its unresolved mealy
pompoms of white or pink (or that awful Easterbonnet
blue made from rusty nails) . . .

Luz grew tomatoes. Okra and beans and lettuce too, but
primarily and most intently tomatoes. She was of a generation which remembered when tomatoes were considered
poisonous; as a child she was warned against the luscious
juicy red balls as if they were love apples. She remembered
sneaking with a friend through the back hedges of a heretical
gardener and picking a tomato off the vine, and forcing herself to eat it. She had dreamed she was poisoned and then
that she had escaped the poison because she was chosen

27

by the devil to poison others. In the dream she poisoned her whole family. She even hid a piece of tomato in bits of meat and fed it to her dog; the tomato fell out onto the ground uneaten but the dog, with a dog's wet reproachful eyes, picked it up from the dirt and loyally ate it nevertheless.

"How did your tomatoes do this year, Luz?" Su asked just as a wave of heat sparked from her uterus, rising rapidly to her face which began its blush immediately after the question was asked—a blush strangely appropriate to Luz's vestigial shame at being so intensely involved with a vegetable that was certainly redder and juicier (when ripe) than any other.

"The green-tomato relish turned out better than it ever has before," Luz answered, delicately steering the subject onto the tomato's virginal childhood. When Su didn't answer, Luz's black eyes grew round and helpful. "Are you flashing, dear?"

"Yes." Su patted her forehead with her napkin. "You know, I don't mind flashing when I'm alone and can relax into it as if it were a hot bath; it makes you feel a little faint but not at all unpleasant, really. It's when the flash comes in the middle of a conversation that it is so distracting. I simply can't remember what anyone is talking about until the flash is over."

"Distracting, yes." Luz frowned in sympathy.

"To say the least," Bettina said. She was forty-six and had lost no estrogen yet, or so she claimed. Su did not believe her. "I don't see how you can stand it."

"It's supposed to be worse for you young women who have never had children, isn't it? Or have I got it backwards?" Luz wiped her mouth in unconscious imitation of Su and rang the buzzer with her foot. "I barely remember going through it, in fact. Although I'm quite sure I *did.*"

"Miss Su, you feeling all right?" May asked from her pause at Bettina's place. Su's hair, which she wore short and close to her head, was wringing wet in spite of the air conditioner. "Is it your flash?"

"That's all," Su said. "Wetter than usual, for some reason."

"You're a head sweater," May said. "So'm I. And when I had it, I didn't have any hair on my head to speak of—no more'n I got now. That sweat covered my scalp with beads the size of marbles—why I remember Clarita was staying over with me one time when she was a little bit of a thing and she say, 'Grandmama, your head is all blistered.' And she reached up and stuck her finger in one and they all started running down my scalp then and it scared her. Didn't scare me none. I tell you I was glad to see it. I had enough of that other and plenty of children." May stood, momentarily having forgotten why she was there. "Now what was it I was supposed to be doing, Miss Luz?"

"You can take the dessert plates, Miss May. And just leave the coffee on the stove. If you children want coffee, you don't mind going in the kitchen and helping your-selves, do you? Miss May can't carry that heavy tray any more." Every month Luz said the same thing; every month Su went into the kitchen for her coffee and Bettina went in for a fresh rum and Tang.

"Just like we did last time, Mummy." Bettina, usually pleased enough to be the youngest, now felt menopausally neglected.

"Now don't you bother to come in until lunch time to-morrow, you hear, Miss May?" Luz held the arm of her chair to steady herself before beginning the walk into the living room.

29

"Yes'm, I hear. That's one thing I can still do. I hear and I hear good. I hear you coughing in the morning and choking."

Luz reached for her old-fashioned glass and drank what was intended to be a last watery sip; suddenly she stiffened, her face red and tight, straining muscles pushing the red outward for long seconds before a huge wheeze of a gasp came out followed by an exploding cough: Luz was having an attack of choking. May hit her between the shoulders with the hard flat of her palm, hit her four or five thumps, her other hand holding Luz's shoulder to steady her aim, her face bent into Luz's straining red one. Two plump almost white-haired women of the same height, balanced on inadequate legs beneath cotton skirts hemmed well below the knee, Luz clutching the chair arm, May holding Luz's shoulder and thumping, Luz finally able to cough the one longer deeper cough that came from a normal chest, that signaled that the windpipe had closed itself off from the esophagus once more and the spasm was over. Luz coughed a few more times, wiped her eyes on her napkin and turned, putting her hands on May's upper arms in a hold of tenderness and affection. "Thank you, Miss May."

"You all right now?"

"I'm all right."

"You sure?"

Su stopped in the hall, midway between May's ritual dressing down of Bettina in the kitchen and Luz expectantly arranging things for them on the porch off the living room. Su stood before the oil painting of Foremother, waiting for the coffee in its Spode cup to cool, staring at the face made to look matrician by a loyal artist and at

30

the strangely elongated hands after Roualt's "The Cardinal." This white-haired aristocrat looked back at Su the commoner with a cold gray eye; her daughter's black ones had come from *her* mother and Bettina's gray ones from her other grandmother; Foremother (as she was called by everyone in old Wilmington) had taken her Confederate steel to the grave with her. In life as in the portrait, she approved of nothing.

Her daughter, Luz, fat from childhood and blunt-footed, had chosen her build from the short branch of the family and her husband from the wrong side of the tracks—a large handsome man who had made a lot of money in middle-class business ventures (seldom spoken of in Foremother's presence), Luz's late husband had somehow managed to intrude his own genes and thoroughly block out Foremother's aristocratic heritage. Bettina, her sister Adele, and her brother Furious were as fat and stubtoed, as round-faced and pug-nosed, as prone to disorders of the gall bladder and liver (as opposed to the heart and brain) as the most average grease-eating, beer-drinking citizens of nontidewater North Carolina. Foremother, alive until two years ago, had lived to see it all—see her dearest values vanish even unto the fourth generation: her own commonplace great-grandchildren out of Adele and by Furious.

Su herself, lower middle class and one-quarter Jewish, nevertheless looked more like Foremother than any of her begotten women and for that reason she had alternated between ignoring Su and peevishly questioning and requestioning her upon possibly mistaken facts of her ancestry.

But Bettina had inherited the most persistent attribute of the aristocracy: sloth. Bettina was an optimist when it came to money. She expected money to be provided while she shifted positions on the couch. But she was a complete

31

pessimist on the subject of work: she had no faith that work would produce any benefit whatsoever to anyone whomsoever. She had been made to work—by use of coercion, threats, or guilt—but she had never been convinced that work had value. She was as far from the Puritan ethic as an adult can be. She felt her father had made money *for* her and her mother was stingily holding on to it (or meting it out a drop at a time). She knew that she worked only to use up the time before she would inherit that which would buy leisure back again. She waited (although she did not admit that she waited) for her mother's death, meanwhile borrowing from the bank on long-term loans.

Her sister Adele, with her three little boys as alike as triplets, did not bother to wait; she asked her mother for money at every birthday, holiday, or everyday greeting; even her mother's, "How is everything?" drew the reply, "Short of money, as usual."

Her brother Furious, the most placid man alive, was called Furious because he'd gone briefly into the used-car business and paid an old college friend to do his public relations for him. The friend had called the car lot Furious Fred's and had thought up a number of slogans dealing with how furious Fred was because his cars sold so fast he could never sit down, or see his family, or eat lunch—he was always running out to sell another car. Needless to say the business failed because Furious would do anything to avoid an argument, even agree to the prospective buyer's lowest offer, most expensive demand for pre-sale repairs, post-sale guarantees. Furious could with justification be furious at his friend for putting out an image so unlike the actual Fred as to seem mocking but Furious, the most placid man alive, had never been known to raise his voice.

They had all been left behind by a booming new Wilmington foreseen and nudged, kicked, cheered, pushed, even spat on its way by Bettina's crass father; a boom begun by Uncle Sam in World War II; the country had placed Camp LeJeune adjacent to Wilmington. Su, on her one grant and one trip to the cultural centers and back-waters of America, sometimes concluded that real estate was behind World War II, that the war had been engi-neered by chambers of commerce in the nation's small towns who found the army/navy/marine/air force bases placed abruptly on their outskirts an eyesore but a palm-liner devoutly to be wished.

Su had come here after the war, as the town stampeded itself into a two-paper city and then in the slump of 1960, back into a single daily and double Sunday, medium-sized town. She had been drawn by Wilmington's past not its future and had stayed. She was attracted to decadence in all its forms, including extreme old age, she realized as she stared at the unloved and unloving face of Foremother at eighty-seven.

Mamie Carter Wilkerson's manservant drove her up from one direction just as May's husband Robert came from the opposite direction to pick up May. The two men were cou-sins. Robert, white-haired and bent with age himself, po-litely waited for the other, older, also named Robert but called Captain by Mamie Carter and (almost) everyone else, to walk Mamie Carter up the driveway and see her into the screened porch before he, Robert, walked up the driveway and escorted May back to the sidewalk, to open the car door and help her inside.

Su watched the performance from the window flanking the front door. Mamie Carter wore a beautiful shade of dark red through the soft pearl of a tidewater twilight, stepping up the crushed shell of the driveway on her still

33

sturdy legs, chin up defiantly while Captain followed behind according to custom to see that she didn't fall, head up for an audience she assumed was always a possibility. Both women, at almost the same moment, with a quick arm gesture shook off the offered physical assistance of the men.

Su left her coffee cup empty below Foremother and went out onto the porch—the reality of its warm multi-fragrant, real air a shock after the air-conditioned house. Su, a flash, and Bettina occupied the doorway simultaneously. Su turned in defeat back to the living room, experiencing this flash as a final wringing out. She felt wet and ugly.

3

"ARBARA Barbarachild is here." Daisy's soft graygreen eyes looked as if they'd been slapped.

Su fought back to wakefulness. "Who?" Looking up, the light made her frown. Her voice was querulous and sharp.

"Barbara Barbarachild . . . Washington Women's Media." Daisy's face closed up as if Su were an unforgiving parent.

"I'm sorry." Su tried to rub away the frown. She had been saying "I'm sorry" for two weeks. Daisy had recently moved up from classifieds; her ambition was to be Su. *I'm sorry* was nowhere near enough for *her* and Su's real need was unthinkable: she wanted to scoop Daisy into her arms and breathe again through that curtain of lightbrown hair like seawater holding some miracle of energy. "Daisy?"

"I should have reminded you this morning," Daisy said. "The appointment was made so long ago, it's no wonder you forgot."

"I forget a lot lately. It's not your fault." She shook off the tugging memory of Daisy's in fact reminding her this morning. "It's this thing I'm going through." She didn't want to use the word *menopause* to someone whose hair was like seawater. "I just hope Barbara Barbarachild is fifty, too." She grinned at Daisy, hoping the joke at her own expense would make up for . . . she saw too late that the remark implied that Daisy was too young to understand. Daisy looked quickly away before Su's eyes could show that she hadn't meant that. "I'm sorry," Su said once more in a voice gritty with irritation.

Walking down the hall, she suddenly woke up and could not remember feeling sleepy. She breathed deeply several times, needing air like a gasping fish. She couldn't remember why she was walking down this hall, where she was going. She stopped and forced her mind to concentrate, try to remember. She began laboriously at step one, like a person trying to retrace a preoccupied path in order to locate a misplaced object.

Her mind was as vacant and impenetrable as a grave.

She stopped at the water fountain. Gulps of ice water hit her stomach with a sharp pain. Suddenly she jerked erect.

"Barbara Barbarachild?" With her smile and hand outstretched, Su approached the woman standing by the long counter which penned in the women who worked in the open lobby (away from the men in their cubicles). Momentum carried the social period through its preliminaries:

"Barbara Barbarachild! What an original name. Do you like seafood?" Habit let Su steer Barbara to her car, turn the car into traffic and toward the beach. She longed for a cocktail like an addict.

They were the only women in the Neptune. Su ordered a Bloody Mary set-up, placing her brown bag covering a pint of vodka on the table.

Barbara Barbarachild slid into focus after half a drink. She was direct and immediate, having carefully thought out all she wanted to say. Unfortunately Su heard none of it. From a lifetime of being able to remember almost verbatim the words of the person she interviewed, she had not brought along her notebook. She found an envelope and pen but, after so many years remembering, she no longer knew how to take notes. Her usually precise and tiny handwriting smeared across the paper. She decided to gamble on listening. She smiled at Barbara's gray-streaked hair—she might at least be forty.

"Your publication will be an alternative to *Library Journal* which is owned by Xerox?" Su said. "The whole publishing world seems to be owned by unrelated businesses now. We can understand that here, you know. We're owned by Flack's Auto Stores. No, seriously. They're our biggest advertiser. They also own two movie theaters, a fleet of soft-ice-cream carts, a chain of racehorses, a mortuary, and Apartment City—the 'Inn' place to live for a thousand people. A Flack daughter is married to our editor-in-chief, a Flack son is on the city council, a Flack grandson is an all-night disc jockey on the local radio station. And a Flack granddaughter sings. I wrote a mild criticism of her thin flat styleless voice once and almost got fired, even though the copy editor knew enough to pull the review and run a 'critic on vacation' slug." Su drained her

Bloody Mary.

Barbara laughed. "That's just exactly what we're fighting against. We . . ."

"But what will you be able to do? Xerox can push you out of business by refusing ever to review you, in *Library Journal* and *Publishers Weekly*. And you know they own . . . do you want another drink?"

"I didn't have one. Remember?" Barbara smiled hesitantly. "That's why I came. If women not connected with New York, on papers like yours . . . let me show you something." She took out a booklet and Su pretended to look at it but she was really looking peripherally up and out to catch the waitress's eye. She signaled another set-up. She turned to Barbara, unable to recall a word she'd said.

"If you think you could," Barbara finished expectantly.

"Well, it depends." Su shook her glass, looking at the red-flecked ice for a clue.

"On what?" Barbara's smile had disappeared and her eyes were not as warm now.

"On what?" The second drink arrived, and lunch. The table was rearranged slightly and everything put into position for eating. "I'm not really a member of the women's lib movement, of NOW or anything." Something like disgust closed up Barbara's face. "I mean, of course I'm for some of the things they're for. It's just that I'm not a political person. I've never been much interested in politics at all."

Barbara put her knife and fork down together, lined up, to indicate she'd finished eating. Her plate was empty, too. Su was still holding a bite on her fork—a second or third bite, apparently. There was very little food gone from *her* plate. She must have talked straight through lunch, with sips of Bloody Mary for periods. "I mean, *commas*," she said quickly.

"What?"

"Oh, nothing. Sorry." A small flush filled Su's head, radiated beneath the skin of her face—not an intense flash whose sweat brought some relief from tension, was a peak which was followed by a plateau, however brief, of nontension, almost normality. This flush was barely noticeable, as if it were a tiny discharge of a small overload after which the load would build back up almost immediately to the same intolerable pressure. The back of her head was hurting as if a curved skullshaped iron had thwacked it.

Su saw that she had eaten half her lunch. Therefore she must have let Barbara talk some. She was so grateful for her own good behavior that she turned with a warm smile to Barbara and said, "I'm really *so* glad you came down to visit us. So I could hear about . . . everything." Barbara looked startled. "It's just . . ." Su felt the ineffectual flush returning, suppressed an overwhelming desire to yawn. "I am really so incredibly sleepy! I don't know why. Would you like some coffee?"

After lunch Su said, "You must come back to the paper. I want you to meet my assistant—I hope you brought copies of your journal and press-releases or statements of what you want to accomplish. My memory works better if it has a few facts written down to work on. I *am* looking forward to writing a piece on you all."

Su thrust her to Daisy and hurried into the bathroom. She took a vitamin E, B12, B complex and two Cs, and splashed cold water on her face until she could hear no more echoes of lunch.

"Bettina, where are you?" Su spoke in a voice Bettina

39

could not possibly hear through the television noises of her six o'clock perch in front of the news.

"Hi!" Bettina's standard greeting reached through to Su like an explosion of shore to one rumbled inside a wave. Su sat beside Bettina and held her hand, grabbing it. Bettina looked up and immediately took Su into her alarmed arms.

"Hysteria," Su said, tears finally covering her eyes. "What the Greeks knew. I'm having an attack of hysteria in its true meaning—undulations from my uterus. I'm going insane."

Bettina shifted now and put her arms properly around Su. "My goodness, baby." She patted her back with a strange repetitive patting while trying to think what to do. "My goodness." She was afraid if she suggested a drink too quickly Su would be insulted. "Poor baby," she said, still patting.

Su pulled away. "I'm all right. Maybe a drink . . ."

Bettina held up her glass. "I'm having one, I'd be delighted to fix you one, What would you like?"

"I feel like I'm going crazy but I know . . ." Su reached for Bettina's glass and downed two big gulps, wincing at the sweetness of rum and Tang. "My aunt thought she had a brain tumor when she went through menopause. I can see why."

Bettina returned with two drinks and a huge grin. "My aunt thought she was going through menopause but it turned out she had a brain tumor."

"Do we have any birthcontrol pills?"

"I don't. Why would we . . . what are you getting ready to do?"

Su slammed the door and started her car. An hour later she returned with a disc of pills. She revolved the plastic wheel until its window was opposite . . . "What day is it? Tuesday?" She dropped out Tuesday's portion and popped it in her mouth.

"Dammit, Su. If you take those things without seeing a doctor I'm really through with you. Don't you know you can get a blood clot?"

"Birthcontrol pills have estrogen in them." Bettina stormed out of the living room.

"People use alcohol to make them want to eat, to cut the fat in what they do eat, to digest the excess they have eaten, to help them sleep, to wake them up, to warm them up, calm them down, but I am the only one who needs alcohol to create urine!" Su shouted after her.

"It's just not natural," Bettina said much later. "I know it's better to just go on through menopause and get it over with naturally."

"We don't do anything else that's natural," Su said. "We don't get fuzzy when the weather turns cold."

"The least you could do is see a doctor. You'll die of cancer at sixty."

"I'm not so very alive flashing and flushing you know."

"Please, baby, please go see a doctor." Bettina's eyes were puddles of pleading and concern and Su wanted to smash them.

"Don't you tell me to go see a doctor!" Su's own face disappeared behind a half-smile of pure vindictiveness. "You were supposed to go back to the doctor once a year for a checkup after you had that tumor removed and you haven't been once."

The first time Bettina had ever gone to a doctor for a gynecological exam had been just after she and Su became lovers. Bettina was bathed in guilt because she knew the doctor would necessarily know—have to know something as profound as what had happened to her body, especially the very part he was looking at. That part had gone almost unnoticed by Bettina until she had known Su; but then (now) it throbbed and hugged itself at the merest thought of its discoverer . . . because Bettina thought of Su as in fact its discoverer. Surely the doctor, looking so closely, would be able to see the imprint upon her soft silk-like insides of Su's touch, particularly Su's rougher touches. Probably there were new mounds where parts had reached up for a caress, new creases formed by the stroke of Su's finger. Besides, the doctor's mere look at her, there, would produce in her such a swamp of memory of Su that all her parts would blush and give everything away. Or, worse, make the doctor think it was his look which caused the blush.

Bettina closed her thighs tighter. "It's different with you. You're thin."

"I've just lost everything." Su lay in the curve of Bettina's arm, not bothering to exclude Bettina herself from the catalog to come. A sudden meanness came up from inside and let the hurt stand. "Everything," she repeated. "I talked the whole time. I didn't let Barbara Barbarachild say one word. And when she did anyway, I didn't listen, don't remember one thing she said. I can't concentrate. I know I am old and have only more age to anticipate, that sexually I'm losing not only my own attractiveness but even desire, that the last two times I rode horseback I threw my elbow and shoulder out of joint and they both still hurt—I can't pick up a heavy book any more with just my left hand. All this is unbearable and humiliating and impossible to live with but I'd live with it gladly if I could just have my concentration back. Every time I think, I re-

42

alize how stupid I've become, how each thought of value was thought *then*. Before."

"You're not stupid. You're the . . ."

"I can't write any but the simplest column. It falls apart if I include anything complex. I'd lose my job if it weren't for Daisy. She does all my rewrites . . ."

"Daisy's nothing but a child." Bettina scowled, hoping it wasn't Daisy.

". . . she's covering for me all the time. I can't remember who I'm supposed to meet and even after she reminds me, I forget. I'm just like all the old women the books are written about, just what everyone always says old women are like . . . forgetful, distracted, silly old biddie chattering on a mile a minute trying to hide the fact that I don't remember what I started to say."

"I still love you," Bettina said.

Su didn't answer.

"I really do."

Su got up abruptly. "Oh, what do you know. There's nothing to love, for godsake. I'm not even here . . . just a bad-tempered old bossy. Don't you see? I *am* the person I used to make fun of!"

4

O R BECAUSE each moment contains its own memory, this glisten of wet road and sound of wet tires and smell of old September eight o'clock ... Su was fifty years old and remembering Kip who would be almost sixty if she were still alive. She had died halfway out of bed, slanting headfirst from the bed toward the floor, caught on an outstretched arm and the knob of the bedside chest, died either from a heart attack or an overdose of liquor and pills, accident or self-determination: Su was as close as any legal next-of-kin and Kip's then-grown

44

daughter, Sherry, had told the police that Su was her legal guardian and Kip's half-sister. No one wanted an autopsy. Kip had the right to leave her survivors in doubt as to what her final choice was, death or death.

Su was now past her middle age of prejudice and into the age of tolerance

memory slid her down lavender strips of smell as if she were smelling for the last time, nose given just this scent reprieve and then forever ceasing to be among smells . . . how could she possibly be interested in whether one smell were purer than the other; how could the last smell on earth be other than magical. Equally, the last color her eyes were permitted to see before they were forever closed to color would be a color most precious itself, certainly not to be compared . . . to white or black or her or her. Age then, producing the absoluteness of infancy, turns its back upon the syntheses and contrasts and comparisons and judgments of middle age or pre-middle age.

Kip said, "What an unusual name—Sece?" She looked closely at Su's handwriting. "Oh, it's *Sue*. Maybe you won't mind if I call you Sece?"

"I'm the only one who can write Sue illegibly."

"Gifted." Kip stared at the face of the woman she would ask for an hour—in a minute.

45

Su felt drenched with sexual currents under her scalp. She decided to give passivity thirty seconds and then break. At second twenty-nine she said, "See you," and swung scarf-out in an arc toward her car.

"Wait," Kip said.

The air was damp through every piece of plastic or metal which stood between them and the other cars poked into the drive-in like pigs into a trough. The damp came unchecked through sneakers left from summer and inadequate sweatshirts; only Su's excess of health kept the damp from chilling her soul. Health plus beer alternated with Kip's real silver flask of pure bourbon, warm and golden.

"You're a healthy animal," Kip said.

Su responded by a stare. "What do you mean?"

The flat of Kip's hand sat like an interrupted pat on the side of Su's head gently. She meant—a hope. She flicked the lights for the carhop, started the motor, and put money under the ice bucket; she drove to the next corner where beneath a brief tree shadow she kissed Su with only a hesitation in neutral.

Su had known her body from the outside, known its shape of grace from what her audience's eyes said when she moved across a stage. She had known her body from inside too, although mostly in pain or frustration: she had felt prevomit shifts and posteliminative emptiness, predinner emptiness and postmenstrual shifts, and sensations of cramps, spasms, stitches, sore throats, and sore muscles. She had studied anatomy from a dance teacher and at one time queasily understood how insides arranged themselves.

She had never felt the inside and outside of her own body as one, indistinguishable, as if skin were gas containerless and everything solid were fluid in flux taking positions at caprice. Her heart nestled between her underarm and Kip's shoulder, her lips wrapped themselves around Kip's entire body, her spine grew long and curved like a tree over the bed, her palms grew teeth she had to restrain from slashing Kip's back, and her cunt stood high as the head of a young horse seeking a patting and praising hand, felt so tall that she thought, it is shameless, it can surely be seen from the street.

The door opened. Light from the hall threw a slice of proportion over the bed and Sherry's voice a child's fear to her mother. "Kip . . .?" she wanted to know. Kip got up and knelt by her; Su lay as quietly as possible, her skin a solid without doubt now.

Sherry peered into the bed. "Oh, it's Su!" She laughed and her voice relaxed back into the midnight whine of small girls. She wanted to be carried back to bed.

"It's all right," Kip said, returning. "Unless the interruption ruined everything."

Su's selfconsciousness tried to push into the background the still-lustful horselike part of her, unsuccessfully. "It didn't ruin anything," she laughed into Kip's breast, nuzzling her other half around Kip's thighs. Kip stroked, beginning again from the middle.

"You're just a healthy animal, aren't you?"

"A fuzzy bay," Su said.

"A horse?"

"Feel my perfect soft muzzle."

"Velvet. Real velvet."

"Mmm."

Su spent all her spare time at Kip's and the happiest three weeks of her entire life. Three weeks of perfection are eternity. Three such weeks would endure fullstrength forward and backward and last a lifetime. She felt sure

47

that even Sherry was wrapped with love.

At four Sherry straddled surliness and fear. Every night she had a nightmare; usually she was being chased by a cow. "It's me then," Kip said, pride strengthening her concern.

"I don't believe that," Su said from loyalty buttressed by ignorance. "Sherry is an absolutely happy four-year-old and has been all week. I think it's because happiness frees her creative dream-maker; she goes wild on a great dream which suddenly turns upside down and scares her. I used to do that when I was writing plays . . ."

Su's face showed that she wished she could have made that claim in the present tense. Kip touched her hand. "Prepare for fear. I intend to muse you to work right after breakfast."

"Real playwrights skip breakfast."

After lunch it rained. The screen porch was as dark as a cave and noises of rain surrounded them like curtains. Smells of rain made them gulp at memory. Su wanted to include Sherry, spread the magic she felt onto her.

"Sherry," she said.

"She's gone," Sherry said, taking her thumb out of her mouth just long enough to speak.

"Oh. Well, if you see her would you ask her if she wants me to tell her a story?"

"I'll ask her but you must be very gentle with her."

"Are you her friend?"

"I'm her tiger."

"Oh, stop that tiger nonsense, Sherry!" Kip stood up so abruptly that her chair fell backward onto the floor. "You're not a tiger and you don't have a tiger for christsakes."

Sherry sucked rapidly.

"Well, how do you think it makes me feel?" Kip explained to Su's shocked face. "I'm a mother whose daughter needs a tiger to protect her from her? Am I supposed to let her believe all that horseshit?"

"Tiger," Sherry whispered during an instant's withdrawal of her thumb.

It was the first time Su had ever seen a real parent show real anger to a little child, the first time she had had broken for her the myth that those angel faces provide their own deterrent to evil, the first time she had ever questioned the assumption: why, you look at that darling little baby and you just know no one could possibly want to hurt it. Su stood paralyzed in the pose sudden truth had found her, and she would forever after assume that pose each time this scene was remembered as it was to be often like a scar across her own inner forehead. She stood thus, Kip there, Sherry like so. Hours passed. Su knew she should rescue Sherry from her mother but she could not move—not to take action against her lover. She knew she should say something to Kip, that Sherry was only kidding about the tiger, but she did not know Sherry well enough to belittle her. She knew that at least she should disappear so mother and daughter could hate each other purely, without the distortion of an audience, but that would be an admission that mother-child angerhate was real and even commonplace if it could be so swiftly recognized and acted upon. Su was still too clutched on disbelief to become verifying agent.

She stood for hours and hours, listening to Sherry suck against the rain, watching Kip's face gather more and more fury unto itself, feeling her own chest swell with fear like milk boiling over in a cauldron of white.

In what must have been only a few seconds, Kip lunged

for Sherry and carried her screaming and kicking from the room, carried her belly outward on her hip as if to protect her from her arm's crush, lunged for her before her fury could mount any higher and she would kill.

She explained this to a shaking Su when she returned. "You don't need to worry," Kip said. "There is a built-in mechanism that tells mothers when to spank their children or put them in their rooms before the mother's anger becomes too great and the child might really be hurt."

"Really?" Su knew in her toes that she was acquiring knowledge that would take a lifetime to justify.

They made love in the rain all through the rainoise coming through the old screens with wetsmell and the summer sounds of rain on heavyleaved trees and bushes and mud and plops through open windows. All afternoon until the darkness of the rain seemed to be the darkness of the invisible sun setting and still Sherry hadn't waked up: as if she knew that they claimed the afternoon for love and her life depended upon her sleeping, she slept.

"It's six o'clock," Su said, coming back to Kip from the kitchen with a beer apiece. She wanted to go quietly to Sherry's door and look to see if she were asleep or hiding there pretending a game to herself. She wanted to look but she was afraid of Kip's anger, that it would erupt again at the name Sherry and take for its object this time the one who said the name. She waited for Kip to suggest it.

They stood in the doorway together. Sherry lay, her head pushed against the bars of the cot's foot in what would have seemed a positive force of pushing except that her whole body was as limp as a worn balloon. Suddenly she opened an eye and stood up, clutching her mother about the legs and hips and holding her arms to be picked up. Kip sat on the cot holding her in her lap in the posi-

50

tion she insisted upon—Sherry's arms around her mother's neck, her face in her hair, her legs wrapped around her lower waist as if it were a pole. Su said a meaningless well-meaning sentence and left the room with a shiver.

I am going to take care of them both, Su said silently eating her hamburger's combination of lettuce, tomato, mayonnaise, mustard, pickle, meat, and bun which activated memory upon memory, flavor by flavor. She could not say it aloud because she was afraid Kip would laugh at her presumption; Kip had laughed once when she had jokingly replied to something Kip said: "We'll be each other's mothers." The laugh let her know that she was and was supposed to remain, as far as Kip was concerned, a healthy animal, young and nonparental. Kip liked to think of herself as the old one. She said she was older than Su would ever be and other unarguable but unconvincing statements like that. In the past week alone Su had seen Kip's need to think of herself as old as a need to be expert, as a helpless reaction to unwanted responsibility, as an excuse in advance for the day Su left. There were doubtless other facets of it, including truth: Kip had worked in an aircraft factory during World War II when the older sisters of Su's friends were comparing photos of their uniformed child-husbands.

Su grinned at Sherry above her flavors and winked. She grinned back. Su swore she'd love and protect her until the day she died.

All through the long fall and short winter Su lived with them and wrote her play. She kept house for Kip and took care of Sherry in return for her life's dream: time and a table on which to write.

The play was intellectually sprung in the current fashion, after Arisophanes. The situation: in the play the men were constantly waging war, year in and year out, and the women were very tired of it. They decided the only way to deal with war was to limit the number of men allowed on earth. The two nations met and all the women agreed: boy babies were to be allowed only by applying to the allotment bureau, a small number each year (less than a battalion). The future was settled. The problem now was the present large number of men/soldiers. The two countries met. It was decided. The men also agreed: the women were to kill all the men except x number decided jointly by both sexes of both countries.

Why did the men agree? They were raped into submission by logic. Each one was asked if he would lay down his life for his country. Each soldier returned an immediate *yes*. Unqualifiedly? Without questions? You will follow the orders of your government for the good of your country?

Both countries, drained and demoralized by war, needed peace.

The women were trained into firing squads and each took a turn at eliminating war from the land. Soon the agreed-upon male remainder was all that remained.

The women met and voted to reduce the remainder a bit more. It was argued that what had seemed a small number of men when there were many soldiers milling all over the land, now seemed an exhorbitantly large number (because of their loud clumsiness) upon a warm earth of women.

Soon the second agreed-upon male remainder was all that remained.

The women met and voted to reduce the remainder a bit more. It was now argued that there were too few men to form a real community of men, but too many to pro-

52

tect as an endangered species.

Soon the third agreed-upon male remainder was all that remained.

The women met again. They didn't bother with logic this time. They had discovered in the killing that they liked to kill men. They had never felt so in touch with their real selves as when they were forming firing squads, practicing, exercising their duty to their countries, and, afterward, sharing the companionship and conviviality of their womenmates.

But now men were an endangered species under the protection of the government.

Kip was furious. "How can you babysit for my daughter and write like that about men?"

"It isn't . . ."

"How can I go to work and leave Sherry here with your hate? You want to turn her into a murderer."

"My play has nothing to do with Sherry."

"All writers say that. Artists are the most irresponsible people alive. And never admit it."

"You think Sherry doesn't have her own violent side? How . . ."

"Don't give me that repression shit. Violence is *habit*." Kip's hair was dark and red and smoldered under the kitchen overhead bulb. Her angular face was tightened into *v's*. "Besides, that's not art, it's diatribe!"

Soon after, Kip was instrumental in getting Su a job on the Wilmington *Commercial-Appeal*, church page. She learned to write book reviews instead of plays. She dropped the final *e* from her name. She read every book in the library on children and solemnly committed her sober energies to Sherry's chance. She had learned to drink and to say, "I love you, Kip," on beer-muddled Saturdays, to which Kip always replied, "I know you do, Su." Her handwriting improved, growing smaller and neater and smaller; soon her signature bore no resemblance to *Sece*. And somehow, in a sequence Su was unaware of until it was over and could not even then retrace, she and Kip drank away their sexual attraction and focused upon fortifying their private unit against the conventional world.

Remembering, Su felt more tenderness for Kip than any other feeling except The flash got her straight on the pretension. She spoke out loud and heard her voice tinny, her words bland, deceitful, oblique. She reached for a kleenex as if sopping up her sweat would restore concentration enough to drive.

Women, someone once said, are water-shedders. Women's bodies collect and dispense fluids. From tears over love lost to flashes from absenting hormones, we drip onto the ground, wet our surfaces, slip and slide through our race to grab onto each other on a layer of fluid more alike than not. We fail more often than not. We sweat more than we drool, vomit more than we feed, let loose a greater volume of tears than birthwater, more waste urine from bar drinks than menstrual blood from refused pregnancies —we drip and piss and sweat it out from one year to the next in hopes that we are really growing more beautiful, less fat, more brilliant, less mean, more talented and famous, less left behind. Until the year when we see that we have dripped away our energy and we can only weep for the past and ask, is this all there ever was?

Su pulled the car off onto the breakdown shoulder because she could no longer see to drive, there were so many tears so fast.

An hour later she drove the same misted way back in a wet and glistening rage. Mustang tires screeched the semicircular shell. The car door slammed with inadequate noise; she re-opened it and reslammed. Standing by the grass-and-tree planted island which was the front lawn, she pushed her face toward the misted moon and screamed.

Inside, Bettina had the dishwasher on and didn't hear her; Mamie Carter couldn't. They received Su's rage visually first, saw her fury before they heard—throbbing in white her face hit the kitchen like an explosion.

"I hate Kip! Hate her into the grave, hate her rotting corpse, sodden memory, hate her red hair which she was always combing in the sunlight, does anyone understand?"

Bettina set down her glass with a plop. "Suzy! What happened?"

Mamie Carter, who heard her very clearly, smiled and nodded approval.

"Nothing *happened*. I was supposed to be her pet. I was supposed to stay put. That was what happened: nothing. As soon as something began to happen, she fought it like a bull whale, flapping her flukes down on my head." Su stopped on the incongruity of Kip, bony even through alcoholic pudge, as a whale. "I remembered tonight because her counterpart was at the party. Peter Lyon." She laughed. "Roaring."

"Roaring drunk," Mamie Carter said. "How is he Kip's counterpart—besides the fact that they both scorched their hair?"

55

"He praised me." Su's fingers were stiff, arms angular, face atwist and reddening around the nose. "He praised me for balance, calm, dispassion. He called me a palliative upon the quarrels of the nation's culture. Not knowing what that polysyllabic word means," she shouted, "he used the one word from his own polysyllabic ignorance . . ."

"If he didn't mean it," Bettina said, "then you can't be angry . . ."

"Palliator!"

"What other compliments did he offer you?" Mamie Carter said with a twinkle, hugely enjoying the circumstance that she could hear every word without straining a bit.

"I'm neat!" Su screamed at her. "I'm as trim and tidy as a Whitman's Sampler, in mind and body. Not a bulge bulges its unspeakable stuffing into the circle of politeness. I explain but not too much. I object quietly. I laud in Latin symmetry. I am a poet of critics because he thinks poets are rhythmic little box-makers. I am too young to be garrulous, too old to shout. I am shouting now!" she shouted.

"You sure are," Mamie Carter said happily.

"I'm shouting because I am fuzzy, immature, obscene, excessive, loud, and . . . not even drunk." She fixed a splashed-together gin and water, splash on the counter, splash running down her hand, upraised for all to see. "See that splash sloppy Su made? Dribbling all over herself. Messy! I'm a palsied old woman and an impetuous young one, I'm skipping the middle altogether. Middle," she sneered. "*Middle.*" The word came out like liquid rot. Her top lip pushed up over the *m* as if it were a hump of rotten mush. "*Middle* him."

"Oh good," Mamie Carter said.

56

"Now, now, Suzy, calm down," Bettina said, putting her hand on Su's shoulder.

"No. I won't calm down."

"Oh good."

"And you too, Bettina." Su turned with such force that Bettina froze in her palliator pose. "You're always on the side of my bad half. You're always telling me that I'm tactful or that people like me. The highest compliment you have for me is that I'm attractive or poised or have taste or can talk to strangers or stand up straight or have a nice voice or like people or am never boring . . ."

"I fail to see what's so bad about that."

"That's the half that be*haves*. If it is half. More like three-quarters or ninety percent by now."

"But shrinking rapidly," Bettina said, her mouth narrowing.

"Good." Su closed her eyes and drank half her drink down fast.

"Good!" Mamie Carter said. She handed her glass to Bettina, who had to get up and refill it. After a pause, Bettina got up and took the glass, expressing through her clumsiness how unjust she thought it was that she be made drink-fetcher at forty-six just because she was youngest.

Mamie Carter's eyes were so bright and round that a child would have laughed with delight on the spot. Su stopped screaming. "I wish I were you," she said, her voice catching on *were* as if unused to the elegant subjunctive, stumbling over *you* because what she said was true.

"Oh, poopooh," Mamie Carter said softly. "Now you don't mean that, Su. Why, you wouldn't even have time to enjoy it, supposing you could be me; you'd hardly get used to looking alive when someone said, Mamie Carter,

57

before you'd be cold in your grave."

"Better cold inside my grave than freezing on its edge."

"Here you go, M.C.," Bettina said, putting her freshly-wrapped drink before her.

Mamie Carter, who had turned toward Bettina to thank her, therefore missing Su's last sentence, now looked straight ahead, pulling her chin up to point at the last row of a small theater. "I simply can't hear you when you speak behind my back, Su."

"Oh," Su said. "Oh. I've always known that; why do I behave as if you were pretending to be deaf?"

"Good," Mamie Carter said.

"Do you want to know what I'm really angry at—if I speak to your face?"

Mamie Carter settled back in the only kitchen chair with arms, snuggling her freshly-wrapped drink into her lap, and expressed her *yes* with a wideopen listening face.

"So do I," Bettina said.

Could she say . . .

In the mirror, from her eyes looking down at her crossed right knee, from her eyes looking down and feeling themselves looking down, sight tracing like fingers a path on each side of a nose she suddenly saw on another face; from hearing the *urhm* which unexpectedly cleared her throat—this instant but echoing through the hollows of her hearing as the identical sound she had known all her life . . . followed by a *clckclck* halfway

down the throat which only her
mother had been able to do: her
self had gone back and forth between her mother and her own
one all day.

today in the mirror . . .

Mother's face making its eyes
round as if Su weren't past fifty,
using a face to express her answer
like a girl whom everyone wanted
to watch, Mother's nose grown
long and bulbous, Mother's
pursed lips whose purselines remained etched beneath her pale
lipfuzz even when she relaxed
her mouth . . . Mother whom she
kept watch on all alone now and
would forever, because her
brother was dead and there were
no other children and none of
hers to keep watch on her face
and know it.

her face

watching her mother without letting on that she was watching
had occupied her childhood. Her
brother's too. Children knew
every tiny detail and change of
the face, knowing for their own
opportunities, protection, and
awesome love . . . until the face
was forgotten, lost among the
faces of a lover or child or animal

or stranger, covered over by the denial of your own busy grown-up life of looking and being looked at.

"Children are mother-watchers," Su said.

"Yes?" Mamie Carter said.

"All children. Mothers know that. If the mother doesn't talk, she gets her face watched even more. Constant attention." Su knew the surge of power that came from walking into an autograph party and having every eye turn on her, every smile settle on her lips alone. "It's the only attention my mother ever got so she stopped talking altogether."

"Now I have to disagree with you there," Mamie Carter said, hating the thought that *her* daughter might hate her like that.

"You couldn't know, Mamie Carter. You were an actress; you got other watchings. You didn't have to stop talking to your children." She waited until Mamie Carter's face resolved its frown and accepted her own blamelessness.

Bettina availed herself of the pause. "I don't know what you're talking about, Su, and I don't think you do either. Your mother talks to me at the drop of a hat."

"Tell her we're living together."

"She knows *that,* for petesake." A flush spread over Bettina's face and she hastily lit a cigarette.

"I watched my own face all day today . . ."

"I bet your boss liked that," Bettina said.

". . . it's turned into my mother's. I made my own face into hers so I could watch it to my grave and behave. I have her frown and disapproval shake and pursed cautious lips. It keeps me from talking to myself, too."

"What a shame," Mamie Carter said.

"I decided to tell my mother that Bettina and I are living together, I mean, that I like women ... that I'm a ... a ..."

"A lesbian," Mamie Carter said.

"Yes," Su whispered just as the flash caught her face in a prickle of clammy sweat.

5

SU THINKS she's the only one who's different,
Bettina said to the mirror inside a harness-yoke
which still smelled like mule sweat, hanging in
the front hallway. What about me? she said,
turning into the living room's gray ordered half-light. I am
not talking to myself, I am talking to you, she chuckled,
tapping her forefinger on the top of the console color
television.

It wasn't just that I couldn't go on in that office, among
the fall specials and children's programs, where I pretended
so smoothly to have accepted the family world that pretense made it true. She liked the sound of the last sentence and repeated it. Pretended so smoothly to have

accepted the family world that pretense made it true. "Pretend so smoothly," she said a third time, smoothly taking long dipping steps across the living room floor. Graceful inside, she poured one perfect jigger of rum into a red glass.

I don't know exactly how I am going to pretend that you are not in love with Mamie Carter, though—I am talking to you now, Su. Bettina poured in Tang and didn't watch, letting Tang rise over the surface tension rim of red glass, run over the edge, down the sides onto the *Su & Bettina* cocktail napkin.

It is certainly good to be alone . . . Nefertiti! Bettina hurried to the door to the back yard. "Oh, poor baby!" She cuddled the clipped head of her fat dog, avoiding the mouth's slobber. She patted Nefertiti's curly back, stroking while aware of stroking, speaking and hearing too quickly, insisting to that spaniel age that they were both perfectly sane. Together. "That's the word these days, Nefr," Bettina said, gratefully straightening up from the unbalanced patting position the short dog required. "Together we'll go fix your supper." She walked purposefully across the oak expanse, rattling all the unstable pieces in the room.

I am certainly not afraid of being insane, she said to the dog's dish, placed in the dishwasher in such a position that it would not get washed, cupped (again) too close to the plate ahead. I can calmly pick up your dish and rewash it, take out the steel wool and get the hardened food from last night off—I am not even angry at Su because she deliberately refuses to put your dish in the dishwasher in such a way that it might get clean. She does that to needle me . . . Bettina stopped to cough; smoke had caught on the chuckle. Need to needle! Su'll like that . . . cough replaced

63

chuckle entirely. Bettina coughed in huge gasps of cough, coughed to her belly, coughed as if the sides of her chest had to be pushed out of her body. Between spasms, she unzipped the large canvas bag she carried with her everywhere and reached into its interior, deftly reading the surfaces of the bottles like braille until her fingers closed around the one which contained her cough medicine and pulled it up. She knew every bottle by size, every packet by texture of paper, every bit of medicine she took by color and shape. Every bit of medicine she took? She took fifteen pills, three liquids, and four chewup tablets daily, counting vitamins, not counting an extra dose of hangover cure or the penicillin she kept always handy for a real flare-up of her bronchitis.

She waited, standing still, while the medicine calmed the cough and her body quieted down. Then she resumed washing Nefertiti's dish and promising the dog hamburger tidbits and her own array of pills and vitamins (she had heartworms).

The doorbell rang.

"Well, as I live and breathe!" Bettina grinned at the small fat boys grubbily present when she opened the door. "Howdy, howdy!" She stepped back to let the boys and the fat woman with them enter the house. "What a pleasant surprise! What'll you have?" she said to Adele, her sister, ten years younger. "How's my favorite baby sister?" She grinned at Adele, meaning it, and gave her a kiss on the cheek.

"Do you have company?" Adele tried to look beyond into the hidden living room, preparing to meet at least Su.

"Not a living soul. Nefertiti and I were just having a little drink. Welcome, welcome."

Bettina watched Adele as she talked, watched while fol-

lowing the ball game on television with one ear, watched
as Adele's face went through circles of memory, pleasing
Bettina, causing her to smile inside at a plump five-year-old
singing, ringlets cuter than Shirley Temple's; watched as
Adele used adult muscles, twitches unknown to Bettina,
frowns which shut out her sister, made her ache to comfort Adele. She was frowning now.

Bettina waited, hearing the score, missing everything up
to "hospital."

". . . hospital. Did Mummy tell you?"

"No!"

"It's not serious." Adele bit her lip, leaving lipstick on
the bottom of her front teeth. "I'm having a polyp removed from the mouth of my uterus. It blocks the uterus
apparently."

"My goodness. Is it serious?"

"No. It acts like a flap shutting off the womb." Adele
shook out one of Bettina's cigarettes. "I wish you didn't
smoke mentholated." She lit the cigarette stiff-fingered,
facing Bettina with half-manicured white nails. "It just
means I can't get pregnant."

"Things are tough all over," Bettina said with a chuckle,
having just caught a nose-wrinkle from Adele the toddler.
"However much you make love, you just can't get pregnant? Some people have all the luck."

"I want another baby." Adele the petulant adult pouted, plumpness looking less adorable, more self-indulgent.

"Well, if that means that Doug has finally got a job, I'm
glad." Bettina kept her voice reserved; she was the oldest;
she picked up both their glasses and refilled their drinks.

"Mummy has plenty of money and you know it. She's
just full of poor talk—all that business about taxes. Why,
Doug said Fo'mother left her half a million dollars."

Bettina returned with full glasses. "And what did Fo'mother leave Doug?"

"Everything that's mine is Doug's and you know it!" Adele half rose as if testing her instincts: was the insult to Doug such that it demanded she leave? "I love him and if he had money he'd certainly share everything with me. I know it." Adele drank three fast swallows as if swallowing tears. "If anybody's going to insult Doug I'm leaving."

Bettina's heart could not bear what her mind insisted upon, but with enough rum and Tang her mind could accommodate itself to her heart's most outrageous request. Adele, her face puffed from something other than either food or tears, pouted with lips like Betty Grable and eyes much rounder; Bettina saw the little girl she took everywhere for ten years and chaperoned for another five; Bettina saw the child she felt she had had when her mother indicated that she didn't mind at all if Bettina, then ten, took over baby Adele in all her manifestations. Since a roundfaced roundeyed instantly responsive and happily adoring baby was Bettina's idea of what a baby should be, Bettina often said, even after Adele become ten and rather tall and overweight, "Tell'em you're *cuter* than Shirley Temple."

She closed her eyes and drank three gulps of her own drink. Everyone drank more these days. Su would say it was because of cultural apathy but Bettina thought it was Watergate. Vietnam and then Watergate. Why single out Adele?

If that face was going to fall apart, if that perfection of memory was going to acquire bourbon scars through rosebuds—if what should remain a circle under the eye was going to take a bizarre downward swipe through the bone, a diagonal dent of drunkenness . . . Bettina held her anger in by contracting all the muscles of her mind. At the Country Club the drink was called a Shirley Temple. Bettina had never tasted it, had ordered it for Adele with exultation: it came pink with cherries and a mint sprig in summer, a long striped straw, and was probably gingerale underneath.

"I just saw a picture of you putting vodka in your Shirley Temple. Vodka drinkers think you can't smell it, but you can. It doesn't still smell the next morning, that's all." Bettina reached to hold Adele's hand. She wished she did not say things like she was now going to say. "Baby, *please* watch your drinking."

"Don't you tell me—don't you ever tell me about what to watch when you're the original drunk of the family, the family drunk, the town drunk . . ."

Bettina felt swamped by that violent face. She shivered and closed her eyes. Su was going to leave her because she was a drunk. It doesn't take x-ray vision to see that, that's for sure, she cried inside. Maybe you never did love me, Su; just accepted my gifts of costumes and props. You played those parts, my paper doll with black hair and blue eyes— you let me put you on every stage I found, you fit into all the cardboard boxes I cut into theaters and you swayed in every position in your paper dresses, scarves flimsily tabbed around your neck, onto your wrists, triangular off your hair. Queen of Scarves. I'm a fat slob dreaming of a woman who can wear scarves, whose neck is slender and chin high above it, over whose beautiful shoulders a scarf fits with motion and grace . . . every woman with a short neck and a sloping chin, with upper arms like clubs and a walk that rearranges the body at every heavy step, wants you to love her, so do I, Su.

"Are you crying?"

"Yes." Crying, Bettina felt like a puddle of blubber.

"Have you eaten today? You know you should eat."

"Let me eat as little as possible for jesus sake, Adele!"

Adele's mouth froze half-open. "Sister," she demanded of the past. "Sister, pull yourself together."

"I'm sorry. Dell, I'm really sorry. I didn't mean to be such a crybaby." Bettina's apology was barely whispered, barely audible, half sigh, half sob of apology.

She let Adele urge her into the kitchen; she fixed them a bacon and cheese and tomato sandwich and a glass of Carnation Instant for vitamins. As soon as she was finished, she put the dishes in the sink and fixed another rum and Tang.

"I'll wash these later," she said, running water onto the cheese-spotted rotobroil pan, their plates and knives and forks. "If I wash up as soon as I've finished eating, I feel like I haven't eaten at all. You know?"

Adele laughed. "Yeah." She found an oreo to eat with her drink, and another. She made a stack of oreos on the counter and sat back on her stool. "It's like brushing your teeth right after eating. If you clean out the frying pan, you take away all the taste."

"It's good to see you laugh." Bettina sat below her in a chair. "Really good."

"I know it," Adele said.

6

NSIDE the drawer that morning there was a typewritten
sheet from Sister Gin:

You are smothered by Bettina and her mothering, her
breast which works in reverse to suck back juices
from your mouth. Her reassurances leave you filled
with rage, to vent into soft air.

The best women do not see beyond their daily pleasures; what makes them feel good is no more than
what has always set women up—flattery, prettiness
and smiles, attention. In the new wave of women,
everyone tumbles over each other like periwinkles
racing to get stranded on the sand. Us old periwinkles
who have been beached before shout with a mouthful
of salt. Salt is full of savor here in the breakers;

wherewith shall it be sweetened? My thirst . . .

Oh, S.G. Your thirst is legion. Have a salty dog then, briny bitch.

. . . has hands. My . . .

Your thirst has hands? Sister G., those are purple words. A blue periwinkle whose thirst has hands is a metaphor that carries many colors on its back. You are coated like your tongue today, Gin.

. . . has hands. My words may make you laugh from your height, Su, but they race from my right brain faster even than periwinkles in a fast surf and I leave you to edit. You locked your drawer last week and shut me out. You use wooden means to block me. Take my thirst's hand. I am your friend, S.G.

Su's heart soared. "Wooden means to block you? Very sound language. Shouting in the wave hasn't dampened your spirits, sister dry gin. There's proof in the old bottle. Limp messages and hard stuffing. Sis, I think I'll leave you a letter tonight."

Dear Friend, it is Mamie Carter that I love and how preposterous it is I know from my beginnings. That she with all the world behind her could let me stroke her parchment skin—I would sand the whorls off my fingertips to avoid scratching that silk. But how bored she would be with being adored, now. She is only interested in a new adventure, and I am so sodden with admiration of her I could never dare even frame a sentence without endlessly questioning my brain to see if it would offend. My dream is to sit at her feet and hers to be pulled to standing. It takes a strong woman to turn her dream inside out to love her lover. Dreams hold their tender side in. You are the only strength I know, Sister. Can you help me before the callouses come? Yours, Su.

Su sailed into her driveway that evening and glided to rest at the door, where her feet took over and skipped. "There is only one perfect joy in the world," she said aloud. "Only one perfect one. To put a letter into a—well, mailbox, the letter to your future."

She packed her car for a weekend in the mountains at her cabin, now the retirement home of her mother and father.

"Are you going away?" Bettina wanted to talk about Adele.

Four words from Bettina was too much intrusion; each syllable scratched the image of Mamie Carter hanging in her mind's image chamber, six gross cuts marring that face perfectly scratched already by time. "I know I told you last week I was going to the cabin." Su softened her voice to a flat whisper. No scratches from there.

"Did you? I forgot. Adele . . ." the name screeched ". . . Adele came over today."

Adele was an inchwide gash on a five-inch surface. "Oh?" There was nothing to say about Adele that would help. To Su, she was either the human experiment that was the final damnation of god or the test case to prove salvation, depending upon one's despair-hope ratio. Su pushed despair away from her perfect joy. "Are things improving, I hope?"

"Not a prayer."

"But not worse?"

"She wants to have another baby."

"That is worse."

"Well, *you*'d think so." Bettina turned her massive back and strode to the bar. "It just so happens that she is the only one of us daughters likely to have any grandchildren for Mummy and she's thirty-three and if she wants to have another baby she should have it now and not wait and have a Mongolian idiot when she's forty." It was true that you could hear Bettina the length of the living room with her back turned better than you could hear most people in the next space over.

"Nothing in her current offspring indicates that she is prejudiced against idiots." Su's voice carried three feet at night.

"What?"

"I said, she's a dedicated mother. Maybe she'll have a girl."

"Dedicated?"

"Accepting. Look, I just meant she doesn't force her kids to grow into a mold. She lets them be. They'll fit perfectly into the world." As it is. Two can be the devil and the other two the hindmost. "Adele will be fine. Don't worry," Su said, running up the stairs.

What does reassurance cost me? Mamie Carter's image, battered, striated, gashed, fading, faint now, spotlight tactfully off, could be restored in the car. Fifty miles out of town, the outlines reappeared. Mamie Carter smiled snugly behind Su's eyes. We are going to the mountains, love, Su said. Brush your perfect eyes into my inside forehead. We have hours among the pine trees before you meet my mother. Well, I rented it to them, in a sense. They retired and appeared. They wanted to be my dependents. Better in the mountains than in the house. Parents can't live forever, Mamie Carter, Su said aloud, knowing they could.

Then we will have the cabin for our own.

Mamie Carter, Bettina's Mummy, and Su's class-conscious mother were exactly the same age: seventy-seven.

Slowly her mother's and Bettina's Mummy's faces appeared at opposite sides of Mamie Carter's image, pushing against the middle like two men crowding a beautiful woman for a penny-arcade photo. Her mother's face, full from the front and angular in profile, horrifyingly like her own, pushed with the sharp hostility of its pursed mouth with radial lines, its gaunt but dewlapped cheeks, its five frown lines fighting into its nose which, dominant from birth, had grown as noses do long after the other human parts had had the good taste to stop. Su forced her mind to see her mother's eyes as color not disapproval. Blue like her own, unmixed with gray or green—startlingly blue among the cornflowers of Montgomery once. Su widened them and sent them back to the flower patch. They were eyes that could cry and crinkle. They were once . . . too vivid now, all Su could see of her mother's face was the eyes. Blue eyes can't hold the wells of sadness that brown eyes can, but these eyes represented on her mind were as sad as their blue allowed. Su felt a shudder inside her ribs. Mother! The date. Today is . . . Hubertjunior's birthday and tomorrow the anniversary of his death.

She saw from the junction of Route 52 that she had forty miles to go. We had two hours, Mamie Carter, before they came. Now I have to decide whether I should pull off and bring Mother something; I won't—it is time enough after thirty years to let lapse commemoration and decently forget such a day. Although Mother won't. I could stop for —a birthday cake with black icing? a case of beer to get through it? a nonfunereal plant that no one will mistake

73

for a wreath but Mother will put in her Hubertjunior window along with the others?

All the faces were gone. Bettina's Mummy's, barely noticed, had disappeared with the rest. Her mind simply reflected the pine trees, exuberant now, crowding the air, smelling up the road with their pitch.

From the bend, her cabin nestled like the fantasy she had copied when building it—low down like a cave into the pines. That fantasy had won over its rival—a shelf high up in the pines—partly because of the huge expense and the nature of pine trees, partly because she had needed to snuggle at the time, and less to soar. If the treehouse, the soaring, had won, her parents could not have considered renting the house and it would still be hers. If she had been less realistic, reality would have rewarded her.

From the inside, the cabin was unrecognizable as any fantasy: carefully tightened and made efficient for two other people, the walls and floors hidden by her mother's plants and rugs and shelves she had insisted upon her father's building—to occupy him, make his retirement therapeutic, its appearance said the occupants planned to endure for a very long time.

"It's Suann," her mother told her father. "I told you she wouldn't be here before nine."

"Do I have the only father who can't recognize his daughter by sight?" Su kissed her father first and her mother twice—that cheek was down, its smell bottled, its age the same as her love's; that face was as female as the other, as deftly marked by a life of being in charge of unimportant things—children, a hat department, dying. Her mother's cheek withdrew the second before the second kiss was finished.

74

"Mother, you look wonderful. Are you . . ."

"How's Bettina?" Her mother was quickly at the stove. "I declare, that girl's a sight. We sure enjoy her, Dad and I. She makes you feel so good with her funny tales—she could make the devil himself die laughing. I guess you're lucky to have such as Bettina for a roommate."

"We're lovers, Mother." Su tried the words very softly.

"Course it keeps the men away—a roommate, I mean. I know I've told you this, Suann—if you want to get married you don't want to appear too set up already. Better to live alone and let them see you're available." A plate of pork chops and grits and sliced tomatoes appeared on the table. "Sit down, Suann. We've eaten—Dad gets hungry up here pretty early and I guess it's pretty near our bedtime at this hour, but you eat. What will you have to drink?"

"I'll have a beer—I brought some."

"Well, let me see if I can fit it in the frigidaire," her mother—Shirley—said. "We only go to market once a week if we can help it and it's pretty full in there. Maybe I can just set it outside? You can drink that little bit tonight— Dad'll probably help you some." She put the two six-packs out the door like dirty shoes. "Well, you look tired, Suann. How are you feeling? And how is Bettina? You should have brought her with you."

"We're not lovers, Mother."

"Su*ann*!" She stood behind Su's father with her hands on his shoulders like an older sister. "Your dad and I don't listen to gossip like that. Wait, I'll get you a glass for your beer." Shirley poured a glass for Hubert, letting foam fill the upper half. She saw no need to drink beer at all—there was something about the amount of it that seemed gross, as if there were a large belly to fill up, as if it could only be drunk in gulps followed by belches (a noise, among many others, which she still thought was a personal insult).

"I'll get a glass," Su said. "The pork chops are really delicious."

"Well, you know how I feel about pork chops but your father had to raise a pig this summer and now we're stuck with all that pork." Her distress at being so close to the bottom of the class larder made her finger her hair, a thing she had always pulled Su's hand away from if she caught it. She caught it herself and laughed. "Well, at least it isn't horsemeat. Suann, remember that time when you ate the dogfood?" She turned to Hubert. "Remember, Hubert? It was when frozen horsemeat came in and a big skillet of it was sitting on the stove the summer Hubertjunior had that police dog and Suann ate it for lunch! I'll never forget it. And you thought it was good, too, didn't you?"

"A little strong." Su's stomach swayed at the memory; as a lover of horses, as a horse herself in girl's skin, she had felt like a cannibal.

"I'll never forget it," Shirley chuckled.

"You know, other countries eat horsemeat regularly," Su said. "It's a delicacy in France."

"Well, this horsemeat was probably from some old spavined mule who just fell down one day," Shirley said. "I guess even a jaded Frenchman would think twice about that. But now, this is nothing to talk about at the table. You go on and eat now before everything gets cold."

The room was so hot Su could not tell whether she was flashing or legitimately sweating; every chink of the house was plugged against the crisp mountain air, holding in the room's own smells of pork chops and motherscent and bottled gas and beer. After dinner they discussed the house: built three years ago by Su, occupied one and a half now by Shirley and Hubert, certain areas of responsibility were still mingled and they went over the insurance and the utilities and the roof leak and a recent trash-burning law and the new linoleum they wanted to get to cover the bare floor in the bathroom. By nine-thirty Su felt like a prison guard making endless cell-checks. Each corner was flashlighted for a possible leak, each wall for a foreboding message, each seam for a crack of betrayal.

At ten Su kissed her mother goodnight. In the bath-room mirror she saw the face she had just kissed—her own, drawn, gray, hollow-eyed.

"Mother," Su said the next afternoon, after all the forms had been put in their envelopes ready to mail or file, and the two of them had agreed on a cup of tea. "I want to tell you something. I'm a lesbian, you know." The last two words were included as buffer, so *lesbian* would be surrounded with palatable monosyllables, but after they were said Su wondered if her mother did know in fact.

"Now, Suann," Shirley said after a sip of tea. "You're just saying that because you don't want to have children."

"No, I'm not. Bettina and I . . ."

"What's gotten *into* you?" Shirley's spoon clicked angrily against the china. "I'm not going to listen to that for a minute. Why, Bettina's just a little heavy for most men these days. If she'd lose some weight . . . and *you*. You're just too particular. I used to think you were going to walk through the forest and pick up a crooked stick but now I see you're not even going to do that, and I'm resigned to the fact that we'll never have a grandchild. That's just the way it's going to be. That's all. Now that's enough to say about that on Hubertjunior's death anniversary."

"He couldn't have had a baby for you either." She saw the radial lines of her mother's upper lip deepen as the mouth set its silent answer. "I'm in the middle of meno-pause now, and not just to keep you from having a grand-child. I thought maybe we could talk. How was it for you? I'm finding it pretty miserable."

"I stopped having the curse just after Hubertjunior died. I guess I thought . . ." Her hand stopped stirring in midair. She was looking out the window. "I guess I thought I was going to have another baby. I thought, well, the Lord taketh away and the Lord giveth back."

Su reached for her mother's hand and held it a second before it ran to its own lap.

"No, don't feel sorry. I wasn't sure I liked the exchange one bit. I thought . . . that God was mocking me."

"Mother! I didn't know anything about anything at the time . . ."

"You don't need to, your body'll tell you all you need to know soon enough. I just can't separate the loss of the one thing from the loss of the other, in my mind. It was just one big year of loss."

"I want it to be the beginning of something for me." Su felt too close to those symbolic eyes, as if they would draw her under. "For one thing, I'll never have a grandchild for you. I guess I never was going to, but now we both know it. Like you said, that's the way it is. Can't that be a begin-ning of us being friends—me not feeling guilty and you not hoping and being disappointed? That's why I told you I am a lesbian. I wanted us to be able to talk. I am, Mother. I really like women—their minds, their company, every-thing about them. I . . . we're the only two women in the family. Always were. Doesn't that give us . . ."

Shirley got up and walked over to Hubertjunior's plant-filled window. Her body moved only its legs. Once they stopped, nothing moved at all.

"Why won't you talk to me?" Su whispered. Menopause was going to make her cry. Her estrogen level plummeted. Tears rushed from her abdomen, the uterus itself, poured upward to her head stopping her breathing. Talk isn't obscene!

But nontalk was. The warm surge of fluid through her body, ending as tears, brought the urge to throw herself into her mother's arms and sob into her neck, grip her mother in a hug so tight she would have to say at least *help*. And Su would help her over to the couch and rock her bony body in her arms, crooning I love you, stroking I'll help you, kissing I am you.

Su walked over to her mother and lay an inadequate hand on her shoulder, terrified that that face would turn and confront her. "Mother, don't turn your back on me," she said. No answer. "Please don't turn your back on me." The face turned, surprisingly sad, not at all frightening. "I just want to talk to you, that's all." Su's hand was cupped off-shoulder.

"You call it *talk*. But it's analyze and argue until I'm left with nothing to say—I haven't changed my mind underneath, I'm just whipped down." Shirley walked firmly back to the couch and sat, hands in her lap. "I'll talk—if you *talk*."

"What do you want to talk about?"

"Well, why don't you start by telling me what you've been doing—that kind of talk."

"You mean, let's just gossip."

"Sure. Do you know any good gossip? Now that Bettina . . ."

"Well, Bettina's sister Adele is going into the hospital to have a polyp removed from her uterus. It prevents conception and she wants to have another baby."

"Poor child. What's a polyp?"

"It's a flap, a growth of skin."

"Well, she's right to have her babies while she's still young."

"And I told you I was going to have a radio show? I know I wrote you."

Shirley shook her head. "No, you didn't. Or maybe you mentioned it but tell me about it. A radio show? You always were an actress. Does it pay?"

"Fifty dollars a week. That's not much but . . ."

"That's *fine*. Why. I'm real proud of you." Shirley's sharp eyes pierced their blue into Su's, like hitting like. "What's it about?"

"You know something? I got the idea from you. No, really . . ." Su leaned toward her mother's withdrawing, shaking head. "You remember when we were little, you had those book nights where you all sat around and talked about a book you'd read that week? *I* remember—Hubert-junior and I used to sit on the stairs and listen because you all used to laugh so hard."

"We chose a book we wanted to read, not one of those books we were supposed to be reading."

"That's it. That's what I'm doing on the radio. The listeners choose the books. You must have liked to talk once."

"I guess I did!" Shirley's face was rocking itself. "I never could get used to sitting home night after night while your father . . . and I felt uncomfortable playing bridge."

"Me, too. I hate card games."

"Card games are all right. I just felt uncomfortable. You're supposed to talk and you're not supposed to talk. Well, but we didn't really talk about books either. None of us knew anything."

"Why did you stop—the book nights, I mean?"

"Oh, the books all started to be about sex." Shirley laughed. "We all wanted to read them but we got embarrassed talking about . . . it was too intimate. I think it was *Gone With the Wind* that finished us off. Marietta—you remember Marietta Bowen, she was the lingerie buyer? She went home that night so flushed her husband called up your father! He thought . . . did you read *Gone With the Wind*?"

"Three times."

"Well, there you are."

Su laughed. "That's wonderful."

"Are you going to analyze it now? Tell me what it all meant, that we all had hangups because we didn't wet the bed?" Shirley prepared to get up.

"No, I laughed because I thought you all started feeling love for each other—in a *good* way, I mean," she said to her mother's back. The tears that had gathered behind her eyes earlier ready to pounce slunk back down now, down through her throat and deep into her belly where they froze into salty lumps.

The sound of Hubert splitting logs was muffled through the walls they had tightened last summer; it was sound like a cat's purring, a rhythmic but irregular patting on her ears. It was the only sound in the house now that Su had gone. "Suann shouldn't say that word," Shirley said aloud. "Just listen to me. I won't talk? I talk to myself the whole time. I remember when I first caught myself, talking to myself like an old lady. And then I thought—*said*, well, what's wrong with it? Suann doesn't remember that whole year when she wouldn't say a word, just snarled. Good morning, Suann, Hubert would say at breakfast and Suann would snarl. How was school? I'd ask at dinner and she would snarl. *Unh* was all we ever got out of her. Good morning. *Unh.* How was school? *Unh.*" Shirley chuckled. But she shouldn't say that word. It isn't a nice word. "People don't care what you do as long as you don't tell them about it. I know that."

It was going to rain and her body had its depression ready. She sat back on the couch watching the clouds darken themselves, roll together like huge balls of soot. She fingered her hair. She put both hands to her head and slowly pulled out straight the coarse, kinky gray hairs—not pulling them out, just stretching each one into a long straight hair, sometimes using one hand alone, sometimes both. She stretched the hairs until her arms grew tired but the urge to stretch hairs was still present. It had nothing to do with the way her hair looked; the hairs shrank back to kinks with each washing, but it satisfied her hands, especially the fingers.

"Well, if she's not going to get herself a husband she better get herself a little more gumption. That's what I think. She's her own worst enemy—analyzing everything the whole time, trying to figure out what'll happen before she even starts. I wasn't like that. Was I?" She retrieved the image of herself at fifty—so incredibly young it now seemed that she splashed herself with the memory. "She's got her whole life ahead of her, all she needs is a little courage. Well, not the courage to say that word but the gumption to get on that radio program and tell 'em who she is and make 'em listen." I heard you, Suann. I want to talk to you too, I always have. You're the only one I ever wanted to talk to—but you were so willful! The talk always led to arguing! Never thought I had anything important to say, never agreed with me just to keep me talking and listening, even. You have to agree every once in a while. "Whether you do or not and that's the truth."

Still, I thought we were getting along better these last two years—Suann had softened and I, I just slowed down. I don't know why you had to spoil this weekend too, daughter. Tears rolled down her cheeks and she let them. "I know I didn't behave right but you . . . didn't . . . I did not behave right. It's a fact. I forget how old I am. Everyone who looks at me now has to look at this face, even Suann. When those earnest young faces say something, even criticism is softened because the other person's eyes see such gentleness. Likewise *all* comments are heard as criticism when the other sees the harsh mean lines of an old face like mine. Old people turn into flatterers because that's the only way they can get by. They have to laugh when they make a joke because that's the only way a joke is seen as a joke. And I forget. I look at Suann and I think I still look like that and I don't make allowances for what she's looking at. What happened to those kind old faces I remember from my childhood? Flatterers. All of them were. Well, I can write Suann a letter and tell her how proud I am of her and her radio show." Shirley sat still on the couch. Hubert's chopping had stopped so she lowered her voice to a whisper. "*Gone With the Wind.* Umhmm."

She cradled the telephone in the bedroom like an alcoholic holding an unopened bottle. The telephone number she knew like a birthday sank in a muddy memory. She would not call if she could not remember the number. That was the test, memory her permission—her mind was clogged with four-digit numbers but the number sought had long ago been changed to five and then six and finally seven. There were only ten to choose from.

Minutes later, she dialed the area code and her finger

dialed successively seven digits in an order known to it. If it was the wrong number, she would not try again. She would take only one chance.

"Marietta?" she said clearly, the voice's brief "Hello?" being all the proof and permission in the world. "This is Shirley." . . . "Fine!" . . . "Just fine!" . . . "Marietta, for some reason I was thinking about those book nights we had—do you remember?" . . . "The high point of mine, too. I hardly read a book from one month to the next, now. I don't see how we read so much, looking back on it. Worked all day, kept house at night, and still we read all those books. I guess we really wanted to know about life then." . . . "Fantasy?" . . . "You think so? Maybe we just didn't know how else . . . but here, it's so *nice* to hear your voice right in this room!"

There was the quiet sound of a receiver being lifted on an extension telephone—at which house, Shirley did not know. She broke the connection with her finger the second the sound registered as a receiver being lifted—her memory finger.

7

DR. AMBROSE had changed his entire staff since she had last been here. Shirley sat down after an unwelcome hug from Dr. Ambrose himself, a hug she felt pressed her body unnecessarily close to his. He was almost as old as she was, certainly over seventy, a good-looking man always. She had learned that handsome people were handsome forever, at all ages; however they might worry, they never grew unhandsome, merely an older handsome. The fortunate ones knew that. She sighed and picked up *Newsweek*; it worked in reverse too. Nongood-looking people simply never caught up, never became anything except an older nongood-looking.

Dr. Ambrose's office tended to force such thoughts. It was not surprising that his staff had changed. He was a hard man to get along with—domineering, brooking not one question, expecting (and by bad temper getting) exact compliance. Good looks and bad temper—was it a typically Southern combination? And he chose his staff, as near as she could tell, not for competence but for style. Every woman who had worked for him for the past twenty-five years had been a near-copy of the current . . . not *Vogue* or *Mademoiselle* but—Shirley smiled at the memory—the Sunday fashion ads of Everitt-Buelow's, their Montgomery department store whose clothes interpreted Paris designs in sleeveless pastel linen.

But it was surprising to see the middle-aged woman in Dr. Ambrose's coy white uniform standing in the door-way. "Mrs. McCulvey? Will you come in now, please?" She was one of the nongood-looking at any age. Because she also spoke with an accent, Shirley decided she must be a foreign-trained dentist who could not practice here, thus affording Dr. Ambrose professional skills at a dental assistant's wages.

She led Shirley into the x-ray room. Dr. Ambrose had acquired a machine which moved itself around her jawline. The assistant carefully fitted Shirley's chin into a metal holster which held her head forward of her body as if she were to be guillotined. The blunt nose of the instrument ran around her lower jaw, was raised, repeated its run around her upper jaw. Panic seized her. She wanted to jerk her head back but was momentarily paralysed. She felt her father gripping her head with his knees seventy years before, holding it too long for the joke. Seconds later, the assistant freed her head.

"How awful," Shirley said, shaking her head to toss off

anxiety like gnats. The assistant looked puzzled.

But her hands were cool and delicate. She settled Shirley smoothly into the chair, tilted her to weightlessness and gently placed the mask of laughing gas over her nose, leaving her to tranquilize herself for Dr. Ambrose.

"Tell Dr. Ambrose I don't want to stay under this gas too long."

She smiled. "Just to relax. He likes his girls without worry, not all tense. It's just to calm and relax you."

"Please tell him anyway." The tone of Shirley's voice disturbed the smile on the assistant's face. Her eyes met Shirley's. She nodded.

The first breaths of gas lifted her head just as the plane had as it swooped her airward, leaving her lap pushed down against the seat as if that part of her were in the secure grip of a motherhug. Marietta had said, last evening, soon after Shirley arrived, "So I have your vain hope that you can save those last six teeth to thank for this visit?" Shirley had laughed. "No, Dr. Ambrose has his fee to thank you for. It was the only way I knew how to come see you. Hubert respects health. He doesn't respect anything but that, either." But she hadn't told Marietta that Hubert did not even know she was here. I mustn't giggle, she reminded herself. The gas might make me do that. I don't want to laugh out loud. She giggled out loud but not loud. Let them hear me. Let them say, There's old Mrs. McCulvey giggling on the gas.

They had talked so fast, sitting in the crackling sunshine with the air metallic from chrysanthemums—Shirley's brain was spinning with how much they had said in an hour, in four hours, four years to cover, not a whole minute's halt to leave some part quiet, some experience to come. Tonight they could slow down, they were caught up and could slow down, four years pinned down they could slow up. Marietta's face as a little girl wrapped around her eyes and cheeks in a kiss of brown and white; the brown of Marietta's eyes and hair and the off-white of her nine-year-old skin had fixed those colors into her soul in the fourth grade. No other colors had ever held the beauty of that combination for her; for nearly seventy years that glow of brown and just-off-white ruled her taste and banished all other colors, all, to the realm of the slightly fake.

Marietta's hair was now the just-off-white and her eyes still the same shining birthday-brown of memory. "Actually, Hubert doesn't know I'm here," she had wanted to say, but Marietta was turning down the other twin bed in her own room for Shirley. A cream-colored blanketcover with lace overlay a pale yellow blanket collared with a sheet whose yellow-embroidered hem matched that of the two pillow cases. Marietta's linen shop provided bedclothes more luxurious than Shirley had ever known but more luxurious than even that was the fact that she was sharing a room with Marietta, had not been put in a guest room as she had expected . . . for the first time since they were children they were spending the night together, a treat that having husbands efficiently and wordlessly prevented.

Propped up on down pillows, they talked some more, just as they had years and years ago—Shirley trying to sip a Tom Collins which was her second since dinner and was making her head wild and free and her tongue clumsy, Marietta smoking cigarettes and tapping them constantly into the ashtray. It was too late to say Hubert didn't know she was here because Marietta had just said that she had had to fight depression every day during all those years. In the entire time they had worked together at Everitt-Buelow's, she in the hat department and Marietta in lin-

88

gerie, then she head of the hat department and Marietta
head of lingerie (but it happened in reverse order), during
all their lunches and Saturdays and one year of book
nights, Shirley had felt that her link to being alive was
Marietta, beginning in childhood when Marietta had dared
and Shirley had almost always dared to follow.

Not being born in Montgomery's top drawer, but in the
drawer just below the top one, she was saved from playing
the worst of the Southern roles (but so was Shirley). Just
fifty, her own lingerie and linen shop which served Montgomery's top drawer—filled it—barely a year old, she had
run for the school board (Shirley, still at Everitt-Buelow's,
had not dared admit she was voting for her). And won.
Knowing no more than anyone else what to do with a city
which paved only its white streets, Marietta had campaigned
on the slogan that education was a business, its inventory
children, and had even had a cross burned on her front
lawn. Shirley saw a fiery cross now before her closed eyes
and shivered. She reached up and took the mask off her
nose. Dr. Ambrose was taking too long. And she was too
old to be frightened so much; there was nothing left but
death and *that* was as near toothless now as herself.

"Dr. Ambrose!" she called.

He came and put the mask back on her nose. "Shirley,
I'm going to take off that front bridge now, okay?"

She nodded.

"What brings you back to Montgomery now?"

"I can't talk clearly to you," she said, her voice furry.

Dr. Ambrose nodded to the assistant who moved closer.
"Open, please." He put the plastic sucker under her tongue.
"Now, Shirley, we're going to cavitron the front teeth."
He reached over and turned up the gas. "And then I'm
going to fit you for a new bridge. This one is broken clean

in two." Several hammer taps and the air on her filed front teeth was an ice of yellow in her mind.

"Oooh, if she only knew! Huh, Doctor?"

Shirley felt his scowl, heard his muttered, "She can hear you." He switched his voice to hearty. "Now, Shirley, this is going to feel like running under the hose."

I've seen them, she said silently to the assistant. I'm not here for beauty. I'm here to see my friend.

"Just like playing in the hose on a summer afternoon. Little naked children without a care in heaven. You know what the little boy said to the little girl when he turned the hose on her?" Dr. Ambrose left the room.

Shirley forced her mind to refuse the image, pushed it back with all her strength; it was crowding in at the top of the screen, wiggling downward. She squeezed with all her might but it came brazenly in and suddenly she felt her saliva gland under her tongue shoot a stream of water like a hose. She opened her eyes in time to see it splatter the glasses of the assistant. She was wide awake now. The gas was without effect.

She stared at the eyes of the assistant until they turned to hers. "Do you feel pain?"

"Yes," Shirley tried to say.

The assistant left and returned with Dr. Ambrose, who increased the gas. "She doesn't feel pain," he said and left.

Shirley held those eyes. They moved on and off Shirley's for five, ten minutes while the cavitron ran deep into the gumline of her six remaining teeth. Shirley's eyes said pain. She gripped that message, held it tight through the assault of gas until she felt her consciousness snap and her head clear with an enormous throbburst of reality. The assistant turned off the cavitron and Shirley's mind collapsed in exhaustion.

She brought Dr. Ambrose back. "I know she feels the pain," she said. Love filled Shirley like a bell. Dr. Ambrose took the assistant by the arm and led her to the window. "Look, do you see those two dogs over there, coming down the sidewalk? The big one is a male and he's a pointer and the little one, what's she called? She's got spots. Do you see that spot? Can you see all of her?"

Shirley concentrated on the assistant's will. "I don't see any dogs, Doctor." She turned from the window. Dr. Ambrose glared at Shirley and left the room. She closed her eyes gratefully. The gas claimed her rest.

Marietta has changed though in the last four years. Shirley saw two different faces of Marietta across her mind as she went back into the chill of nitrous oxide. Bold, her mindscreen answered. Bold—a word used to criticize women during most of Shirley's life. Bold, her ear heard now, played against the rhythm of the machine which sucked saliva from her mouth. She held the plastic sucking end between her teeth, releasing her delicate mouth from its excessive presence. What do you mean bold is beauty, what do you mean bold is beauty, the machine's motor beat into her ear's insides. With a flare of sparklers, she saw that the difference was due to the absence of Marietta's husband. His death had brought her life. Blaze of insight! Shirley wanted to jump out of the chair and shout. Her mind flamed with certainty.

Marietta came close to her then, singing the song that Shirley heard so distinctly yet so infinitesimally faint—a tune she could recognize only as poundingly familiar. Marietta whispered in her ear in tiny gusts of breath, saying, only I am here. Shirley's consciousness lay in the lap of her arrival as Marietta's face grew huge and bent like milk over her mind. Her mouth was glutinous and pressed in on itself

91

throbbing like jelly. Her nose smelled something she could not identify; she understood that it did not need to be identified—the smell contained the touch of all women and came from inside her own nose.

Someone entered the room and opened and closed three drawers with a lot of rattling. Shirley didn't open her eyes. "She's ready now, Doctor. I mean, she's . . . waiting—you can come now . . . I mean, Doctor, in here. *Oh.*" Shirley burst out laughing inside and opened her eyes and had them say, It's all right. "I don't know how to say it," the assistant apologized.

"Open, please." Dr. Ambrose pushed something onto each stub of a tooth, wiggling it with his fingers until it fit. "You know what the fat lady said when she was trying on a girdle?" He pushed and wiggled. Shirley's eyes held the assistant's in victory. Neither of them smiled the slightest smile. In a moment, a mold covered her teeth and she sank back into the semistate of nonpain.

Her mindscreen was now covered with reds and oranges which slowly faded to green. They had won, she and the other woman; the victory was orange and the afterworld green. Against his drugs and jokes, her old battered mind had stood up and now she and the assistant and all women swam in a field of brilliant green, buoyed up by unbelievable green—gathered in a giant sweep all yellow and blue and scooped it into one untouchable safe sea of women.

She felt the mold pulled off with a suck, heard the cement being mixed on marble and smelled the strong sharp gluesmell as Dr. Ambrose moved the old bridge into her mouth. With a shove he fitted it back onto her stubs and held his finger on her palate while the pain brought her back to consciousness for an instant only. She inhaled deeply and cold gas rushed into her nose.

"Now hold it like this," Dr. Ambrose said, with his finger placing his assistant's finger on the bridge. "No, not there. Up farther. You haven't got the right spot." Shirley felt the touch of her delicate female finger press deep into her dream. The forces of joy were massing on the edges of her brain, expanding in a pure and thoroughly sensual happiness; the finger moved slightly and she felt her whole body being rocked inside. She gave herself up to its lulling. "Here, the spot is farther up, not down there," Dr. Ambrose said. "Don't you read *Ms.* magazine? Right here is the spot you want to put your finger on, this little place, see? It's just above the other . . ."

Too late, Shirley forced her mind back into resistance, pushing back the crowd of pleasure that was about to explode, had already built up to such an intense peak that there was no way she could stop it, no way to retrieve consciousness, no way to feel that firm female finger as anything other than . . . *"Oh!"* she gasped as her ravenous blood rushed to her face from her shame at such an orgasm and rushed and rushed until she was totally finished. She squeezed her eyes shut and knew there would never be a way to open them again. She heard Dr. Ambrose finally leave the room.

Dr. Ambrose had grabbed her on the way out. "Hey, not so fast. We need to make another appointment, Shirley." She could still feel his hand on her upper arm, still see his bland face as she jerked away muttering, "I'll call the office." Her knees were shaking but her head drove through the street now packed with afterwork crowds, pushed into and parted the stream of people as if it were a rabid dog dragging her body behind it.

"It was rape," she said to herself over and over, repeating the words like a chant. "It was rape. I was . . ." but *it* was all she could allow the words to say.

She reached the huge square at the other end of which sat the capitol, emptying itself also. The final joke of Dr. Ambrose's must have been a cartoon. She was sure. In *Playboy* or something—the scene was so vivid she was certain the joke had appeared, that everyone knew the joke but her.

She headed for the library, went straight to the periodical section. Aware that people stared, she pulled out *Playboys* and, for good measure, *New Yorkers*, several bound volumes at a time. She licked her finger to turn the pages rapidly; she scanned every cartoon with demon speed. After an hour, she was exhausted. Debilitated. Wrung out with failure. She left the library, knowing the joke was there buried in some magazine, eluding her—maybe even in a dental journal.

She recrossed the now totally empty square and, in front of the hotel, got in a taxi and returned to Marietta's.

But not to Marietta. The shame of her own thoughts left her pale and tongue-tied, which she felt as a lump of death. Metal doors slammed down with a clatter around her head. She barely heard Marietta's anxious supper conversation. As soon as she could escape from Marietta's presence, she went to the telephone upstairs and called Hubert, sobs of guilt making her words incoherent. Hubert thought she was crying because she hadn't told him she was going, had slipped secretly away. She promised him she would be on the early morning plane the next day. She was.

8

FIRST crack out of the box every morning Su says, "Are you going to get dressed today?" She's thin. Does she know what getting dressed is like if you're fat? First I have to take a bath. Fat people sweat in folded places thin people don't even have. It's not so hot taking a bath in this house because the tub is so small that by the time I am in it, there's room left for such a smidgen of water that I smell like soap all day. I really like tubs, though, and I need to lie in hot water and loosen up my chest. But I don't want to smell like soap so I have to take a shower after my bath. I have to stand in soapy lukewarm water around my ankles or get out and freeze while the tub emp-

95

ties. The shower takes all the curl out of my hair—Su doesn't understand that either since she wears her hair short and natural, but my hair is too fine and straight to do that and besides, have you ever seen a fat person with a short flat haircut? I'd look like a pinhead.

But say I've bathed and dried and am ready to get dressed. Now whatever I put on I'll look awful. For some reason fat clothes are cut more angular than thin clothes. They are always in squares so every fat bulge has some limp folds around it. And to look halfway decent in anything I have to put on a lot of underwear. My brassiere, for instance, is stitched and boned and cross-strapped because it really has to hold up the part of me that everybody likes big except on a fat woman. Needless to say, after I have it on I don't feel all that relaxed and loose with those straps cutting into my shoulders. And I always seem to be trying on clothes when I have a girdle on, then having to wear the girdle forever afterwards. I just can't go downtown without a girdle, for one thing. And I can't look in those mirrors with the girdle on and see how fat I am and *then* ask for the next bigger size so that at least when I am home alone I can wear something with just regular underwear. I can only think of how fat I am and imagine that I will go on a diet and then these clothes will fit without a girdle.

Most girdles don't really work without stockings to hold them down. I buy a lot of girdles with tags that swear up and down they don't need stockings, but they do. Even if you're going to wear pants. So I have a great choice: to wear slacks over my girdle and stockings or go on and put on a dress. Since the whole point of slacks being comfortable got lost when I put on all that other, and since my calves and ankles are the thinnest part of me, I figure I might as well put on a dress and look better (you've seen slacks where you could see those little triangles with folds of bumpy stockings over them).

If I'm going to put on a clean dress and all, I might as well dress for what I'm going to do today. And I haven't decided that yet.

But Su says, "Are you going to get dressed today?" at eight o'clock in the morning as if it hurts her that I intend to drink my coffee in my bathrobe and pajamas.

She's really teed off because I quit work. She hates people who don't go to work and plod away hour by hour as if the clock were god and you had to feed *it* time.

Bettina picked up her blue quilted robe off the chair and zipped herself inside. In the kitchen she got out fresh oranges and squeezed two, putting the juice in a glass with ice and a carefully-measured ounce and a half of vodka.

Her step was heavy across the living-room floor. She walked like a man. She was a good executive, too. Not one of those people who have to do everything themselves. Bettina was good at delegating jobs and happiest when there were people around to receive them.

But what Su didn't know was that Bettina had quit her job in order to keep from being fired. Don't be silly, she said aloud now. You know perfectly well Mr. Renfro would never have fired you. But to have given notice! All the office girls had been so impressed. For a month Bettina had been queen of the water cooler. To quit in order to manage a country club . . . they'd never dreamed of doing that. It was her natural talent, even Su agreed; Bettina belonged at the Country Club because she really liked people and would have been a great manager if they had just given her a chance.

She poured more vodka and squeezed two more oranges into her glass, believing that orange juice was so good for you that it counteracted whatever there was in vodka that was supposed to be bad for you, leaving you pretty much neutral but feeling a lot better.

Going to the dishwasher, Bettina noticed that Su had once again put Nefertiti's dish so closely backed up against a dinner plate that it could not possibly get washed.

"Come on, Nefertiti. You'll just have to eat out of a regular dish. Su just won't stop putting your dish in all jammed up against a plate." Nefertiti looked at Bettina with a bleary eye and one desultory wag of her tailless end. "All right! Dammit, I'll wash it for you. Just let me have a cigarette please." She gave Nefertiti a shred of chicken from the refrigerator and sat down.

Smoking slowly, she thought that although she had given Nefertiti to Su ten years before, Su barely related to her. She had been Bettina's dog for ten years except when Su felt she should assert ownership to the vet or the photographer. Even the adorable puppy had not seemed as adorable to Su as it had to Bettina. Of course Nefertiti sensed that. She had had fits all one winter, running in a frantic barking circle and biting anyone who moved near her during the fit, particularly small children.

Bettina had told Su a thousand times that it was important to Nefertiti that she eat out of her own dish.

Su said, "Maybe she needs a shrink."

Bettina took Nefertiti's dish out of the dishwasher now, the chicken dried in lumps and strings around the sides from the heat of the drying cycle. She tried to scrape it off under water. One sliver of chicken went under her fingernail.

"Goddammit, Nefertiti!" she screamed into the kitchen wall. She put out her cigarette, picked up the dish with one hand and a fold of her robe with the other, and went upstairs, pausing for breath on the landing. She put the dish on the middle of Su's bed on top of that brocade spread from Spain and went downstairs again.

"It won't do any good," she said to Nefertiti who had licked clean the regular plate and sat waiting for bacon. "She'll never learn. She refuses to learn. She knows that by refusing to learn she gets me angriest. Right, Nefertiti? Are you ready for some bacon now?" Bettina took out a skillet and a package of bacon from the refrigerator. "Yes, now we'll have some bacon, yes we will. Don't you worry. I'm going to make you some bacon. Right now."

9

AFTER LUNCH Monday Su noticed a sheet from Sister Gin sticking to the back of her review of May Sarton's *As We Are Now*. She was just getting ready to send her pages to the copy desk. Her hand pulled clumsily to get it off; she'd be fired if that obscene anonyme ever managed to get herself accidentally printed.

Skimming the sheet Su saw nothing about Mamie Carter and put it aside. Friday was a visit to Mother away, a trip that had so come between herself and last week that she had had to struggle to avoid seeing the old woman in Sarton's book as her mother. She was very far from her first reading of the book when she had loved Caro as all beautiful precious old women wrapped in Mamie Carter.

She checked the review for possible sabotage by Sister Gin. It was as much of a rave as she ever wrote:

> . . . one of the few serious books about female death in our disposall-obsessed culture. Caro embodies the extraordinary virtues of women who have lived in the real world for eighty years—the ability to size up strange situations, the intellect to uncover truth, the sophistication to be able to make contact with all kinds of people, and, finally, as we watch her being stripped in a literal humiliation by the "rest home" attendant whose envy compels her to make Caro die by small days, the courage to choose death.

She skipped over the pages, reading praise of Sarton's precision of language and imagery and her sure touch in pacing her story. "A major book," Su called it, "finally according to old women the honor every other culture but ours . . ." Every? Wasn't there a sadistic people somewhere who turned on their parents at the first sign of frailty? She blue-pencilled in: "every civilization which dares hold its historic head up."

On the way back from the copy desk she stopped at Daisy's desk. "How are you doing on those books that came in from that women's press?"

Daisy's words always came slowly as if she thought before she spoke. Su waited impatiently. "I think we ought to review them all."

"Are they that good?"

"I know we won't though."

"Tell me, are they that good?" Su picked one up, her fingers barely touching its paper cover with their own dislike for amateurism.

"We won't because they deal with lesbianism."

Su laughed. "All five of them?" She held them one after the other, her fingers finding a trace of professionalism in the layout. One had no blurb, just an elegant black cover with red and white lettering. "Selma Lagerlof won the Nobel Prize for literature . . . with a *gay* book?"

"Yes."

Su let the book drop back on top of the others. "If you want to write something up, I'll take a look at it. There's no hurry. They'll be overjoyed at anything we print, any time we can fit it in. If they stay in business that long." Su smiled but Daisy lowered her eyes. "Let me see it when you get something."

Sister Gin's typed sheet was on top of everything in the desk drawer. Reluctantly, she knew she would read it.

"Okay, Su," it began with typical disrespect. "None is so blind as she who will not read the words in front of her nose."

"Oh, bore," Su said aloud.

"Caro has all the virtues of women including horror that she might be thought a lesbian and you hate the word as much as they do. She may have the courage to choose death but she can't stand the word queer. Caro found it disgusting that 'they' thought her feeling for the one woman who treated her with tenderness might be sexual. You found her disgusting for finding that disgusting. You are disgusted with old women anyway. You're not even thinking about love and Mamie Carter isn't going to answer your letter. You'll have to call her up. Please notice that I am talking to you instead of wasting my time writing book reviews you never print. Cheerily, S.G."

"Dear Sophomoric Sister," Su scribbled. "Don't you know the difference between an author reporting her character's feelings and her own? <u>Lesbianism</u>. I hope I never

<u>hear</u> that word again." Su crumpled the page and threw it in her wastebasket, then retrieved it, spread it out and drew a heavy felt-pen black line through *lesbianism* until it was dead. Then she folded the paper several times and put it in her purse to throw it away safely at home.

"I'm leaving for the day," was all she said to Daisy. She called her favorite hair-cutter from the corner and made an appointment for an hour and a half from now. She went to the sportswear floor of Wilmington's best store and bought a yellow pantsuit, an evening suit, very elegant and very expensive. She called Jerry, who said he would be happy to pick her up at seven.

IO

CROUCHED in a pillow of late sunlight spreading over the couch, where not a noise reached this setback living room in a setback house which squeezed the unused back yard into a skinny rectangle against its unknown rear neighbor, Su felt safe. The evening with Jerry had helped her see things in perspective. She could work it out.

When Bettina came home an hour later, Su was ready to express in clear organized language at least the first part of it. She overvalued talk, she admitted. She was simply stuck in her verbal-trained self, linear and oldfashioned; it was a fault in her that she couldn't hear what was being said unless it came in words. She would try to listen also to shapes and movements from now on, really try. But would Bettina, could Bettina also try to communicate in words, say what she felt at the time instead of saying nothing, saving up everything for an explosion which then exaggerated . . . "I mean, when I say what I feel when I feel it and meet a nonresponse from you, silence . . ."

"I wish you wouldn't," Bettina said. She didn't like to be confronted with Su's feelings all the time, every day a cockleburr, no time stretches for the manufacture of romantic illusion, the creation of fantasy which alone made life worth living.

"I won't any more. Or not as much. I'll try." Su's face was so still that Bettina felt confronted with a nondaily Su and wanted to listen.

"Let me get a drink," Bettina said.

Su vowed she would not have one. Can't you talk to me without a drink? she would not say. She would keep a record of the things she did not say when she felt like saying them in order to know when enough had passed unsaid to allow one to be said. She wanted to meet Bettina halfway, not clear across the field.

When she had first met Bettina (her affair with Kip already into overtime although neither of them were admitting it) Bettina had been much too fat to be seen as having a world of her own to offer. She had easily accommodated herself to Kip's intention of viewing her as someone we will feel sorry for and include often. Kip got very drunk one night and Bettina sat up until dawn with Su talking about how it felt to live with an alcoholic. "It must be the living worst," Bettina had said with emphasis. "It's a real tragedy."

But wasn't Su again living with an alcoholic and still not seeing it as a tragedy?

Bettina had been invited to her first Saturday night at Kip's for no special reason. She had a close friend at the paper and Su carelessly asked her one day to drop by the following Saturday night. She was startled when Bettina entered the back yard in full vigor. "Hi!" Bettina thrust the phrase into the grassy quiet like a ship's horn clearing the harbor to its berth. The *hi* seemed to have many syllables as if it were echoing off chambers carefully carved on the inside of that huge chest. Su laughed and ran to her. "You startled me!" she said, totally captivated.

Now Bettina walked on high heels and slender ankles back across the living room, holding her drink away from her best dress. Her walk was as purposeful as that of a stubborn child, each foot occupying its place by will; there was no doubt with Bettina's walk that those feet would reach the spot they had determined to reach when they began, a thing you could not be sure of at all in watching most people walk. She settled herself on the couch with a huge grin.

"Shoot," she said.

"Okay, here comes the first shot, Bettina. I've got both you and me mixed up with my mother who will not talk to me."

"Every time I see Shirley she talks a mile a minute like it was going out of style."

"She talks without talking to me. She always has but last weekend I came right out and asked her to talk to me. I thought menopause would change something, be the change. Now we were both in the same physiological class, at least common creatures . . ."

"What did you want to say to her?" Bettina remembered Su's threat of a previous evening.

"I told her I was a lesbian and she hated me saying it.

More than being it."

"I don't wonder that she didn't want to be common-creature." Bettina took a big swallow. "You must have known she would get in a snit about that."

"Snit. That's the kind of language she uses. Every time I was upset about something as a child, she'd say I got up on the wrong side of the bed, or my nose was out of joint, or the cat had my tongue, or I shouldn't let it get my goat." Su got up and then sat down, remembering she wasn't going to have a drink.

"Why don't you have a drink?" Bettina said.

"All right!" Su's eyes flashed as she got up and walked resolutely to the bar.

Bettina chuckled. "Do it to please me. And while you're there, bring me another piece of ice."

"Don't you see?" Su said, sitting down with a gin on ice. "Language like that says the child's feelings aren't important or deep. She wanted to handle me and I wanted to be taken seriously."

"Did she take you seriously when you said you were a lesbian? I wish I could have heard it."

"She didn't. Hear it, I mean. She pretended she didn't even hear me. Then she pretended I was saying that because I didn't want children. She thought I was going through menopause just to keep her from having a grand-child. She thought when I touched her I was going to seduce her. She's my mother." Su was halfway between rage and tears and Bettina was about to put an arm around her when the telephone rang.

"I'll get it," Bettina said.

"Don't answer it. Let it ring."

It rang.

"Maybe it's important," Bettina said.

"It's only five-thirty. We're not usually here by five-thirty. They'll call back."

All Bettina's sociable urges propelled her toward the ringing; all her loyalty held her firmly still. The telephone rang and rang and rang.

"Maybe it's long distance," Bettina said. "It's ringing a long time."

"*Please* don't answer it."

Bettina was counting. Nine, ten, and then eleven. Long distance was usually ten exactly. She finished her drink. It was too late now anyway; by the time she got there it would stop. "I'm going to get another drink," she said, walking toward the bar and the telephone. It stopped ringing as she passed the dining table.

"You won," Bettina said. "It stopped."

Su's voice was uncharacteristically loud and easily reached Bettina at the bar. "I'm going to start writing again. I have an idea for a play—one I started years ago with . . . before I took the job on the paper. I've got to, Bettina. Maybe I stopped writing because I thought I could talk to Mother, whoever she was inhabiting at the moment. Maybe last weekend was a good crisis. Now I know I'll never be able to talk to her, I can go back to writing, forget about talking."

Su's face was glowing so like a child's that Bettina felt instantly sure that she would write a play, right away, a great play and sure success and show everyone. Bettina was picking out the dress she would wear to opening night when she saw something else: since she didn't have a job, Su wouldn't be able to drop her radio show and wouldn't have time to write a play at all. Her own guilt tightened the muscles in her chest. Pleasure turned to hatred at Su for making her feel so guilty. "When will you have time?"

Bettina said, the words, squeezed between shame and guilt, coming out crimped.

Su's eyes reflected what she would not say before she lowered them. She said, "I could drop the radio show," but the glow was gone.

"You mean I could get a job." Bettina stood up. "Goddammit! Every time we have a talk it always comes right back to what a no-good failure I am. Every goddamn time." She stomped to the kitchen. "All right, don't say it, I'm going to fix dinner. You don't have to remind me. You just forget all the times I fix dinner without your saying anything. You only remember the times I don't fix it fast enough to suit you. You only want to know the bad things about me."

Su followed her to the kitchen. "I didn't say anything about fixing dinner or getting a job."

"But you were thinking it. Don't you think I know what you're thinking after all these years? Now it's going to be my fault that you can't write a play, on top of everything else. It's always me that ruins your life, one way or another."

The telephone rang.

"Goddammit, I'm going to answer it!" Bettina picked it up. "Hello? . . . She's right here." She handed the receiver to Su. "It's your father." Bettina let politeness rule curiosity and went to the bathroom.

"What'd he want?"

"He said Mother has gone." Every drop of glow was drained from Su's face which now looked as guilty as Bettina's. "Just gone. He doesn't know where or anything. She said she was going in to town this morning and she hasn't come back. I told him to call the police—at least they can track down the car. I hate myself now. Why'd she have to do it just while I was hating her?"

"She didn't know . . ."

"Don't tell me that has nothing to do with it. It was Daddy calling earlier. If I'd answered it the police would have been called then. Now maybe it's too late . . ."

"Su!" Bettina held both her shoulders. "He could have called the police without your okay, you know."

"But he didn't! He'd never think of anything."

"Now I won't have you blaming yourself."

"You won't? What will you have?"

"Okay, take it out on me if you want to, but it's just not your fault, you hear? Now you sit down and finish your drink and I'll fix dinner."

"Suppose she left because I made her listen? Suppose she killed herself because she was ashamed . . ."

"She's not dead, for christsakes."

"How do you know?"

"How do you know?"

"Oh, shut up!" Su wheeled around, knocking Bettina's cigarette, laid on the table's edge, to the floor. "You and your endless endless endless cigarettes!"

Bettina's mouth was set during most of the shakenbake chicken dinner, unsetting itself only for clearly-marked bites. Su's face was slumped into ragged despair. Neither of them talked except to exchange food requests with extreme politeness.

At eight o'clock Su's father called back. They had found the car—parked at the airport.

"At least you know she's all right. She just wanted to take a trip," Bettina said. "Su, it breaks my heart to see you so unhappy." Bettina wiped her mouth, glistening from her afterdinner rum and Tang but her eyes were still wet. "Baby, I want you to write your play. I'm going to go

110

out and look for a job first thing in the morning. I don't want you to worry about your mother. I feel terrible when things go all wrong for you. Really terrible. I can't stand it."

Su didn't say, but your feeling terrible just adds to it because now I have to console you on top of everything else. In the nonsaying, there was time for Bettina's caring to get through. Su fought with her guard which was loosening toward relaxing. "I know you do." The struggle to refuse belief exhausted her. "Really? Are you really going to look for a job tomorrow? I mean I want you to for your sake—you're much too intelligent to be happy doing nothing."

Bettina looked grim. "I said I was." Her eyes were on her hand with the cigarette. It was going to be hard to face a jobhunt knowing that Su didn't love her. "It'd be a damn sight easier if I believed you loved me." She didn't dare look up, afraid of seeing the answer in Su's eyes. Su's language was more completely under Su's control; Bettina felt she had a chance there because of Su's politeness.

"I always have," Su said after a moment. "It's just that lately we haven't been very close but that happens, I guess. No two people can live together forever and always be as close as they were at the beginning."

"I see. We'll have an arrangement. I'll go to work and you can go on and write your plays."

"*Plays?* I just mention that I want to write one play and you explode that I am criticizing you for not having a job. I'm not allowed to talk about me, or you. How's the weather?"

"You accused me of not intending to get a job."

"I didn't *accuse* you of anything."

"You just said it then." Bettina's mouth huddled into

her face. You're strong and you don't understand weakness—strong people never do. You mention going out and getting a job just like that, smiling and getting all excited and all I can think of is that you have everything—a good job, a talent for writing plays, and, worse, a new love, while I don't have anything but a drinking problem and bronchitis. Who do you think would hire me? "You said we weren't close any more. I guess we won't be living together either." And that's why you want me to get a job. Too intelligent to be happy doing nothing, my foot.

Su got up and went to the bar. "I'm just too tired to take much more of this, that's all. Tired!"—of being caught in such a cycle of fights and plateaus and fights that tiredness takes center stage and I don't even feel any more, love or hate. I don't even know whether I love you or not any more. I'm determined to avoid a fight now but how can I help but see that we're only postponing it and then the inevitable march of days toward the next eruption becomes worse than the fight itself. "Maybe we shouldn't live together any longer," Su said, returning to the couch but not looking at Bettina. "Neither of us is gaining anything by this . . ."

"Goddammit, I love you!" Bettina's eyes glared their truth through tears. "I love you, Su. You're everything to me." I never did deserve to have someone like you even love me in the first place and I know it. But after loving you, after living with you, how could I ever be satisfied with just an ordinary person? And the worst of it is that I am even flattered that you like Mamie Carter. She's so special that I felt good about being included in the same class with her—that you chose me first and then *her* made me feel really proud. Sometimes I thought that you chose me because you were just plain neurotic—your mother always says that you're the kind of person who can walk through the forest and pick up a crooked stick, and don't think I didn't feel exactly like a crooked stick among all those trees. And the real worst of it is that I love you and since I love you I want you to be happy, to have every-thing—your play, your Mamie Carter too . . . I know I should leave you and let you have all that but I can't do it, I just can't do it. I ought to but I just can't bring myself to do it. "I just love you so much, Su, I couldn't live without you. Please, baby, please don't leave me."

Su sat on Bettina's chair arm and held her head, stroking her hair. "Don't cry, don't cry," she murmured, hugging her to her lap. A wire pulled tight around her chest making her feel breath as pain. If I don't write a play now I never will. Time is getting short for me. I'm fifty. Let me think. If that puts my inner urgency out of your reach, you react by trying to pull me back and I feel that if I really loved you I would let you pull me back. But if you really loved me you wouldn't pull me back, not right now, not when I know I have to write the play now, would you?

"You can have an affair with Mamie Carter if you want to but please don't leave me," Bettina said into Su's skirt.

"What?" Su stood angrily up. "Is that what you've been thinking? Is that what you hear when I say I want to write a play? *Shit!*"

"I didn't mean . . . I know you want to write a play but I . . . Suzy, I see how you are around Mamie Carter, how your whole face lights up when just her name is even men-tioned . . ."

"Well, it's not lighting up now, see? And I'm not going to stand here and be insulted either. You hate me. You really do hate me and you know it. Underneath that shiny red peel of a fantasy of yours there's a poisoned apple . . ."

"You picked it, Eve. You're just a bad picker, like your mother always said. Your mother was right."

"Damn right."

"You picked me and ruined your life. Hah!"

"I sure did. Well, this is one apple I'm not eating any more of."

"Go ahead. Leave."

"You leave."

"Right. It's your house so I have to leave."

"You never even tried to make it yours. You've got clothes all over your room and everything still in boxes even though we've lived here for ten years. You don't care a fig for your surroundings. You're the most oblivious person to surroundings I ever saw. You don't even see your ashtrays overflowing. You might as well live in the bus depot for all the difference it makes to you."

"I never had a prayer of changing anything about this house and you know it. Whatever you and your architect decided was going to be it and every time you discussed *my* room with me don't think I didn't know that I'd better agree with you because that was the way it was going to be. Your house is your status. You've got to have it look artistic so everybody can see how artistic *you* are, that's all a house means to you."

"I was forty years old and had never lived in anything but architectural horrors made into apartments which I had to paint and poster and pretend they were the last word, and I hated it. It was torture to me to live in that ugliness and you never even noticed. The only way I could build it to begin with was because you were sharing expenses. I took all the responsibility, you paid so much a month but the mortgage was in my name and you could

114

always leave and I'd be stuck with it. I always knew you had that power—to leave . . . your room, your job, everything, because you don't even take your own support seriously. You know you can go home to Mummy but my parents have come home to me. I don't have a choice about whether to go to work or not. The house, having the house was my security for my old age—something you don't even think about."

"Bullshit. I can't go home to Mummy."

"You can."

"I'll kill myself first."

"You still *can*."

"Forget that. I'm not going to be a drunken daughter moving in on Mummy." Bettina was silent a few minutes. "Look, I think the house is beautiful and I want you to have it. If you don't want me to live here, I'll help you to find someone else . . ."

"Who?"

"I don't know. Someone."

"I'm not going to live with just anyone."

"You shouldn't. Su, listen to me a minute. I didn't mean that about the house. I just feel so left out of your life lately—I never get to see you and when I do we always argue. That's why I was upset at your wanting to write the play, I thought I'd never see you." Bettina's face suddenly cleared and she stood up grinning. "I've got it! Let's take a trip! I'll go to the bank tomorrow and borrow some money and we'll go away, just you and me, and get close to each other again and have a good time and laugh and then you can come back and write your play. I think it's a fabulous idea! don't you?"

"Borrow money?"

"I can increase the loan I already have."

"Oh, Bettina, it's fantasy." Su burst into tears. "It's always fantasy." She was sobbing uncontrollably and Bettina held her gently. Was it my fantasy that you were ever an oak, Bettina? "And I guess the play is just another . . ."

"Come on now, darling. I'll mix up some martinis and we can brownbag them to Trail's End. We'll celebrate. Come on now. We'll talk about everything over a martini and a two-inch steak."

"The play is just another goddamn fantasy."

Bettina held her close in a grip as firm and secure as their beginnings. Su breathed her hair, her nonallergenic soap, her acid sweat, her twenty years of living together smells as necessary as her own. Su breathed her smells and tried to hear what they were saying. She hated them, she loved them, she hated them, she loved them. Their language made no sense at all.

"Okay. Let's go," Su said.

"I'll just feed Nefertiti," Bettina said happily. "Nefertiti!"

11

"SUPPOSE I run out?" Mamie Carter said in the empty bathroom. "Run out of steam like an old locomotive, run down if battery-powered, run dry if diesel, run aground if nautical, run off the track, run into a ditch, run up too much credit to pay up, pay off, pay out." The bathroom tiles were cleaned often enough by her efficient manservant, the Captain, to show water marks where they needed polishing. Mamie Carter sought them out, found and counted every splash and spollup; filthy bathroom, messy tile, let them have it.

Who? Her former brief son-in-law now suing her daughter for half her property. Clayton Everett Eagle the Third, tracing his New England ancestry as far back as she could her Southern, scion of education and privilege reinforced by heavyduty bloodlines, was suing her daughter Imogene, after a marriage of three years, for half her property.

Mamie Carter's skin, now warmed by reflections off the pink tile and towels, was nevertheless old and cold. "And I am much too old to care about the possessions I have spent a lifetime amassing, which that whippersnapper has decided to relieve me of. Let him have it. Hear, pink tile? Do you imagine for a spotted pink second that I'm going to fight for you?"

Imogene was waiting distractedly on the couch.

"How are the children?" Mamie Carter said, looking around the den to see if anything demanded her attention then arranging herself on the couch, drawing up an ashtray for them both, holding off the details.

Bruce, fourteen, youngest of four, had just scored in the first percentile in the nation on his academic standards' test.

"First?" Mamie Carter said. "You don't mean the very top?"

"I certainly don't." Imogene added, unnecessarily cutting a grandmother's pride, "I mean the very bottom. And that included the deaf, dumb, and blind *and* the upper-level mentally retarded."

"Bruce isn't mentally retarded," Mamie Carter said firmly.

"He will be," Imogene said with a growl.

"Maybe Captain will bring us a drink." She wanted to encircle Imogene as a little girl even though she was now Bettina's age. Imogene's face, padded and pink and here and there dented with age, had the same small sweet downdroop to the mouth and uptilt to the eyes that Mamie Carter had stared at asleep over forty years ago while baby Imo slept. Some adults continue to look like babies—not just themselves as babies but any babies (all babies being similar when asleep). Imogene's light brown hair was fine and curly as a child's.

Mamie Carter reached across her daughter for the four-domed brass bell which she shook, making an incongruous Catholic sound. Her hand on its way back to her own lap stopped briefly at Imogene's arm, squeezed her hand. It was a shock to see that Imogene's was the hand of a forty-six-year-old woman and her own covered with skin barely thick enough to last to the grave, while inside her head she had been a young mother and Imogene a child. As she gave Captain their drink orders, she saw that it was a terrible thing that the mind knew no age at all, could dart from seventy-seven to thirty-two in a fraction of a second without oneself even being aware . . . but what did *self* mean without the mind?

In the same way the past thirty-one years disappeared in a trice and Mamie Carter was Imogene's present age, going through the distractions of menopause which she remembered as being exactly like the distractions of old age. The mind wanders at various stages of life: she had hypnotized her own mind into a buzz on a toddler swing, staring without blinking at an imaginary plane of air. Her mind had gone into halfsleep, just off gear, often enough; it had once seemed important to use every natural gift one had and Mamie Carter had thought of that one as germane to acting—within the haze the character to be presented swelled and grew, having nothing else to push aside or remove, easily occupied center stage (so to speak).

And it was in halfsleep once again. "I'm sorry, darling. You know I can't hear you without my glasses. What did you say?"

119

Imogene repeated. Clayton Everett Eagle III, scion of
noble New England, was going to demonstrate that his
blood had taken root among New England's rocks and he
could properly be called a yankee trader. He had counter-
sued Imogene for divorce on the bizarre premise that he
also had grounds and had won.

"I don't believe it," Mamie Carter said.

"You wouldn't," Imogene said.

"Let's not argue, darling. Is it true?"

In fact, Clayton Everett Eagle III had received a judg-
ment from a judge of North Carolina giving him one-half
of his wife (of three years)'s property, namely an expensive house which she had built with her own separate
money. Clayton, romantically persuasive, had wanted
them to build a new house together for a new marriage;
Imogene had sold her old house and they two had picked
out a piece of earth which cost exactly what Imogene's
house had brought. Imogene, romantically suicidal, had
put the property in both their names. The house, paid for
by selling off everything Imogene had from her father
and her first husband, was built upon land held jointly;
therefore, under English common law, anything built upon
property belonged to the property.

"I was right not to believe it," Mamie Carter said.
"Such a travesty of justice is not to be believed. If one marries a widow with four children one should be paid forty
thousand dollars. But two of the children are full grown
and live away from home. Doesn't that reduce the fee?"

"Of course I know, Mother, that he only married me
for my money," Imogene said coldly.

"He wants you to think that! Don't then. He'd do anything to get back at *you* . . ."

"Even accept forty thousand dollars."

120

"Possibly. Because suing you for half your property makes him look like a drummer. He can no longer hold up his head in polite society."

Imogene picked at her cocktail napkin. "I don't know what I'm going to do."

Kill him, Mamie Carter said silently. "Maybe Captain will bring us a fresh drink and some cheese."

"Mother, I'd like to kill him."

"Oh."

"Really. His life isn't worth forty thousand dollars. His death . . ." Imogene had never been fast at figures and paused several seconds. "His death should be worth about one-tenth of that. So I understand."

"Whom have you contacted, darling?"

"A friend of . . ."

"I don't mean a *name*."

"No, thank you, Captain. I won't have another." When he left the room, Imogene said, "A friend of the man who runs the launderette's brother said he could get it done with no risk for twenty-five hundred. Of course the big risk is blackmail later, but how is that different from what Clayton is doing right now?" Imogene drained the last drop of bourbon off her ice. "I don't feel at all guilty. In fact I feel murderously joyful."

And she had left her mother feeling strangely like a murderer also. A male murderer, single, twenty-six to thirty-two, Causasian, etc. Within the mind there are no ribs.

Mamie Carter called Luz on the telephone.

"How awful!" Luz said when she heard what Clayton Everett Eagle III had done to Imogene. "She should have him shot."

121

"She never could be attracted to a strong man."

"I think a strong man would shy away from her. Because she wouldn't let him have his own way the whole time."

Mamie Carter coughed gently. "You know I can't hear you on the telephone."

" 'She wouldn't let him have his own way the whole time.' Imogene wouldn't. A man can sense that."

"Can a man also sense that if he is weak enough she'll give him anything to avoid defeating him?"

"The men I've known sense exactly that if the she is well brought up."

"What?"

". . .'if the she is well brought up.' "

"Luz, you're not suggesting we bring up our daughters badly, are you?"

"What daughters, M. Carter?"

"We have no more left, that's true."

"God looks out for drunks and daughters."

"There's something wrong with your telephone."

"I said, it's a wise daughter that chooses a young and busy mother to be born to."

"Now, Luz. You didn't say that at all." Silence. "Are you playing tomorrow?"

"No. I'm keeping Adele's children. She's going into the hospital to have some work done."

"Female trouble?"

"Yes."

"Not a hysterectomy?"

"No. I'd rather not discuss it."

Mamie Carter laughed mischievously.

"Not for the reason you think," Luz said. "I'm not embarrassed because it has to do with sex. The fact is . . .

122

Adele wants to get a polyp removed from her uterus. She wants another baby and they haven't been able to get pregnant."

"She's worried because she only has three children they can't support? Has Doug gotten a job yet?"

"No."

"Maybe he could apply to be Clayton's bodyguard. Or is the baby to take their minds off their troubles?"

"Don't ask me anything about young people today."

"Did I ever ask you?"

"They're more than I can understand."

"Adele will be all right. At least she's too smart to put her house in *their* names. Maybe she'll have a little girl."

"Suppose she has another boy?"

"Fathers! Luz, we really want you to play tomorrow. Suppose I ask Captain to take Adele's boys to the zoo?"

"Well, then I could play, I suppose." Luz hesitated. "I hope it's not . . ."

"Good. Captain would like to do that. I don't want him around anyway."

"Twoish?"

"*Two*," Mamie Carter reprimanded her.

123

12

ITH A late September sunset of lavender-gold behind her and the smell of fish and seawater making her hungry all over, Su stepped into the inside of her love's house for the first time. The flat straw rug made the soles of her feet ache through sandals and long to be kissed. Mamie Carter kissed her on the cheek after the custom. Seizing that proximate cheek's smell with her nostrils, Su inhaled her reward and knew better than to kiss back.

They sat on the back porch and watched the sun set over Wrightsville Sound, on that old weathered porch of an old two-story beach house where Mamie Carter had spent her summers as a child (and subsequently her children and

then her grandchildren), one of the few houses to with-
stand all the hurricanes—sat listening to the leftover summer sounds of children's water games and deploring the
increasing number of motored boats each season replacing
the elegant sails. The martini threw a skin over Su's brain
wiping out the city as they sat in the gentle decay of the
day, the house softly decaying behind them, the summer
itself mature and used and gracefully marked, letting out
its last few days with the dignity of a menopausal woman
releasing her last few eggs, knowing that they were for
form only, that the season was over but there was no
hurry about slipping over into the next, it will come in its
season and here, these my last are as worthy as my first.

Su felt ashamed that she had been afraid . . . of Mamie
Carter who was as legal in all her tentacles as old Wilmington itself; of her own passion which, here on this clan-
protected porch, could be sublimated into charm as if she
were a real member of that impeccable clan.

Shaking her olive free from its gregarious ice, Su heard
Mamie Carter's voice off her left ear asking her to fetch
them each a refill, because Captain wasn't here, because
she was alone, expecting no one but Su this evening. Su
took each glass in a grip firm enough to break them—someone could still drop in, would come visit, seeing the lights,
her car, could drop by for hours yet, this being the tradition of the beach, the gregariousness of ice and an island.

They talked of the town's recent rapes and the bizarre
circumstance of the two rapists' being laid out, tied to a
board, one on the steps of the old folks' home, one in the
front yard of the councilman who pulled the largest vote
and was therefore mayor. Both rapists were white, short-
haired, in their middle thirties, and were found nether-

naked and tied outstretched to a piece of plywood in the shape of an x. Since the first rape had been of a sixty-five-year-old woman of color, it was thought that the first man's punishment was the work of a Black Klan group. The rapist had hysterically insisted that the old woman sent five old women spirits after him but no one paid him any mind. The second rape victim had been a junior high-school girl, forced at stranglehold to suck off her attacker; since she was white and since in this case too the rapist had babbled of five grannies who, though masked, had white hands, some of the townspeople wondered if there were witches still afoot.

"Posh," Mamie Carter said. "What kind of talk is that? Black Klans and witches. Next thing they'll say the free-booters are back haunting the Cape Fear."

"What do you think?" Su asked.

"I think the rapists are getting a big fuss made over them. They're not the victims."

"Do you think it was really . . . women who did it?"

"*Old* women?" Mamie Carter's black eyes glinted with laughter. She stood up. "You know, I can't wear flat-heel shoes any more," she said, looking at her medium-heeled sandals below white sharkskin slacks. "I wore high heels so long my Achilles' tendon is permanently shortened."

"Do you?"

Su followed her strong slightly-humped back into the house. "These slacks are from before the war. Would you feel bad if a real shark had given his skin for them?"

The inside of the house was dark after the bright twi-light reflections of the porch. Mamie Carter led Su to the kitchen and flicked on the light.

"You've painted it yellow!" Su remembered to speak loud. "Yellow is my favorite color."

126

"Mine too." Mamie Carter's smile was a caress. "Have you ever thought of wearing a bright yellow wig? Now don't try to talk to me while I'm fixing dinner. You know I can't hear you when my back is turned."

"Now that streak there," Mamie Carter said, nodding at a white swath across the middle of the dining room table, "was made by the yankees. They came to my grandmother's house and took everything they could. Since they didn't have any way to carry off the table, the yankee officer sent to the kitchen for some vinegar and poured it across there. It won't come off. Have some more shrimp, Su." Mamie Carter wiped her mouth delicately and smiled. "Old tables tell old tales."

"Mamie Carter," Su said, her fingers holding the ancient heavy lace of her napkin, her other fingers resting on the heavy stem of the goldleaf wine glass, her eyes staring at that bright elfin face leaning toward her through the candlelight. "I've never eaten such delicious shrimp."

"It wasn't too hot, was it?" Mamie Carter had cooked the tiny North Carolina shrimp with sour cream, wine, onions, mushrooms, and a lot of cayenne. "I don't taste anything without cayenne any more. Besides, it's the only way I can keep my grandchildren from eating every meal with me."

"It made all other shrimp seem bland, diluted, incomplete, wan, and colorless. Unworthy of notice." All unmarked tables, unlined faces, modern clothes, new napkins, streamlined wine glasses, all young or middle-aged things were thrown into a heap of inconsequentiality which, like herself, Su felt to be unfinished, unseasoned, green and smooth and callow. "I think I am in love with you, Mamie Carter."

127

The bright elfin face smiled broadly and did not answer.

Had she heard? In this pocket of the past, within dark wood and the dark saltiness of a September tide coming in and the faint rust smell of old screens and occasional sound of wind flapping the awnings, Su felt herself suddenly dead. She doubted that she had spoken. She had been switched into afterlife where words did not need to be spoken. She had left her amorphous dully-young fifty-year-old body behind and drifted through the definite world of the dead, the epitomized grave, the capsule of self which carried in its concentrate all the love she had ever sought. Mamie Carter did not need to hear; she would know.

A spare hand marbled with a bulging network of veins reached for Su's. "I know."

"Of course you do," Su said, laughing, unable to move her own hand caught in a cave beneath that perfect antique one.

"I've known for a while."

"Of course you have!" Su's smile was as stiff as her body balanced off the touch of that hand. "I should have known you'd know."

"Mamie Carter?" She held that final face taut on a thread of sight. Her hand closed across the silk bones that were Mamie Carter's hand, curled up-reaching on a free patch of sheet in the middle of a Queen Anne bed. Memory was already claiming the sight of her dimpled flesh, infinite dimples winking in their softness, skin so old it had lost all abrasives, rid itself of everything that can shield the body against the world; skin vulnerable, nonresilient, soft forever—Su's fingers had to resist the longing to take some of that flesh and mold it.

"Yes, perfect?"

Su sunk her face into the ageless curve of her love's shoulder and smothered a giggle. "There is one extraordinary thing about us that I have to say, even here on these romantic rainswept sheets, even at the risk of hearing your 'posh' . . . your silk is matched only by our exquisite ability to prolong swallowing, our mutual toothlessness allowing for such a long balance on the tip of flavor: I just never imagined that the delights of age would include the fact of endlessly drawnout orgasms. Did you always know?"

"You like it, too?"

"Without leaving us with a mouthful of cotton wadding. Without wearing down flavor. Without diminishment. With the loss of nothing at all, in fact, except fear."

"I always thought, if old age could be beautiful, life would hold no more terrors. Now if you'll stop talking a minute, Su, I want to get up and put on my negligee."

Mamie Carter swung her legs out of sight, turned her beautiful back, and slipped into a charcoal-red robe—really slipped, but then she had had sixty years' practice. Su saw in her mind her coveted breasts, bound flat to her chest when she was in her twenties to produce a flapper fashion, hanging now from the base of the breastbone like soft toys, too small to rest a head upon, fit for a hand to cuddle very gently like the floppy ears of a puppy.

Memory moved her hand to Mamie Carter's belly—skin white as milk, finely pucked like sugar-sprinkled clabber; memory dropped her hand to Mamie Carter's sparse hair curling like steel—there was strength between her legs and no dough there where the flesh was fluid enough to slip away from the bone and leave that tensed grain hard as granite and her upright violent part like an animal nose

129

against Su's palm. The impact of memory bruised. Su said, to the back that could not hear, "Don't you dare die, Mamie Carter Wilkerson."

Now, as Su was feeling wicked lying in bed while Mamie Carter sat up in her little armchair with the rose-colored skirt, a flash began in a tiny prickling over her upper skin. Last night, just as she had reached to kiss Mamie Carter the second time, reached toward those lips as to a dandelion, she had felt this same beginning prickle and a tear had dropped down each cheek, prewetting the flash with despair.

"You're flashing, Su," Mamie Carter had said.

Tears streamed as if they would flood out the flash and Su had said helplessly, "Why now? Why why why *now?*"

"Why not now?" Mamie Carter had said gently, laying Su back down on the bed, circling her shoulder, stroking her cheek and neck and breasts. "Why not now?" she had said, kissing the shame from Su's flushed lips, sliding her cheek over the sweat of Su's doubly-wet cheek and slippery forehead. Her arm had reached through Su's legs and she had held her in an infant curve, whispering again, "Why not now?" as Su slipped down into the abandon of hotly wetting herself and the flash had raged, burst, and slowly subsided.

Now, lying wickedly in bed, Su ducked under the prickles and welcomed the flash which centered her whole extraordinary body in a fever of change.

"What about Bettina?" Mamie Carter said and Bettina's voice echoed in the room, her blue quilted robe accusing.

I'll always love you, Bettina had said twenty years ago, when always had been forever. Now, with always cut in half, it seemed she had exchanged her mobility for a foundation of quicksand which would suck the house in after it. But still Bettina said it, and even now the words made her feel safe inside their sucking sound.

"*I'll* always love you, Su," Mamie Carter said with a small dry laugh like a kick. "Now Bettina's old enough to know better than to compare her 'always' with mine . . . certainly old enough to know better than that and I naturally know exactly how old she is since her mother and I had our daughters the same month." Mamie Carter held Su's flailing head. "When I say always, perfect, it's an underbid."

"Mamie," Su said to feel the impertinence of using that bare name. "Did you really fall in love with me?"

"No. I just wanted to get you in bed where I could hear you."

"Now you sit among the yellow and read the **paper**. I'll fix breakfast," Su said, wishing Mamie Carter were fragile so she could perch her on the breakfast table in a vase. Her hand met an upper arm as muscular as her own.

"That's yesterday's paper."

"Well, I didn't read it. I was out all day. Doesn't news keep?"

"You didn't read the paper yesterday?"

Su put coffee on to perk and squeezed two glasses of orange juice as if this kitchen were her own. "Why, what's in the paper? How do you like your eggs?"

"Quietly in the icebox."

A bumping along the boardwalk and cry of *o-cree! o-cree! fresh tomatoes and o-o-o-creeeee!* came into the morning. Su sat down with a temporary cup of instant coffee and pulled the paper over. "What's in the paper?"

"What we were talking about last night. There."

131

Clayton Everett Eagle III, Wilmington socialite, was found tied to a board early this morning by a fish merchant, Rowland Livers. Mr. Livers called the police, who reached the scene at approximately seven o'clock.

Mr. Eagle, who declined to comment, was apparently the victim of the same person or persons responsible for similar incidents in the past month. He was tied, partially nude, to a piece of plywood and had been placed in the side yard by the steps leading up to the Cornwallis house sometime early this morning.

The most puzzling clue was a note pinned to his shirt reading, *Shirley Temples Emeritae.* When a reporter asked the police if this might indicate that the gang responsible included some members of the fair sex, Lieutenant Francis Colleton, who described himself as an amateur Shakesperian, replied, "If fair is foul and foul is fair."

The question still unanswered is the reason for Mr. Eagle's pillorying. The previous victims of the gang had been an alleged rapist and an alleged sodomite. The choice of the Cornwallis house might be connected to the fact that Mr. Eagle recently moved to this area from New England.

"Isn't he related to you?" Su asked.

"Connected. Or was. He's kin only to Lucifer."

"Who do you think . . .?" A non-North Carolinian herself by birth, Su felt the reflex of an outsider who would never be able to say *ho-oose* (house) giving the word its full Chaucerian diphthong like a native. Although she was not a yankee, she wondered if Clayton Eagle had gotten himself labelled "outside agitator" and prepared to draw in her liberal skirts against this Temple gang.

"Now that's just damned nonsense, Su. We're not still fighting the War Between the States here. You know we'd already voted not to secede, but when they opened fire on our cousins, then we had to. South Carolina was family —we weren't even separated until 1729. No, I think Mr. Eagle has more to answer for than his misfortune of a birthplace. The Temple Gang. I like that."

Driving back across the causeway that separated land from land, Su threw her words wide so they could skip across the gray glass of Wrightsville Sound: "Change of life by definition refers to the future; one life is finishing therefore another life must be beginning. The menopausal armies mass on the brink of every city and suburb; everything that was is over and there is nothing left there to keep our sights lowered. See the rifles raised? This army doesn't travel on its uterus any more. Bettina, you must see that to stay back in that young section with you when I can reach out to age itself, lust after a final different dry silken life and so much grace and elegance from all that knowledge of days . . .. There is no more beautiful word in the language than withered."

13

KIBITZING from its permanent stand in the middle of the room, the bridge table with its cut-velvet top had been splendid with two scorepads, two gold pencils, and two new decks of cards, one white, one black, bearing the inscription "Make All Checks Payable to Mamie Carter Wilkerson." A small table holding an ashtray had stood at each corner and the bridge lamp had thrown its equal glow from the low ceiling:

Five women (one cut out each rubber to fix drinks) were present: Mamie Carter, Luz, Cad, Puddin, and Ella. None of them sat down; they were looking at a pile of black gowns neatly folded on a chair and a box of blond curly wigs.

"I hope you got my gown long enough, M.C.," Cad said. Her eyes were the open brown of a good child. "You never will admit how tall I am."

"Five seven," Mamie Carter said coldly.

"Five seven and three-quarters," Cad said.

"You've been shrinking just like the rest of us." Mamie Carter held up a cardboard sign: *Shirley Temples Emeritae.* "Do you like it?"

"That feminine latin plural is a dead giveaway," Ella said. "No one would know how to do that in this town but you and Luz."

Mamie Carter frowned—her expression for extreme chagrin and devastation.

"I thought we decided on Shirley Temple *Grad*uates," Cad said. "or was it Shirley Temple Grad*uates*?"

"I thought this was more succinct," Mamie Carter said. "As well as being more stylish."

"It is very elegant," Puddin said. She was trying on her wig in front of the mantelpiece mirror. She was so small-boned that even her plumpness did not bring her up to size and her face was lost under the acrylic curls. "Do you think it's becoming?" She poked the curls to bury the tremble of her conic fingers.

"Puddin, you'll have to wear a mask anyway. You've lived in Wilmington for seventy-five years and *might* be known by now," Ella said. Puddin was getting senile, she decided. Ella, even taller than Cad, wore her dyed black hair cut like a man's and Paris's most extreme styles which she went abroad to acquire at the drop of the latest in hats. Her jewelry was huge—today it was lapis from her eartips to her lean, large-knuckled hands. She could be persuaded to sing at every party and would dance with even the shortest of men. She was the only one who had a living husband, the only one who had never had children.

"Do you have the board?" Puddin asked.

"Are we going to use the board?" Cad's eyes were wide. "I thought . . ."

"Rape can be extended to cover *his* behavior too," Mamie Carter said firmly. "If you look at the laws covering rape you'll see they all stem from the property code. Now Almeta—at sixty-five a woman is not considered of much value as property so her rapist wasn't even indited. And if she is black too she's not even believed. The fact is, people feel sex is obscene with the old, but you all read the tittering between the lines. The fourteen-year-old girl was property not really damaged since her hymen was left intact, so her rapist was allowed to plead to a lesser sentence. If you ever bothered to think abstractly, Cad, you'd see that rape and theft are both classified as property cases; therefore I see nothing amiss in treating Clayton's theft as the only form of rape open to him."

"Exactly," Ella said in her voice as deep as a man's. "Maybe we should expose his backside instead of his you-know to harmonize with the money aspects."

"Is that Freudian?"

"Who wants a little drink while we dress?" Puddin said. Mamie Carter's speech had returned to her memory the fact of the girl's being forced to put her mouth on that man's penis; memory was now stuck on the gruesomeness of it and her hands shook violently as she brought the pitcher of martinis from the refrigerator. "The odor must have been just ghastly. Do you think a rapist would bother to wash? The poor child probably couldn't breathe, her head pushed into that sweaty putrid body . . ."

"Horrors," Cad said. "Puddin, I'd rather not think

about . . .''

"*She* had to. And then he'd squirt all that stuff into your *mouth*." Puddin filled five glasses from the sideboard and quickly anesthetized her own mouth. "Ugh. I think I'd even rather be raped than *that*."

"I feel sorry for Almeta," Cad said. "At sixty-five you'd think you'd be free from even having to think about sex."

"Speak for yourself, friend," Ella said.

"Why do you suppose he picked her?" Cad said.

Mamie Carter took the last martini and held it up."To show his contempt. The ultimate contempt for women is disrespect for age. To us," she said fiercely.

"To us," Cad said, smiling sweetly, clicking each glass in turn.

"You look very handsome," Luz said to Cad, surveying the black graduation gown. "It's because you're tall. That gown is very becoming."

"Thank you. I've always wanted to be a blonde," Cad said.

Mamie Carter picked up the plyboard cut in the shape of an outstretched human figure, a thick x, and handed a canvas shopping bag to Cad who peered inside. "Oh, it's the same old brown leather. Why can't we use bright-colored thongs sometimes?"

"We'll have to balance the board over our heads in the car," Mamie Carter said. "Don't let it knock off your wigs."

"And why would it knock off the blond wigs any faster than it knocked off the red ones last week?" Ella said.

Clayton Everett Eagle III was in Room 514 in the Wilmington Hilton. It took less than five minutes to enter the room, lay him on the floor in surprise, and tie him to the board, Luz keeping him motionless with her valuable weight on his chest, Puddin holding a martini-soaked washcloth in his mouth with manicured fingers trembling only slightly.

"There." Cad stood up. "That was easy."

Clayton lay out like a stick figure.

"Let's gag him properly and take him into the bedroom. Shall we have a game? We have to wait a long time." Mamie Carter took off her gown and wig and combed her hair.

"We should have put him in the bedroom before we tied him," Luz said, visually measuring the width of the outstretched arms at more than three feet. "I don't think he'll get through the door."

"We can tilt him." Ella's arms, still muscular, tilted the board easily. "If Cad'll help me. The rest of you weak reeds can get out of the way."

Mamie Carter let the bellboy in with the bridge table, cards, scorepads, and drinks. All the wigs and gowns were in the bedroom with Clayton; she met the bellboy as elegantly as any visitor in her proper suit and hair. "Thank you," she said, handing him two dollars. "Mr. Eagle asks that it be put on his bill."

"Imogene should never have trusted a man who doesn't play bridge," Puddin said, cutting high. Cad was next high. "We'll sit this way," she said, having seen that the bathtub ran in that direction. She dealt shakily and half-sorted her hand. "I'm a passenger."

"One club," Luz said.

"Is that a meek and timid club?" Cad said. "Two clubs."

"By me," Mamie Carter said.

"We have to try it, partner. Three no-trump," Puddin said.

Luz played the jack of clubs and Cad put down her hand. "Is everyone ready for a drink?"

"I'll get the drinks," Ella said. "I'm out."

"Well, you didn't," Cad said. Ella was staring at the curtains, her frown lines very deep. "Are you upset about Clayton? He'll be all right. He'll just have to lie in there for a few hours. We can't take him to the street until at least two o'clock."

"Well, I am worried. It's damp and he'll catch pneumonia lying outside all night after being strapped to the board all afternoon."

"No, he'll just be a little stiff," Cad said. "He won't die. None of the others did." Her voice was wistful.

"He'll be *very* stiff," Ella said.

"Isn't that a rapist's hope?" Cad said.

Ella refused to laugh. She had been so furious at the previous two men that she had taken part in their punishment with all her height and energy. Now, part of her was tempted to identify with Clayton.

"It's because you don't have a daughter," Cad said.

"Because it isn't your money," Mamie Carter said. "If you have a club in your hand I'll concede," she said to Puddin.

"I have to cut out next rubber," Luz said, looking at her watch. "I'll take Adele's boys home after supper and be back—around nine."

"You be careful driving around at night," Cad said. "You know you can't see at night."

"Shall I bring something back?"

"No, we'll eat here," Mamie Carter said.

"Oh, good," Cad said. "We can order in the room on

Clayton. They have wonderful shrimp here. I wish I weren't allergic to shrimp."

"Who dealt?"

"I did. I'm forced to pass."

"I pass."

Mamie Carter tapped the table twice.

"I open," Puddin said, calling attention to the score by peering at it over Mamie Carter.

"We all know you're vulnerable," Mamie Carter said.

"One heart," Puddin said.

"Suppose he has to go to the bathroom?" Ella had taken off her Jourdan walking shoes and was exercising her toes on the carpet. "Clayton, I mean."

"That's my long suit, partner," Cad said, laying down her hand again at two hearts.

"Grossly underbid," Luz said.

"Speak for yourself, friend," Mamie Carter said, taking the first trick and returning Luz's lead for her to trump. "No diamonds, partner?" she said, scooping up their second trick. Luz returned a spade and Mamie Carter took her second ace, returning a third diamond to be trumped.

"It's time to get the children off the streets," Puddin announced, getting in with the king of spades and leading a heart to the board. Luz showed out.

"Many a woman has walked the streets of London cold and hungry . . ." Mamie Carter said mischievously.

"Can't help it, partner." Puddin conceded a trump and the spade ten to Mamie Carter. "Down one. If Luz had opened anything but a diamond . . ."

"What if he has to go to the bathroom?" Ella missed the bidding and had it reviewed twice before she bid.

"I do feel mean drinking in here with Clayton lying in there alone," Puddin said. "It *is* five o'clock."

Cad said, "You're on the board, partner. This'll be the first five o'clock he's missed in I don't know when."

"*I* know. Since he was knee high to a duck. That's a trump," Mamie Carter said as Ella started gathering up the trick.

"Ducks are trumps?"

"That duck of spades is."

"Oh. I'm sorry." Ella dropped the cards and swept them toward Mamie Carter with the backs of her fingernails. "He must be suffering in there."

"Now don't you go feeling sorry for a Black Republican," Cad said. "A little dry spell will do him good. He can ruminate on his evil ways."

"Chew his cad," Mamie Carter said. "The rest are mine."

"Chew his *what*?" Cad said.

"You use the name, you don't own it."

"What if he does have to go to the bathroom?"

Cad lay the cards for Luz to cut and then dealt them rapidly and expertly. "Let's don't think about that, Ella," she said, picking up her hand. "You'll just upset yourself. There's nothing we can do about it. One no."

14

EXHILARATED as if she were suddenly fat with air, the formerly conservative book-review editor of the *Commercial-Appeal* put a normal yellow piece of paper into her typewriter and wrote the following review (with a few changes):

A pink cover, a naked woman, and a Bourbon Street penny-arcade title: <u>Do With Me What You Will</u> . . . but: the pink is not shocking, the woman's nakedness is humbly presented bowed back first, and the title is a come-on.

Everything on the front leads a woman to believe that Joyce Carol Oates has written a book about a woman; both she and her publisher state it: "Elena . . . heroine." The <u>Me</u> in the title, one assumes, means

Elena. We will read about her . . .

Occasionally. The first quarter of the book is about her father's perverted lust for little girls (sort of Elena) and her very strong—though cliched into the whore with the heart-throb of gold—mother. Elena, as even Oates's admirers admit, psychically disappears beneath the brutal thrust of the (real) world of men and women.

The second quarter of the book doesn't even mention Elena. She has disappeared in fact. For 150 pages two men, old and young, lawyer and murderer's son (husband- and lover-to-be of Elena) act out their primal attraction to and identification with each other. God the father and God the son, ruthless law of the Old Testament and civil-right's humanity of the new: Freud to the spirit of the Holy Ghost.

The third quarter of the book allows Elena to hover backstage as Lawyer Father presents her as his wife and Lawyer Son covets her as the father's presentation. Elena herself is described merely visually, including her handwriting: too perfect to indicate intelligence, says amateur graphologist lawyer-friend (p. 260). We know by now that Elena is perfect looking too but, curiously, we haven't the faintest idea what she actually looks like.

In the fourth quarter Elena re-enters, steps up center stage: she has an affair with lawyer-son while lawyer-father tapes, photographs, omnipresents. She has her first sexual awakening. Her eyelids flutter. She wonders how come she slept away her life . . . but unfortunately we know why: so Oates could write about what she is really interested in—men and their big doings in the world of politics (but not feminist politics, of course).

The publisher's attempt to cash in on feminism with a book which is not even remotely feminist (even in opposition) is standard male commercialism. Oates's attempt to flatten her women so stringently (to get them beneath her men) that they are no thicker than paint on the floorboards is par for the fifties where busy, productive, educated women wrote novels about idle, passive, ghostlike females as if they, the writers, were not women also. The writers spoke their intelligible lines through their mouthpieces: lawyers or prophets, I AM THE WORD.

Busy, productive, educated, and parched and starving readers who were also women knew in their wombs that such writers were pulling a fast straddle and were, in fact, writing male fantasies in a female hand. As Sister Gin, that fearless critic of those who cry "woman" too often to be believed, succinctly puts it: In the new wave of women, everyone tumbles over each other like periwinkles racing to get stranded on the sand.

Oates's refusal to see women shows up in the hollowness of her writing: unable to relate to the drama and tension of life by the moment, she relieves the detached descriptiveness of her novels by using the only resource of the unimaginative—violence (or, in its polite version, surprise). Like male novelists, she adheres to the describe-and-shoot school of literature.

Oates's unwillingness to take her own womanself seriously makes her insensitive to other women: she calls a black woman's fingernails "flesh-colored" when she means beige; she defines rape by the woman's resistance because otherwise there is no crime (p. 276), it is called "love"—a bit of logic straight from the Bible's mouth: I AM THAT I AM.

Which is doubtless why the male literary powers have elevated Oates to the pedestal of woman-novelist-to-get-the-praise. We understand all about pedestals down here in the tidewater. But us old periwinkles who have been beached before are getting ready to shout . . .

Not until she had finished, made her changes and copy-desk marks, did she look for a note from Sister Gin. There was none hidden within her stack of yellow paper, nothing beneath her typewriter, no page stuck behind yesterday's review.

Sister, where are you? Su scribbled across a yellow sheet before she left her desk to hand in the review.

She grinned at Daisy on the way back and received a startled laugh in response. At her own desk, there was no note. Sister Gin did not appear on call like a tv genie.

Dear S.G.: I will love Mamie Carter for the rest of her life. Since you choose to absent yourself, I will write your lines for you. You said: No one believes in monogamy these days.

You missed this time, Sister G. Su gulped air with abandon. This time you are way off the mark. No one is perfect —my mother said often enough. I wanted to love you and now I can, imperfect sister. But I certainly no longer have to reverence your surreptitious word.

S.G.: Monogamy is the old-fashioned arrangement whereby one partner profits at the expense of the other. It means only possession.

It means to be possessed by love.

And assurance that the offspring of the fickle woman is also the offspring of the named, will-writing male.

Spring on off that, S. Gin. This is menopause and after.

Okay. Now monogamy—when I say monogamy, I mean a long-term relationship. I assume nobody believes any more in a till-death-do-you-part kind of thing.

You know what ageism is, S.G.? It's that sentence. Suppose you are at an age where the rest of your life isn't a long term?

What?

I hear you gurgling. You heard me.

Sister Gin smites her forehead, gnashes her teeth, groans and gurgles, beats her breast, clenches her fists, stamps her foot, tears her hair. You got me, Su. I'm ashamed.

145

Good.

I'm going to die.

From shame?

I'm humiliated. How could I have been so thoughtless, so insensitive, such a total prejudiced clod?

Sister, nobody is perfect; you heard my mother. You don't split wide open from one fault, plummet to earth from one *faux pas*, landslide from one slip-up, shake apart from one sob, dissolve from one dash of cold water . . . *et cetera.* Do you have anything else to say?

Yes. What about Bettina?

"Where the hell have you been?" Bettina's bulk was a push of fury; Su lost her balance in a start and sat in the concave white plastic of the dog dish. Bettina was a shouting open mouth in a red face, her words of rage so familiar that Su heard them as sound only, the sudden roar of an angry impersonal ocean.

"Where the hell were you?" came clearly through at intervals. After one such Bettina stopped, momentarily out of breath, leaving the question, accidentally perhaps, last.

Su shuffled her choices warily; a discovered lie would produce an explosion so overwhelming as to make this one seem the lapping of a pond's waves but the truth would destroy all of love's aftertaste. She stared as Bettina turned her back in search of a cigarette, lit it, and wheeled back—an animal on guard between thrusts.

It would have to be the truth; acid was already rising into her mouth. "I was . . ."

"Never mind. I know exactly where you were—you don't have to scratch around for one of your clever lies. You were at Mamie Carter's, don't deny it! Why can't you just admit that you were at Mamie Carter's *all night!*"

Su moved the dog dish from under her. "Why do you keep putting Nefertiti's dish on my bed?"

"Because you don't care enough about her to bother to remember to put her bowl in the dishwasher so it'll get clean, that's why. You don't care enough about anybody but your own precious self to bother to ever think about the other person ever." Bettina dragged on her cigarette as if it gave her air; angrily crushed it out. "The world has been right, right along—lesbian affairs are just plain rotten. Sick miserable things, rotten to the core. I'll never fall in love with another woman as long as I live." She sat on Su's straw hat, raised up, and pulled it out from under her and flung it across the room. "How do you think it makes me feel when Mummy calls this morning and says Puddin said she saw your car at Mamie Carter's early today when she drove by and Mummy wanted to know if we'd gotten sick and had to stay over or if your car had gotten stuck in the sand . . ."

"In the driveway?"

"How do you think it makes me feel? And I have to think fast and tell her we'd gone there in two cars and you hadn't felt well and hadn't wanted to drive home . . . I had to think of all that while all the time you were feeling just fine, having the time of your life and I was even *worried* about you."

Ropes of guilt wrapped around Su's chest and squeezed her heart down to her stomach; love's aftertaste was completely obliterated in the nausea from that crowding.

"The fact is the car wouldn't start so I spent the night, but that's all."

Bettina's face balked at the edge of tears, clung there between belief and belief, hesitating in reverse.

"That's the truth. I just slept there." Su stood over Bettina's slowly changing face, wanting to make it believe her.

"That's all?"

"That's all." Because Bettina's face believed too easily, Su added, "Is *that* so important between us?"

"Not if you're in love with her. And I guess you are. Aren't you?"

"She's changed my life."

"Are you in love with her?"

"Yes."

"And you're wearing the see-through shirt *I* gave you for your birthday, for her!" Tricked and betrayed, Bettina welcomed the return of doubled rage. She yanked the shirt collar, ripping it. She seized Su's lip gloss and threw it through the open bathroom door, then her mascara, then a jar of foundation cream which smashed with a heavy plopping thud.

"The roar of the greasepaint," Su said.

Bettina came close to strangle her, breathing heavily into her face.

"The smell of the crowd." Su ducked under Bettina's arm and ran to the bathroom. "I am in love with her!" she shouted, quickly closing the door, her hand nervous at the bolt, unable to turn it at first. Once safe, she felt her back and neck stiff as hardened plaster. Over the sound of water running full force into the tub, her ear by the thin door, she heard Bettina shout through the walls as if they were air: "Then I'll leave!"

In Bettina's voice was the razor strap of her childhood, dark coarse-grained hide lashing out at her, pressing her back against the tiles. "I think that would be best," she said, not knowing whether Bettina heard her or not. She was shaking as she sank into the tub, taking the last of Mamie Carter's irreplaceable smell into the water with her to be obliterated by the soap.

Bettina sat in a corner of the living room, welts of sunlight through the venetian blinds streaking her face, while
Su told her about the book review she had written that
morning—had the courage to write, told her that she would
not ever again live a lie in any part of herself. Including the
two of them. Whatever happened from the review, even if
she got fired (because she would not withdraw it, change
it, soften it—whatever they said) she intended to go forth
into the sunlight from now on, having spent too many
years crouched against the stovewall grimy.

"That's me, I guess," Bettina said.

"It's not your fault . . ."

"Just my person. I always wanted you to speak up for
what you believed in but it has to be Mamie Carter who
gives you the courage to actually do it."

"I guess that's true. You didn't seem strong enough . . ."

"I'm not. I'm as weak as they come." Bettina's face
quivered as she insisted that Su was right to leave her, she
was a loser, and nobody in her right mind would take the
advice a person gave if she could see that the person was
nothing but a coward and a drunk. "I guess I thought that
I couldn't be strong unless you loved me, that if I was
weak enough you would have to love me, save me, or that
I would punish myself because you didn't love me, by
wallowing . . ."

"It's not your fault!"

"I know what you're saying: shut up and don't make
me feel guilty. All right. I'll shut up. But you'll see. I will
become strong. I'll pull myself together . . ."

Su held her head tight as if she were afraid it would fly
off. "*No.* It's too late. I can't go through this one more

149

time, this leave and unleave . . ."

"I didn't mean that. We'll part—I'll leave. I meant I was going to pull myself together." Bettina stood up. "What about dinner?"

Bettina wanted to fix it together, a last ceremonial laying out of her foremost pleasure. She was determined to begin being strong this minute—and keep the conversation going, forcing that voice she longed to hear many times before it left her, postponing the silence which would be ultimate if merely filled with all other voices in the world but not Su's.

("Would you like to eat in the kitchen or at the dining table?" "I don't care; whichever you prefer." "Either is fine. You choose." "Well, maybe the kitchen would be nice. Easier." "The dining table isn't too much trouble, if you would like that better." "All right. Let's eat there." "Are you sure you wouldn't prefer the kitchen? It *is* cosier.")

Good manners were molded into the special tenderness a woman feels who has at last said: I want to be free. Now, at just this moment, the love which was held in abeyance by the need to express hatred comes forth, threatening freedom like a soft paw on the shoulder threatens anger, covering the draw of freedom with memory (which pulls back the hand from the garlic on the shelf—it gives Bettina indigestion), with absence of tension (which slides off the edges of the paring knife), with jealousy (which measures the exactly perfect amount of butter and flour into a cream sauce), and loss. Loss pours into the rice, fluffing it; slips with the cream sauce around the onions, coating their shiny white into a center; holds the chicken thighs high up in the grease, letting them lightly cook.

150

The telephone rang and Bettina, signaling that it was the man about the roof leak, began a long happy conversation, the receiver in one hand, a cigarette in the other, alternating with a stirring spoon and a highball. Su felt the problems of the house crackling through the telephone wires, oozing into the kitchen, reminding her of Bettina's inestimable value as a telephone warrior of genius and the future with that black tormentor stabbing her ear alone. She motioned Bettina to forget about the roof leak until tomorrow. Bettina mouthed back, "No, he's going to fix it." She talked for another ten minutes, letting so much outside into the room that Su left it, shutting the door against it, and turned on Sibelius. The thirty-minute conversation would be repeated word for word, in dialogue form (then he said then I said) by Bettina grabbing at all possibilities of conversation. Su sat facing the windows; a streak of sunlight hit her eyes like a whip. She fixed herself a drink, dependent upon its sugar, and calculated how many days they would still have to spend together. Sibelius scratched her mind like a dry pillow between her teeth resisting her attempts to case it.

At the table Su saw only division. The chicken on its platter seemed separated into two opposing armies, breasts against thighs—white meat for Bettina, dark for herself. The rolls pushed at their saucer's edges, one against one. The onions fell too neatly into two servings, the salad hunched equally on either side of the wooden servers; only the rice fluffed together as a unit and Su reached hungrily for it.

The table itself would have to be divided since they had bought it together; each could have an end table to rest on a wall ledge. The chairs were six, the silverware would come out more or less even, most of the dishes were Bettina's . . . but what of the washing machine and dryer combination and the built-in dishwasher? All their goods of twenty years marched past her mind asking her to be Solomon himself but she would not be; the rug could be cut in two as easily as the table and the portrait of Bettina and herself would gain a lot by a median division—one the artist had painted into it even though at the time of their posing they had been most in phase, the artist (a friend of Bettina's family) more likely acting from innocence or delicacy than from prognostication. Su hated the portrait; it showed her in squares.

"Suppose I take you and you take me?" she suggested.

"Take us where?"

"You take my portrait half and I yours. We could re-frame them."

"Won't we look crowded against one edge and awful?"

"We could cut the other side down to match and mat them."

Bettina considered the portrait. She hated herself in it; it showed her flowing in circles. "I'd much rather have you. Do you really want to cut everything in half?"

Su thought so, if Bettina didn't mind. It was a way, at least, of making this parting final so they wouldn't have to go through it again. Neither of them would be willing to put all those halves back together.

Bettina stood holding the cheese cake up off the table. Her mouth was slipping but her voice was firm: "I'm not the least bit worried about you. You'll be so much better off without . . . alone. I'm really proud of you for writing that review this morning. I can hardly wait to read it. Tell me what you said."

Su stood up, her arm reaching for Bettina's shoulders. "Piglet," she said, using the silly name, one of the words their love affair had begun with, feeling it tug at the present like a bossy child. "You're so *good* . . ."

"Don't say anything." Bettina put down the cheese cake, hugged Su. "Now tell me what your review said." She listened to a verbatim repeat of Su's review, laughing between mouthfuls at each joke, chuckling during mouthfuls at every successful hit—all were, she said, grinning at the football images, the game she knew so well, accepting Su's credit to her for that language; hardly able to eat, she got up and poured more wine for Su, asking her to go more slowly, finally, beaming, she said, "I'm beaming from ear to ear. You've done it. You've gotten your memory back. Anyone who can write that and remember it . . . Su, you'll be famous."

"Or fired."

That didn't matter, Bettina was sure. The book would be a smash hit; she could write her play—I'll always be in love with you, her gray quintuplet eyes insisted.

"Now you've got to promise me that you'll call me Monday the minute you get the word from Frank," Bettina said, hovering in the doorway, postponing, postponing goodnight.

In the middle of the night, Su came downstairs to water her plants, stood by the fiddleleaf fig which she could never get to hold more than three leaves at a time. Her hope each time a new tiny leaf began to unfurl to become the pattern-breaking fourth was smashed within one or two days by the thin beginning edge of brown on the oldest of the fullgrown three, telling of its sure dying, however carefully she watered, fed, tended. There would be no problem with the plants if . . . when they split up; Bettina hated them for the unrequited care they demanded, hated all demanding things as reflections of herself. A twinge of pity for Bettina lodged in Su's fingers, the ones reaching out now to the fiddleleaf fig; did Bettina have a thin beginning edge of brown on her too? Pity fell off Su's fingertips with the ball of dust she had wiped from the oldest leaf (of three); Bettina's refusal to care for plants was metaphoric of her inability to clip, prune, stake, or turn herself in any way at all. Her talk, her love, her hatred grew wild in all directions, spilling over her own pot and into the air and light of everything else in her vicinity like those vines in Mississippi which can cover and strangle a whole forest.

part two

15

J ANUARY'S excessive sunshine brought the crocuses and jonquils out and then left, abandoned them to February as if February were as toothless as the old women. Jonquils and crocuses and then azaleas stood and blazed in their fragile colors and everyone knew they would get it, any day now the temperature would drop to freezing; still they popped up one after another thumbing their little cuplike heads at the calendar—all over town, yellow and white and pink and white and yellow spotted lawns and walks and foundation-hiding beds until the young women were saying that the weather had permanently changed because of those astronauts walking on our moon and the old women were muttering that the little things were going to to get it, mark their words.

They got it. February fifth frost came. The next morning the flowers drooped, wilted and crumpled, some still in buds, grew limp and brown and withered in such a total and useless way that even Su would not have found beauty in the word.

Su found beauty in nothing now. The cold matched her need and the gray days that strung out February made her feel closer to nature than she ever had; her flashing finished, she was now as wet in her soul as the rains of a cold coastal town could ever be.

Only anger sometimes flared.

"Goddammit, are you going to sit around the house all day again drinking yourself to death?" Bettina, fifty pounds thinner, stood in a regular size sixteen pantsuit accusing from the entrance hall of the house they still shared—inhabited, according to the census, under one roof.

Anger wasn't going to flare this time. Su took her gin bottle to the garbage can, reached under the sink, and took out a fresh one. She was a long time opening it because she was concentrating on her play. Creativity requires drinking, Mamie Carter had often said.

But the cause of Su's cold gray inside wetness was not Mamie Carter, although that had finished shortly after it began, shortly after she had been fired for refusing to pull her Oates's review, for insisting on running Daisy's outrageous write-up of the women's press books, for telling the office that she would not lie again for old Wilmington. The day she was fired was the happiest day of her life; the day she heard flatly that her book contract was off was the second happiest.

Her love for Mamie Carter had not ended but their affair had when Su realized that Bettina needed her. Mamie Carter was a fantasy, she explained to all three of them—a wonderful life-giving fantasy which had made her see herself and her life whole, see that her choice (Bettina) had been real and that that above all would be her commitment. She would never leave Bettina because she would always love her.

"I'm not against a little drinking, you know that, Su. But you're going too far lately. Don't you think you should see a doctor?"

"Doctor?"

Bettina took the bottle and opened it for her, setting it down slightly out of reach.

"The whole year is out of whack." Su reached for the bottle, sloshing ginperfume on her wrist. "I didn't do it. You think I made the jonquils bloom in January and the doctor can cure me and put them back inside their onions?" She licked her wrist, sucking it around the little knob of bone on the outside. Laughing. "I bloomed too" laughing "the crocus and the jonquil and I . . . all the white turgid underearth bulbous onions and me." She took the paper and a pencil, writing above *your family newspaper.*

Bettina said, "I didn't . . ."

"Shh. Maybe I did do it. I made—what did I say?— *underneath onions?*"

Bettina turned in her svelte knitted-for-mature-women pantsuit and looked for Nefertiti's food. "Under*earth* onions."

"Once we have sprouted out of our onions there's no coiling us back. Too turgid in there—every mite of space filled with cells no gin can touch; cells jampacked around

159

a jampacked center so tight you can't even see a pattern. I think the character here wants fame. Poor character."

"Are you still on the first act?" Bettina looked pointedly around the kitchen which, though not clean, showed no trace of dinner. Since she had started to work for the Wilmington *Commercial-Appeal* (television page), it was Su's job to fix dinner, hers to clean up after. "The before-dinner cocktail, as it were?"

"Poor character. I remember when I wanted fame." Su tore her writing off the front page and took the gin bottle back to her first act, covering the dining table and floor beneath. "Don't I? It was the attention. When I walked into an autograph party they rushed up to embrace, surrounded me with smiles at my jokes, covered me with kisses of response. I knew, as I wrote, that someone thrashed about all night waiting for the words I was writing, rushed out while I slept to read my . . . *opinion.* 'Su says . . .' 'Did you see where Su . . .?' 'She liked it!' When I was a child I was surrounded by a school of goldfish every time I went into the lake, covered by flecks of sunshine which came especially to make *me* warm, gathered themselves together like feathers around my cold. And birds opened up a trail of music (and closed it in a wake behind me) as I swept through the woods. And when there were nightmares there were eyes in every round irregularity looking at me, hands on every branch reaching for me, potential boos or shouts of triumph keeping silent until *my* ears were near."

"You're supposed to cook dinner," Bettina shouted. "Midge and Belle are coming over at eight. That's the arrangement."

"Some people are committed to their work with their life. Some people only with their temper." Su blew a kiss at Bettina who winced. "You think the difference between right and wrong is the difference between correct and incorrect? Poor character. She gets all the answers right—except a gentle few which she misses so people will like her."

Bettina disappeared into the kitchen, returning a few minutes later with a sandwich and a glass of milk. She hated sandwiches now; she had lost fifty pounds by eating lean meat and vegetables; the sandwich would mean no loss at all today, and with Su drunk it would be hard to keep her own drinking down to the carbohydrate level she had set herself. She gritted her teeth and felt their strength.

"You'll always love me, Bettina. Right?" Barely focused eyes hardly looked blue now they were so dull and bloodshot. Su smelled of soap from a recent bath, sandalwood between her pores battling gin from the pores themselves. Her hair needed cutting. Her clothes seemed not so much put on as there—cloth which somehow found a connection around her body one way or another. Her body no longer looked the correct weight even though it had changed little; there was something about the way it padded after Su's head or fell into a chair below her elbows that made it appear not to be correct in anything at all, although Bettina couldn't put her finger on . . . she shuddered. She no longer wanted to put her finger on Su at all. "You know I love you," Bettina said roughly, shuddering again at the lie. As soon as you get that play done, Su, so help me I'm leaving . . . a rat deserting a sinking ship? What else can the poor rat do? she hollered at her meddlesome conscience.

"Midge and Belle? Are we going to play bridge?" Su laughed nonsensically, dragging her laughing slowly through the air in front of Bettina's face.

"Hell, Su." Bettina slapped down the sandwich and stood over her former queen of scarves. "How long do you think I can take this? You're either laughing maniacally or crying like a fool. You can't do a damn thing right. You've been sitting here at this table for three months, drinking and laughing and crying and writing that . . . you're about ten years old."

Su scowled at her rubber band, concentrating on the fingers of her left hand. She held it up. "Look, I bet you can't do that. This end is looped around this finger through itself and so is the other end! See? It's very hard to do. You have to work one loop through the other loop without letting it unloop and since it's elastic, the one thing it wants to do is . . ."

Bettina left the room.

Ten years old was the age when the poor character had wanted fame badly. Fierce ten, bumping her head against the ever-lowering ceilings as she grew as tall in her mind as a gallery; vengeful ten, she expressed her cramped heart in the words, I'll show *them*; brutal ten, she tied her sexual body to a make-believe stake to be rescued and made queen; duplicitous ten, she learned that lying brought fame from every corner of her world, renown running to her feet like mice bringing her all the crumbs she could eat— you are clever, good, brilliant, our leader.

At five times ten the poor character still wanted all those things until one day she learned to humble herself with gin, the equalizer, the bringer of youth to the old. Mamie Carter had said, "The brain is very different in the young and the old. The old have successfully eliminated a large number of excess cells and grown over the years many increased clusters of idea-cells; their brains therefore

162

have a quite definite topography. If you can imagine a tiny wanderer among the brain's interior, for example, she would be climbing up quite a lot of hills, which we old women call *knowles* . . ."

A terrible glinting giggle appeared in her eyes and pink spots flushed both cheeks. One day Mamie Carter would die of a suppressed giggle—like a clot of air suddenly blocking the brain, the giggle would lodge at an opening and hold back life, like space, even better than a vacuum.

". . . old brains are defined, laid out, patterned, are in fact pitted and scarred and swollen into a million prejudices. It's the hardest thing in the world to stop a series of messages once the first one sparks off; therefore it goes without saying that old people need alcohol. Only the killing martini can reroute the series by opening up a sudden new path, only the deadly gin and tonic can free enough space for a new idea to take encouragement and grow. Old people without alcohol are like streetcars in San Francisco which *will* plod on down the hill, if something gets them started, in exactly the same creaking way they always did."

"Dear Mamie Carter," Su wrote somewhere on Act I. "My brain no longer creaks. Is that the origin of the expression for drunk: well-oiled?"

Bettina was still out of the room so Su answered the door, admitting Adele who lowered her eyes.

"Welcome, sister, welcome." Su bowed her inside. "Come have a drink with me. We're going to play bridge and you are welcome to play too. In my place, in fact. I am writing about a poor character who *still* wants fame at five times ten years old." Su pulled her to the pantry-bar and lined up bottles in front of her one after the other. "Your choice. Tell me, how did you avoid wanting fame yourself? You did, didn't you? Avoid it? I can tell by the happiness on your face that you never wanted what you didn't have."

Adele, her next baby barely plump beneath a dirndl skirt, sat down in the chair Su pulled her to and looked at Su for the first time. "Seriously, Su, I want to say something. I know it's none of my business but don't you think you've been drinking a lot lately?" Adele's ten-year-old eyes were really serious.

"I humble myself by drinking. That takes a lot of gin. I wanted fame very very very badly once, like a creaking streetcar wants to get to the bottom of the hill. Do you understand that?"

Adele shook her head, her eyes still serious and fixed on Su.

"My poor character grabs after fame but fame is like a speck of yolk in the middle of eggwhite and keeps slipping away from her. It's like eggwhite itself and takes the nearest vessel's shape—it slides like attention, or bunches up like renown, or divides like approval, or sticks like a compliment, or, if you whip it well, it peaks like money—or falls like love." Su drank from the bottle now and Adele lowered her eyes. "But it doesn't matter," Su said. She'd lost her image.

"I always thought you had a lot of talent; I know you did. And I always thought it was real mean the way you were fired. I mean, that talk about you and Sister . . . you all didn't do that and I know it."

"Yes, we did."

"No, you all didn't. I know it!"

"We did . . ."

"Now there's just a difference between *writing* about something and doing it and you know it. And a lot of my girlfriends feel just the same—all of us. It was because you

164

were a woman. Just because you write a review of those women's books doesn't mean you are the books. I . . ."

"Wait a minute. I wasn't fired because I was a woman. I was fired because I tore *Fear of Flying* apart and its publishers had paid for a big ad. You're not allowed to goose daddy."

Adele made a face. "I wouldn't want to either."

"But you are allowed to lick his ass." Su started laughing. "It's just your finger you can't stick in his pie."

"Su!"

"I'm an old warmare on the warpath, Adele. With a dirty mouth from all that licking. A foul tongue from always being behind, a forked tongue from trying to do two asses at once, a pointed tongue from serving those real tight ones . . ." Su ignored Adele's frozen face. "A thick tongue with shitty taste; a coated tongue with you-know-what; a loose tongue sinking ships on their way in—my own, and a native tongue when my oil is near." She patted her gin bottle. "My baby. When is your baby due?"

"August first. You sure have changed."

"Do you blame me? Wouldn't you have changed if you had been me?"

"Now just what answer is there to that?"

"You're tongue-tied?" Su put a hand on Adele's arm. "I'm sorry, I know I'm being bad. But I'm having such a good time."

Adele's vestigial ten-year-old face relaxed into a grin. "I don't mind. You go ahead. You deserve it." She swung her shining hair across her shoulders. "I think *I'll* have another drink and catch up."

"Right. You don't want to get behind."

Belle was the most talked about woman in Wilmington.

165

People spent more time talking about her than they would ever have spent talking to her: there was a tenacity to her problems that clung to an irritated mind long after she herself had gone home. Su thought it was because the problems were her personality—they were always just serious enough to involve a listener and Belle knew better than to solve them, diminish them in the slightest and thereby lose her audience.

"Belle, I want to talk to you." Su cornered her at the bar, blocking her retreat. "My poor character wants fame and I can understand that. I always wanted the ribbon from the judge when I rode in a horseshow—the winning blue silk from his own hands. What difference did it make whether my friend said I rode a good show? None. None at all. It was the blue silk from his own hands. The horse beneath me could run him down but that little scrap of shiny blue rayon with gold approval . . ."

"Are you riding now?"

Belle's face was strangely horselike and Su examined it carefully.

"I know I haven't seen you lately. You never call. I thought you might be riding now that you don't have to . . . are home a lot. I don't blame you for not calling me, though. I'd just talk about my problems. I can't help it but I know it's really boring for everyone else."

Very tired and horselike, especially around the mouth. Su looked under the mare's muzzle, the satinsoft space between the nostrils, to the strange mouth curved like a shark's. Isolated, a horse's mouth, closed, was a crudely-drawn slit, lipless. Yet it inspired its phrase . . .

"Nothing comes from the horse's mouth but green strings. It's the judge who has the ribbon." Su half-closed her eyes to focus upon the horse in front of her, daring it to open on anything but green strings.

Belle laughed nervously. "Claudia has taken up riding lately . . ."

Midge appeared behind Su behind Belle. Midge was beautiful. She had brown hair and brown eyes and skin the color of a Palamino's tail. She had always been beautiful and always would be; everyone agreed including herself; it was boring. Su turned back to the tired mare now squeezed close against the bar in the tiny hallway by her flanks. "Belle, tell me the truth, now wouldn't you rather have the blue ribbon than the green strings?"

Midge pulled Belle away, leaving Su to the arrival of Bettina.

"What's gotten into you?" Bettina hissed.

"Gin, I think." Su gave her a glazed sparkling smile. "Do you still love me?"

"You're *drunk*."

Su widened her smile winningly. "Do you?"

But Bettina was gone.

Leaving Act I and the poor character wanting fame strewn over and under the table, Su took her bottle upstairs so the others could exchange their sober glances undisturbed. Mamie Carter had given her freedom from fear and now she missed fear. Fear had provided a faithful spurt of adrenalin every day, loosening her muscles, letting her slide like lard through women like these, her friends once—fear making her able to please, think of the contact things to say, leaving her feeling warm and satisfied and shared. Fear had let her run up the stairs, if she had, excited by what they might say in her absence, not heavily plodding one indifferent step at a time as now. Could a woman live without fear and find anything to live for?

167

Would any woman beside herself know?

An hour later she had found the scrap of paper she was searching for with such concentration she had forgotten to drink from her bottle. She dialed.

"May I speak to Barbara Barbarachild, please?" Her enunciation showed little improvement from the abstemious hour; she repeated, "Barbara Barbarachild."

It was Barbara herself, surprised.

Does the brain hold a quantity of fear which it uses up with the years? Does fear grow slack with age like muscles? Fear narrow its range like the appetite, content with an unvaried diet? Is fear a casualty of menopause? "I thought you might know, Barbara. You're the only practicing radical I've met." Su's own practice had been brief: two stands against the *Commercial-Appeal*. She was too far from perfect.

Barbara had read Daisy's review of the women's press books, with the mention of Barbara's own group. Someone had also sent her the reviews of Joyce Oates and Erica Jong's *Fear of Flying*. Barbara had a clear analysis: on the one hand, it is good to review women's presses (an A for Su/Daisy); on the other, it is risky to attack women right now—there were reasons, we are not yet strong enough, there is support to the enemy, we spend our energies pulling each other down; however, on the third hand, some women are not "us," we are naturally interested in women, most involved when *they* uphold a male-dominant culture or sexuality; Barbara understood; and besides, since Su was fired for it, it may have been rightest of all. A conditional pass? "An incomplete," Barbara said. "Depends upon how you finish it off."

"I am finishing myself off."

That was bad, Barbara was sure.

168

"I am very bad." Su heard a knocking just off her skull, a vigorous demand for entrance. She heard a sudden friendly growl from the room's corner. A brief unidentifiable strain of music near the window. "What can I do, Barbara? Listen, I apologize for that lunch we had. I don't want to be famous any more. I just want to belong. How can you belong to your sisters in a town like Wilmington? There's nobody here except wives."

"You should have told me that you were going through menopause." Barbara's voice was northern cool. "You Southern women are so . . . funny. What's the big embarrassment? After all, it's just a natural phase."

"Who did tell you?"

"Daisy."

"She's from Memphis."

"But she couldn't tell me she was having premenstrual tension. I thought *I* made her cry."

"I could have told you." Su stood up to give her voice height. She sent her words out from her diaphram to minimize their blurs. "We are funny. We have to speak for each other. We've been practicing that for years now. Thanks, Barbara. I just found out where I belong." Su added a paragraph of conventional politeness. After she put down the receiver, she said softly, "Y'all come back now, you hear?"

She put the gin bottle on the bookcase, paired with a pre-Columbian head. "Sister, you've done your work for now."

16

OW MANY did you get?"

"I threw them in the shopping bag without counting," Daisy said. "A dozen or so."

Su peered at the red light as if it would try to escape. "The Hilton?"

"Sure. I'm dressed."

The man running the newsstand appeared to be trying to look less fatherly than he was. Daisy lingered at the woman's magazine section; in a few minutes she placed three magazines by the cash register.

"Excuse me, sir," she said softly, barely nodding at Su leaning over the newspapers wiping her forehead. "My aunt is having an awful hot flash." Daisy looked embarrassed. "It's terrible to bring it up like this, but could you possibly get us a glass of water?"

The man glanced at Su, lowered his voice. "Why, yes, m'am. I'd be glad to. Why, sure. My wife . . ." He darted a look at Daisy and rushed to the back of the store, hoping she had not noticed that he was about to—had given his age away, in case she liked slightly older men. "Here you are, miss."

Su accepted the water with her eyes downcast and whispered to Daisy. They quickly left, Daisy waving goodbye to the man with a look of great gratitude.

"Hey!" he called but they had gone. "Poor girl was so embarrassed she clean forgot about her magazines," he said to himself, replacing them on their racks.

"There's not a girlie magazine left in town!" Daisy dropped the last stack from the car on the floor of Su's living room, cover down. Glossy cigarette ads shone from every exposed surface of the six by six pyramid sloping like laundry. "You really did those flashes great."

"Practice. And natural sweats and shakes from gin withdrawal." Su smiled wanly. "I'd sure like a beer after all that water."

"Should you?"

"Maybe I really should."

"Now how can we do it next month?" Daisy stirred the pile with her foot to change the pattern. "I could put some blood on the back of a white skirt and you could . . ."

The pile of magazines hit Su's eyes with their gloss like slime; she saw behind them her pure flat black and white pages of Act I, still spreading like a frozen puddle over the floor; behind them were Bettina's newspapers from Sunday, Monday, Tuesday, Wednesday; behind them, a fiddle-

171

leaf fig with four leaves, one browning at the edges; behind that, a couch which could comfort her in its crumpled corduroy. Beside it, a telephone which rang.

It was Mamie Carter. Su's voice grabbed at an earlier lilt. Could Su come by for a drink tomorrow?

"I'm not drinking!" Su shouted, liltless.

"Good. Come at seven."

"Wait. How are you?"

"You'll see for yourself and you know I hate telephones —let me get off this thing. If you have an adventurous friend you can bring her."

"An adventurous friend?"

Daisy jabbed her chest with her finger, her face a grinning question mark.

"Are you getting deaf?"

"No. Yes. A little. I think I do have an adventurous friend here."

"Good. Tomorrow at seven?"

Driving home, Bettina thought of her job as her only present real happiness. Not because she liked working—she certainly did not like getting up every morning and working eight hours every day—but because the job coincided with and gave validity to her belief that she was America's touchstone. She had long felt that this was her unique value: her averageness. Whatever her natural tastes led her to, she believed that so would America's. As she laughed, so laughed the nation; as she cried, raged, outraged, or was bored. Any television programmer could count on her instincts. She did not need to analyze why a program would succeed or fail, she need only feel it for it to be true. Infallible averageness—in this lay her superiority.

And it was superiority, she argued with the spectre of

Foremother. Any ordinary thing that was perfect in its ordinariness was extraordinary. She viewed pilots and wrote her opinion. Polls followed. She applauded and audiences soared. She turned thumbs down and, Bettina-says-thumbs-down, viewers turned thumbs down. (Those who did not, those few—she said it like a dirty word, rimed with phew—those *few* could read a book.)

She had not slipped once in three months. Along with the happiness this brought, following along like a mangy cat that will not scat, thinning her exhilaration with increasing wakeful starts in the middle of the night which left her eyes gritty in the morning, was the fear now of even one miss. Only perfection was extraordinary. One miss, however trivial or soon forgotten, would unperfect perfect. A marred record is no record at all.

She had held the record for driving from Wilmington to Chapel Hill in college (although Foremother's car had needed work afterward). She had held her breath longest in grammar school, kept her yoyo going longest in junior high (nine hours); she had beaten everyone at drinking a jigger of beer a minute for an hour in high school. She held the girls' softball record for no-hitters in the junior Junior League league; she had had a record tumor removed from her abdomen: five pounds; she held the Wilmington Weight-Watchers' record now: fifty pounds in three months.

She kept a record-book of her records. She sighed. She supposed she should record again this year the length of time she had lived with Su—a record among the few women-couples she knew. A record-making that was about to be abandoned? During the middle difficult years, the hope of celebrating a lesbian golden wedding with Su had kept her tenacious; visions of that achievement had

173

blocked out any quarrels they might have had (over what? mainly Su's picking at her for not talking).

Su no longer picked at her at all. She hugged. Or she shouted. Both were invasions and Bettina would say that lately she was becoming nervous had she not firmly believed that only thin people were nervous. After the next fifty, though, she would sure lay her claim.

She lit a Kool from the present stub, stubbing out the old one.

Su no longer made fun of her records, either, and Bettina missed that. Records were her idiosyncrasy, her jolly fat personality, and she liked to be kidded about them. It made her feel special, like the tag-lines people put on their friends to tell them apart. Yearbook mottoes. Nicknames. Pet goofs. Hair colors. Dog tags.

"To hear Su talk these days, you'd think she was just plain against personality," she said to Nefertiti's rheumy adoration waiting for her at the door.

There was no bottle on the table this evening—on any table. She looked suspiciously at Su's hungover face, drawn, gray, tight with pain. Sudden fury invaded her. How dare you put me through all you've put me through for months and sober up now? she said silently, her teeth gritted against sound.

"I'm finished with gin," Su said. "Aren't you glad?"

Bettina sucked in rage and turned her face to the paper-strewn floor. "Does that mean you're going to clean up the house too? One careless match and we'd go up in smoke. Aren't you getting curious to know what color the rug used to be?" She jerked the cigarette from her lips so they could be widened to what she hoped was a smile. "Of course I'm glad." Teeth showed but no pleasure.

"You look like a cartoon," Su said.

"Of God? I was just thinking about the progidal son. After all that trouble, God was supposed to smile when he repented."

"Who's repenting?"

"Do you know what you said last night—to Adele, to Midge, to Belle, not to mention me?"

"You mean people do pay attention to things drunks say, after all?"

Bettina took the groceries into the kitchen. She would have to cook dinner and clean up tonight. She fed Nefertiti from a paper plate, the extra heavy, very expensive kind supermarkets sell for runny dinners. Although she had given up on getting Su to wash Nefertiti's dish correctly, she was still determined to make Su pay for it—halfpay, at least. The dog pushed the plate all over the linoleum with a paper-scraping noise every night before she would leave off licking its coated surface. Bettina waited irritably for the licking to cease, saw Nefertiti's ears gummy with dogfood as usual, as she sat at the kitchen table totalling her carbohydrate count so far for the day.

At a hundred seventy pounds, she felt much too thin. Her stomach, still a mound, gave her no pleasure—it was just an average-sized mound and the juices behind it constantly reminded her of its insides flat against her backbone. Too much was missing. She had shifted her fantasies to visual ones, nothing like as sweet as the ones of touching. She looked at herself in the mirror, shop windows, or down aslant at what she could see—often, more often, all the time, hoping to seize with her eyes what had been so rich to her palms. Enjoyment was pale and fleeting, nothing to build on, no rising swelling crescendo of overwhelming sense of self, no total immersion into being flesh, nothing but a little tweak to her vanity, quickly vanishing.

She crossed her legs—a two-week-old accomplishment by now—and figured she could have two drinks tonight. Four half-drinks. She mixed one and turned on her kitchen Sony to watch the news.

It's just too late, Su, she said to the anger rising from her vacant stomach at the sight of Agnew's face. And for you too, Spiro. Some things can't be forgiven. You think you can wipe out all those months of *wrong* with one day's sorry? And you're not *even* sorry. "You ought to be in jail," she said to the tv screen.

Su's hand jumped and she spilled the milk she was pouring. The puddle got the exposed ends of Bettina's Kools. "For stealing a few piddling magazines?"

"For *what*?" Bettina stared at her haggard face, more crumpled than Agnew's. "What?"

"We just took the porn off the streets. Daisy and I. We were talking for each other. I'd think you'd be glad now that you're working for our family newspaper."

"Su! You can go to jail for that."

A tiny current of fear returned, lapping her pleasure points. "Really?"

"You can't just *do* that. You just *can't*."

"What are you drinking?"

Bettina pulled her glass in close. "Where'd you put them?"

"They're the southwest part of the rug." After Bettina left the room, Su opened her rum bottle and inhaled until her head quieted down.

Past midnight Friday Bettina was startled awake by the telephone. It was Su, calling from jail.

"I knew it."

"We're here. Mamie Carter, Cad, Ella, Puddin, Luz,

Daisy, and I. "

"Mummy? Mamie Carter? Cad? Ella? Puddin? You and Daisy?"

"The whole kit and caboodle."

"*Mummy?*"

"See if you can find a lawyer who can get us out to-night . . ."

"You ladies aren't going *no*where tonight."

". . . first thing in the morning. Don't *worry*. We're all all right."

Su, especially, was more than all right. She was exuberant. Her blood, freed from its chore of creating uterine linings she had to then slough off, charged through her veins like spring torrents from grandmaternal mountains. Her brain's electric charges jumped easily·over the network of vacuums left by months of gin. Only her knees ached from the dampness of the cell.

Fortunately, they had gone under no disguise last night and there had been seven of them, so there were important differences separating them from the other incidents. Fortunately, they had been seen before they had done more than seize the three young men responsible for gang-raping the woman in a downtown shop, so there was no real crime on their part. Fortunately, they had not brought a board because there were three men. Unfortunately, they had chosen George Davis's statue, intending to tie the men in a circle around its base and let them be judged by the Attorney General of the Confederacy himself (and all passers-by); the statue, perhaps because it was near the Cornwallis house and police depend upon repetition, caught an officer's eye on well-traveled Third. Unfortunately, they had been caught. But fortunately, these men were known by Daisy as the ones who had forced her car off the road last summer; she had escaped by rolling up the windows and locking the car but she stayed imprisoned there while they rocked the car and taunted her until another car stopped. She had, with terrified boldness, taken their pictures; the raped woman had identified them. Fortunately, the raped woman was young and white and the police could imagine (although she was to blame, tending shop alone in the afternoon) that she was the woman they were supposed to protect. Fortunately, as usual, the rapists were white; the woman would not be offered the grim support of Rights of White People (pronounced rope).

Unfortunately, they could not agree on the next step.

"Get Davis, Dickinson, Bordon, and Boatwright," Luz said. "I know Jim Davis. He'll take the case."

"That old fool?" Mamie Carter snorted. "I'd rather defend myself."

"Well. His grandfather was attorney general of the Confederacy. I think his genes speak for themselves."

"In a hoarse far-off whisper. I'd rather have the old man's statue speaking for me than that tall drink of water. I don't know about you, friends, but I'm defending myself." Mamie Carter's mouth closed firmly around her decision.

"Me, too," Cad said. "I also filed to run for councilman this morning. Councilwoman. I never told you this, but my great-great-great-great-great—is that five?—grandmother was one of the citizens of this town who kept the British from unloading their stamps for the Stamp Act. That was eight years before the Boston Tea Party, Ella."

"Ella?" Ella said. "We may have landed in Boston but neither of my grandmothers poured anything but sweat."

"You've always been brave, Cad." Luz could not understand why anyone would willingly expose herself to public view, but public criticism? Examination? Digging into your private life, your past? Or even your present.

"I will, too," Mamie Carter said.

Mamie Carter's house, white, classical Southern, on the oldest street in Wilmington sheltered by huge live oak trees dripping with moss, protected all conversations. While Puddin mixed the drinks and Daisy carried them, Cad and Mamie Carter, the only two actually willing to run for public office, planned their campaign. Su, eager to be campaign worker, offered Bettina's services to arrange television time; offered her old friend at the paper, Mrs. Dibbs, for news coverage (although it would appear on the Life Styles page, formerly the Woman's Page). Daisy had heard in Chapel Hill that women referred to the North Carolina license-plate slogan as "First in Freedom—for Rapists;" a question mark was all it needed for their campaign slogan. Ella offered five thousand dollars from her husband on the spot. Puddin said she would speak to the League of Women Voters, unless they were too radical? "After all, they did speak out for the Equal Rights Amendment . . ."

Luz withdrew into her fear and spent the afternoon unnoticed. At five o'clock she got up to say goodbye. "I guess this means we won't be playing any more?" Reality struck the faces of her four best friends. No more bridge?

"We'll be so busy we won't even miss it, Luz," Puddin said.

17

"YOU'VE ALL lost your minds!" Bettina slammed Nefertiti's dinner to the floor, splattering the linoleum with juice from Particular Pups. Three half-drinks, finished in a few gulps, did nothing to cool or dampen her fury. She just wouldn't have it. She wouldn't have them making a spectacle of themselves pretending to be lawyers in court, she wouldn't have them exposing themselves to public ridicule by running for council, she wouldn't have had them spend the night in jail if she could possibly not have had it. They might as well stand on the corner of Market and Third stark naked, they'd fare better if they cut off a breast apiece and charged New Hanover County on horseback, they might just as well dig Bettina's grave. "Just take out a gun and shoot me," Bettina said in a glum pause for breath. "Just dig my grave and put me in it. I never thought I'd live to see the day."

Bettina's anger-power had not fallen off at all in her recent loss of other padding. Placed square at the head of the kitchen table, commanding the room, she left no doubt that she felt that all their actions, especially Su's, were tantamount to inviting the entire population, the dregs of the population of Wilmington, into the very house, the very bed she slept in. And of course she would lose her job—a minor point. She would never be able to get another one in Wilmington—a petty detail to Su naturally.

Opened up by belonging like a trellis of morning glory to the breakfast sun, Su felt the impact of Bettina's tongue as if it were an icy hose. "You don't have any coherence!" she shouted back. "You just have no coherence. You wanted me to review *Patience and Sarah* and lose my job when you didn't think jobs mattered because you didn't have one. Now that *you* have one . . ."

"You didn't do it!"

"I didn't accuse you of murder, either."

"So I've *learned* something."

"You've switched from one absolute concentrated position to its opposite. You'll switch back easy as pie. Anyone who puts her whole self of forty-six years into one blast of steam is bound to have all the power. You have to think to learn. You have to keep things around, make room for them, fit them into a pattern in you. You dissolve everything you ever *learn* in one day's boiling. That leaves you perfectly empty for the next thing you *learn*. And so on and so forth and so on and so forth until I feel cooked to nothing but mush. You have to have some co-

181

herence from day to day for christsakes."

"You don't." Bettina's face fell at the mouth like Nefertiti's saddest one. "You're an upstanding reporter, then you're a drunken playwright, then you want to be Texas Guinan. How's that coherence?"

"That's progression. Anyone can see that one leads to the next. Texas Guinan?"

Bettina smiled first. "She smashed the saloons with her ax."

"I bet she didn't do it and then forget she did it."

"I bet you won't forget what you're planning to do, either, if you do it." Bettina finished her last-allowed half-drink, decided she had miscounted, and fixed another.

"Are you going to get drunk now?"

Su stood up and breathed as much oxygen as she could find in the smoke-infested air. She turned her back and drank two glasses of chlorinated water from the tap. She concentrated on relaxing the convolutions of her brain until she felt them grow slack and smooth. She said, "I am going to do it anyway. All of it. Defend myself in court, campaign for Mamie Carter and Cad, and that's just a beginning. I'm going to write up the whole story and find out from Barbara where to send it. I'm going to start fighting and assume I have nothing to lose. Soon I won't. That's the only strength an old woman fighter has. So I guess you had better find another place to live and pretend you don't even know me. You don't have any other choice and neither do I."

Total loss threatened to drag Bettina under quicksand. She could give up Su as she could give up eating, but she could not bear to have the very food she was about to bite snatched from her mouth. "Are you making me choose between you and my job?" she accused.

"You're making me choose between your job and my life."

Su had seen Bettina as very strong when they had met and was unprepared for the weakness that masked; Bettina had seen Su as fragile and soft and was not at all prepared for the strength that that became. Su's love for Bettina had been enough in the beginning to allow Bettina to admit, express, even indulge her prior secret flaws; Bettina's love for Su had nurtured the stalks that sprung easily from soft pliable earth into strong trunks. Now they faced each other, seeing the product of their love so alien to the impulse that had set it in motion.

Su drove around in the rain for an hour, bringing her car to a halt in front of the house two down from Mamie Carter's. She had driven down this street four times, twice pretending to be looking for a number, once very fast as if pulled by a destination, once at upper-class neighborhood speed. She was afraid another pass would cause the quiet curtained houses to call the police. Her stopping might, also. She watched the side mirror for a patrol car, prepared to move up if one appeared and knock unannounced at that symmetrical door.

She was caught between habit and possibility, gripped on her right by a halfcentury's training that said old women are conservative, preserving what they have, bottling, jarring their past into rows on pantry shelves, filling their larder for the lean years ahead; simultaneously she was pulled from her left by a longing to smell now the faint combination of smells hovering in the area between Mamie Carter's ear and hair: shampoo and oil, her hair and her skin, perfume mixed, if her hearing aid was in place, with metal and plastic, with its lingering presence if Mamie Carter had thrown it off, irritated by its distortion and static. Within that circumscribed area's smell was the whiff of her answer—if she could just place her nose gently there for a calm second, inhale deeply Mamie Carter's own female underlay and chemical overlay, then she would, like the sibyls at Delphi, pull the exactly proper vapor into her brain's hollows and speak for her own future.

Even though Mamie Carter had said she would never live with Su (it wouldn't do), had said that living together had nothing to do with loving (but it does! Su had cried); even though she had accepted without a ripple Su's decision to stay with Bettina; even though, now more than ever, Mamie Carter had her life full; even though . . . no, especially because Su's own name was clouded by the town's tongues, she knew she would find out the truth in that chamber of air caught between Mamie Carter's ear and hair . . . *if* she could thrust her long, quarter-Jewish, lowclass nose out and sniff. If she dared.

Crouched in the moss-blurred shadow of a five-hundred-year-old tree, the street a tunnel of dark glistening green—among it the green of camellia bushes which would flower tomorrow if the sun came out, her car a cavern of metal receiving rain filtered through the tree's umbrella, she experienced the sudden certainty that she had always been here, right here—all her life with her shoulders hunched beneath age, her eyes pointed down tunnels, her ears pelted with the wet leftovers of the most desirable block; always here—pushed and held, pushed and held, longing and self-preservation squeezing her in a clamp, concentrating too much of her in her middle while perfectly balanced houses drew their curtains and spoke their inside words behind them, ignorant even of her presence.

It was a moment of absolute selfknowledge without

184

measurable duration.

She was suspended in it weightless, and it in her.
Her heart was a vacuum and she was its center.

It certainly isn't necessary to act now—there is always
tomorrow. It is late—almost nine o'clock; she might be in
bed already. The rain will drench you on the way to the
door; you will look bedraggled and old. At least you could
telephone first; where are your manners? Every impulse,
if it is a true one, comes again; second thoughts never
stopped anything but mistakes. Go is a good dog but hold
fast is better: her own mother's favorite. She could hear
the exact intonation, see the slightly-turned away face as
her mother said the phrase, often, very often—she said it
herself now, exactly the same, the face turning away after
go to avoid seeing the chagrin in the face receiving, the
shameful acceptance, the speechless deflation, for who can
answer the mistress's evaluation of her dogs? Go is a good
dog but hold fast is better go is a good dog but hold fast is
better go is a good dog go is a good dog go

She went, running through the rain with short steps to
avoid slipping on the sidewalk, up the front walk, walking
up the steps, and rang the bell. Rang and rang and rang.

Mamie Carter opened the door with a smile of welcome
and no surprise, but that meant nothing coming from a
trained Southern face. "Come in, Su"—but that meant
nothing because she was already in, dripping on the Oriental rug. She patted her hair with a kleenex quickly soaked;
rivulets ran into her eyes. "Su, you're sopping wet!"
Mamie Carter brought a towel from the downstairs lava-
tory, placed, for male guests, just off the entrance.

"Come in and have a visit. I'm so pleased you dropped
by." Mamie Carter's voice pretended it was tea-time.

185

"Won't you have a drink?"

"I'm not drinking still."

"Good. You know I never drink during Lent. I'll make us some tea."

Su followed her close, her head forward so she could get a glimpse of that corner of her head where hair and ear met; so close she could have, by darting her head a foot forward, thrust her nose . . . she felt her nose to see if it was still wet and Mamie Carter had already turned to fill the kettle.

Comrades for future battle, they talked of strategy for an hour. Su passed on Bettina's fears, lingering over the image of their cutting off a breast apiece and charging New Hanover County on horseback.

"Doesn't surprise me a whit," Mamie Carter said. "I've known her mother for some time now. Luz would never have given us the time of day if it hadn't been Miss May's little sister Almeta who was raped in the first place. She was so damn furious when a policeman hinted that Almeta made it up that she wanted to tie *him* to a board. But we had a time with her on the next one. Tell me something, Su—you've been out in the world—what makes women so frightened?"

In the middle of a gold couch on an Oriental rug with an ancestor in oil overseeing her answer, Su said cautiously, "You're not, Mamie Carter."

Mamie Carter was leaning her head to one side, exposing half of the triangle containing Su's future, unobstructed by the tiny button from Nu-Tone. If the roles were reversed, *she* would find the courage to insert her nose into Su's space—find it ready on the top surface of her heart or even standing tall, jerking its hand into the air eager to be called on.

186

"No, I never was," Mamie Carter said. "Even when I was a little girl. Mother used to tell the story about the time I ran into the ocean—I must have been about three or four. Mother and I had gone down to look because the waves were higher than a house and before she knew it I ran in and disappeared into the stomach of the wave. The next wave picked me up and deposited me as nice as you please back in the shallow by Mother's feet. Mother told the story that she ran into the ocean knowing she could never find me there—the wave took the child and only the wave could give her back. A little more tea, Su? Yes, I remember another time—I was older then—when . . ."

The muscles of Su's face ached from the effort to hold her nose in check. Once the stories started they would go on until bedtime, which would be her go-home time because she was as inert as a winter fly. She opened her mouth. At first no words came out. Then she shouted, "I don't want to hear any more family lore!"

Mamie Carter drew very erect. "Now you just listen to me, Su . . ."

Su seized the bend of Mamie Carter's right shoulder with her left hand, the left bend with her right hand equally, and put her face against Mamie Carter's hair, inhaling to her toes.

"Stop that nuzzling at my ear."

She pulled away and Su let go simultaneously, Su sitting back with a smile which spread all her escaped muscles. "I had to sniff out the answer this time."

Mamie Carter snorted. "Funny place to put a question."

"I threw it into that spot behind your ear and the spot threw it back. No more fear."

"Fear is one thing, rude another." Mamie Carter stood up. "Well."

187

"I'd better go."

"You're welcome to spend the night but it is getting late. I can't stay up all night on tea."

"I'd like to tuck you in if you'll allow it, then I'd better go home. The people in this town are car-spotters."

"Certainly not."

Su waited for the reference; none came. "Certainly not what?"

"Of course you can go. But you certainly won't tuck me in. I never heard of such a thing."

"I could rub your knees."

"My knees don't need rubbing."

"Mine do."

"At your age?" Mamie Carter's eyebrows made a grooved seashell of her forehead.

"I'm on my last legs. Out on two limbs—is that better or worse than one? Does love temper the race to the worn knees or will you run me ragged. Am I trying too hard? I want to catch up. I understand that love is not living together. I think." Su's face was wistful.

"While you're making up your mind whether you're going or staying," Mamie Carter said, reseating herself, "you better sit down and listen. I'll tell you one reason women are so frightened all the time—they listen too much, start listening early like all little animals and by the time they're grown they make up their minds they'll never listen to anyone again, just when they might hear something different. They get stuck with the things they heard when they were helpless and little. Now you can't tell me the women I know have anything in common with the rabbits in the forest. Obstinate, that's what they are. Stubborn as mules. What makes them still think of themselves as rabbits? They sure aren't listening any more. Haven't got time, they'll say when they have all the time in the world—the time of their lives, you would say." Mamie Carter chuckled. "It's the special quality of age that it alone has available to it, to its brain, its recall, the majority of the person's life. Only in age can one brain be all ages. Because a woman in the middle can look forward and backward, she will naturally see that youth is to anticipate, to expect, and age is to possess, to claim, to have available."

"A decade in the memory is worth two in the hope," Su said.

"Because the life of the mind is more intense, more complete than the life of the body everyday and because the novelist creates by rounding out, filling in, and rearranging everyday, the old mind is the complete novelist, or the completed rounded-out filled-in novelist is the old mind, with every past age and day at its mindtip. The truly free is she who can be old at any age. Now you know, Su, that it's not necessary to be old to think old. It has been said that geniuses are forever old. And it is true, you're only as old as you feel. Or as you look."

My darling's face has been walked on by life, Su said silently, a kiss at her mindtip. "What about Bettina?" she asked aloud.

"Bettina will be all right when she reaches menopause. She will be old again as soon as her body stops being under the moon's dominion. The child and the old don't go by clocks and don't know fear. Time took away the child and only time can give her back."

"I guess I'm not as old as I used to be," Su said, taking Mamie Carter's hand in hers with total affection.

"You have plenty of time."

"I'll move the car," Su was at the door in no time.

"You'll get soaked to the skin!"

189

"I'll just put my car on someone else's block. Spread the wealth. Sow the rain and reap the gossip." Su turned briefly from the door opened into a downpour. "I'll be back in two shakes of a duck's tail."

"I'll have a duck-towel waiting."

Su woke up a few mornings later wet between her legs. Spotting. She had had that before. Bleeding? On the toilet she wiped and wiped and still the toilet paper showed red—not brown, bright red. She was menstruating again.

Really menstruating? How could she accept the joy that whipped through her whole self, carrying the vivid proof that she was young again . . . reprieved from old age, youth restored, possibilities magically given back to her—was it her daring in letting her love for Mamie Carter be that caused this churning in her uterus, reward, proof that love is life-giving? Her face in the mirror was plump and glowing, a mere forty. She ran down the steps like a child.

"Bettina!"

Bettina had left a note: Daisy called.

Daisy lived on Wrightsville Beach. After they picked up their unemployment checks, Su drove her home: February twentieth, the temperature was seventy; they took a lunch and walked on the beach, letting the sun beat the winter chill out of their heads and backs. Staring at the crystal green of the winter sea all things seemed possible and spring, for the first time, inevitable.

Daisy's vigorous lightbrown hair and sunlit youth reached out for Su, including her, as they schemed confidently, laughed, caught shells, scratched at the sand. Lying on her stomach, Su felt her belly flat and concentrated. She was remembering Lumina, which had been torn down

190

before Daisy got here—a huge winking pavilion which the electric company put up to induce people to ride the electric railway to the beach. "They decorated it outside with thousands of bulbs, that was why it was called Lumina, and had free dances. I remember one Saturday night I was there with Kip, pouring gin in our orange crush, and we danced together. We didn't dance close, we jitterbugged, but it was the most daring thing I'd ever done in my life. I could hardly go to work next day, I was so sure I'd be fired." She thought a minute. "Do you think my mother is right—in the South at least people don't care what you do, it's what you say that counts? You can be a lesbian but you can't call yourself one. Or, words act louder than peeking?"

"I've never thought about girls—women that way before . . . until recently. I guess. I mean I'm not sure I'm . . ." Daisy looked as if she were expecting to be chastized, criticized, rejected.

"Looks are deceiving, books bereaving? Daisy, you don't have to feel *guilty*."

"Shouldn't I? I'm already twenty-four."

Closer to my age from the bottom than Mamie Carter is from the top? "You have plenty of years left for women," Su said. "You know, I'd like to play tennis again." She saw her legs tan and muscular again, her skin oiled by the reappearance of her eggs. "I'm having my second coming. Men would call it, a new lease on wife. Would you like to play now, on Bettina's Mummy's membership?"

It would be going down instead of up, back instead of forward, Su argued with the sun-streaked grimy windshield in Wilmington's ugliest afternoon traffic through the billboard underbrush. Or starting at the beginning instead of the end. Not me, she said aloud. However much I like to talk into that healthy face. One little jigger of blood isn't enough to make me go through the twenties again, or the thirties or forties. One perfume-bottleful of blood isn't enough to wash away the smell of my darling's ear-by-the-hair. Not me. Tempt away, uterus. Red as a camellia on the first day of spring—that is, February twentieth. It's only blood, you know, that's all; don't you worry, Mamie Carter, I love with my heart not with my eggs and gin is thicker than anything, our cement, our sharp, clear inheritance of courage, as the witches knew: her brew.

18

PUDDIN WAS the only one of the group who did not live in town. Her family house, where she had been born seventy-five years ago and now lived in all alone, was on Masonboro Inlet, southeast of Wilmington. The house like its neighbors was set so far back from the road, at the end of a drive which cut a path through centuries-old live oak whose moss hung nearly to the ground, that it was visible from the gateway only as a suggestion of a house, a partial picture of doorway and some adjacent porch and wood which the mind had to construct into a full building.

Su nosed her Mustang into the driveway with a sense of violation and drove gently through the crimson azaleas and camellias which glowed against the fall of gray moss, slightly lavender in the twilight. The house, behind that curtain, sat squarely in its clearing and assumed no other space. The white of the house and a small, rundown building which was the old summer kitchen had a quality of whiteness hard to identify; Su stared at the paint which was not exactly flaking, was not even clearly in need of a new coat; the texture of the wood and the layers of paint was soft, antique, porous, pricked over by decades of salt air which gave the white a depth, a dimension not often possible with white.

Inside the house, age was repeated in the entrance hall— really a parlor-sized room containing stairs and a French-door view of the other half of the yard, a long moss-filled rectangle leading to the misty water of Masonboro Inlet. Age pervaded the living room bordered on two sides by a porch whose ceiling was at the floor of the upstairs bedrooms (providing them with their porch) which sheltered the west and east sides of the house from the summer sun. In Februaried twilight, the room was thick with shade and harmony.

Except for the children's wall: the photographs of Puddin's eight grandchildren, taken by modern photographic techniques, glared with the gloss and color of perfect young faces. In an attempt to accommodate that youth, Puddin had had two chairs recovered near the wall that held the children; they too separated from the rest of the house like curdles of sour milk in coffee, holding youth at arm's length away from the strong faces of age.

Puddin greeted Su with the customary kiss on the cheek, laying her sere silken skin on Su's for a fleeting instant. Inside her own house, her small frame expanded as if magnified by the seventy-five years collected in these rooms. Su had barely listened to Puddin's voice before and thought she might be hearing it for the first time.

"Look around," Puddin offered to Su's expressed admiration of all that beauty. "Take a walk down by the water, anywhere you want. If anyone asks you what you're doing tell them you'll tell them later. That's what I always say: I'll tell you later."

A terrible anxious trembling had seized Su at a glimpse of Mamie Carter, sitting well away from the children's wall; Mamie Carter, fitting in here like azaleas among the moss . . . Su accepted the invitation to take a walk, to let the air of Masonboro in more gradually—to ease the shock produced by an abrupt entrance into old gentleness. She could not bring herself to call the woman before her, whom she hardly knew, Puddin. Was her name Pudding? "Thank you. Thank *you.* Very much. I will."

Maybe I am just not old enough, she said to the largest tree she had ever seen, dominating the back land. The blood of her unseasonable menstruation was a blaze of bad taste against the moss—the red of the camellias was right, the same red of blood clashed; the new rose of the azaleas right, the children's cheeks plastic. Moss encircled its own.

She leaned her back against the biggest tree she had ever seen, on the side away from the house, hidden like a child in a game, facing Masonboro Inlet where pirates used to find cover in their own games. She could be found easily. Then she would be It.

19

VICTORY AND defeat followed November's elections. Cad had won easily, was elected councilwoman of the city of Wilmington by a conservative electorate because of her age and standing in the community. Mamie Carter had lost heavily, running for the newly constituted Board of Commissioners for the newly consolidated government of the county of New Hanover, defeated by the vastly increased conservative majority interested in opposing everything on either side of its private middle.

Her defeat had been magnificently aided by Su, who discovered her anger just after she began campaigning. March first anger rose into her brain, seeped into every

196

cavern left by the sisterly gin, took full possession of every vacuum and wiped-out cell, dug in its toes, and waited. March third a chivalrous remark from a newspaper reporter brought the first lashing from Su's tongue. Every subsequent occasion, to the initial delight of Mamie Carter, brought the same boisterous fury expressed in words Su had never had so ready, oiled, honed, cooperative. After two weeks, Mamie Carter's own anger asserted itself, at Su: "We're going to end up with fewer votes than McGovern if you don't control your tongue," she told her co-worker. "I'm sorry," Su said. "I promise not to get angry again in public."

Until the next remark seeded another full torrent of anger—flowing, pouring, cascading down from the speaker's platform like a mountain waterfall, sparkling and shimmering and clean as glass, glistening and fresh and pure as spring. "I promise," Su repeated each time. "How can I believe you?" Mamie Carter said in disgust. "I promise. I really promise."

But Su was at the spout. There was no way to let out a drop of fury, as if a geyser could refuse to drag its rushing tail after the first gallon was spat. The push on the geyser's water was from the bottom; the top was merely material sitting there, that is, Su. She was sitting on the spout of herself; the force was from her own bottom; once she, spout's cover, was knocked off the opening, the entire stream of scalding water escaped at once, scalding her too.

Wise women say we hold back anger, sit on our spouts, because we are afraid our expressed anger will result in loss of love. Su could tell them that it does result in loss of love, yes. And votes.

Love. She tried to explain to Mamie Carter that the anger came from a lifetime of deception. She had spent fifty years longing to be inside the rich, moss-grown world of upper Wilmington and now she saw that all her energies had been wasted, there was nothing here. "Maybe you're not as inside as you think," Mamie Carter said, firmly closing the door.

Su felt deceived by her mind. She could imagine love, beauty, being another, but she could not have it. She said to Mamie Carter, "Imagine our minds mingling into each other, interswirling, contact at every point so permeative that touch would be a ridiculous word to describe it. And then allow me to touch your mole." "Which mole?" Mamie Carter said with a snort. Su reached out and touched a mole at the base of her neck. "Don't expect me to accept touching your mole," she said. "After I touch it I will put a hand on your arm, another over your heart, an arm around your thigh. Then you'll draw back and claim the mole was touch enough. Then I will eat you and devour you." "Su, control yourself."

Control Su tried. Sitting on the spout, she could become a steam engine if she could learn to raise up and down in regular squats and if she had something for the resultant power to turn, a wheel of some kind, however tedious. It would be a way of falling in line with the mechanized rest of things. With regular squats. The regular-squats alternative.

But the geyser had already known the freedom of eruption and Su, spout's cover, was growing old and fit loose. The next encounter brought the next eruption:

"Supposin you ladies planned those rapes just so you could conduct this here campaign?"

"What?"

"Ya gotta look at whose benefiting from the publicity of them rapes. Looks like to me it's you all. Getting folks all upset and afraid to step outa their houses in the evening, naturally they want to vote for the fella that'll stop it. So I say, the main benefits are going to you all, seems like it's possible you set it up in the first place."

"You mean you think we got those people to agree to being brute and brutalized just so . . ."

"*If* it happened. Ain't nobody been convicted yet. Ain't no proof any of it *happened*."

"You *man*," Su began screaming. "You primitive, proof-hungry, cell-clogged, mechanized, will-ridden, eye-proud, unqualified male human . . ."

Mamie Carter stepped in front of Su, hearing the last few words shouted from her back into her overly-sensitive hearing aid.

Mamie Carter sent Bettina to talk to Su in June. Bettina had moved out of their joint house March first and had not seen Su. She was amazed at how well Su looked.

"Su, you look marvelous," Bettina said over and over. She was re-experiencing the strong attraction she had first felt for her queen of scarves. She thought she could fall in love again, partly because she knew she too looked marvelous—another thirty pounds gone, Bettina felt skinny and desirable.

"Don't get too thin now," Su said, alarmed at how little was left of her second and longest love. "You be careful now, you hear?"

"I hear you're spouting off at the mouth everywhere you go," Bettina said. "That's what I hear."

"Spouting is right." Su's eyes were flashing like sapphire. "I have to make up for so many years of letting things go by. I can't help it. I don't really want to. Every time I speak up I hear a pair of tiny hands clapping inside my head. They belong to a woman who doesn't dare say anything, who can't yet. But she claps like the devil. You know I always wanted to be an actress. And each time, if I think, no, I won't say anything, she pokes me. In my head. I imagine her as a little femina, two centimeters tall. My microscopic sister on the whatnot shelf."

"Mamie Carter isn't clapping," Bettina said.

"Yes. I know." Her face dropped into sadness.

Bettina's heart fell flat from what that sadness meant. She shook herself in an attempt to scatter nostalgia like water in fine drops. Their lives had changed so much in three months. Her own, living on Wrightsville Beach now with students and young outsiders, was more nearly bohemian than any she had ever experienced. Su's, crowded into a garage apartment between a huge couch never meant for this space and her collection of reviewed books and half-written plays, jobless still, seemed to be a fall forward into the abandonment of old age. Her unemployment was about to run out. She had no car. She bicycled everywhere and claimed she would not work again until her anger was twenty-one.

"I'm dedicating my life to her, whatever the trends of the times. No more anger-sitters. No more camps or schools. No more lollipops. She's going to get all the advantages my expanse of years can provide, every opportunity to become whatever she wants to become, even if she just wants to get married and have lots of little angers. And Mamie Carter will just have to accept it."

"I guess it would be asking too much to wait until after the election?"

"Push my baby back inside the womb? Hold her head when she's already pointed down the chute and keep her stuck there for six months just to please *voters*? Oh, no."

Su squeezed between the couch and the books and looked in her cupboard. "Have a glass of gin, Bettina. I don't have any Tang. It's all dye, you know. Gingerale, tomato juice, soda, ice water—soda and lemon?"

"Thanks," Bettina said. The sharp slap of gin's first taste made her worry quiet down. She had delivered Mamie Carter's message. She had done all she could. She took off her jacket. It was much warmer here than at the beach; the fear of being too hot invited the close heat of June right in next to her skin. With the smell of gardenia and freshly-cut grass from the open window rubbing her nose in summer, she felt exposed, barren. Her birthday was last week, her forty-seventh.

"How's your job?" Su asked, sensing her envy.

Bettina smiled. "Thanks for asking." Everything was in great shape at the paper. They really appreciated her down there. She told Su an office operation, an office triangle, an office vendetta. There was just one thing, a rumor really . . . *The New York Times* was going to buy the paper, they were saying, and syndicate all the columnists. Bettina drained her glass and held it out.

"Help yourself," Su said.

"I don't know how you fixed it. It was just right." Bettina saw Su unmoving and got up. "How much lemon did you put in?"

"A half."

"How much gin?"

"Ten gurgles."

Bettina drank half her drink before she sat down again, pulling at the too-clinging material of her pantsuit on her knees. Su, cross-legged in baggy cotton, clucked in mock sympathy.

"Well, anyway, as I was saying . . ." Bettina paused to

light a cigarette.

"You've already got one lit."

"Oh." She put out the fresh one, picked up the forgotten one, and pulled a half-inch into her lungs. "It's just a rumor really and I know they just wouldn't do that to us —I don't mean to me but some of the feature writers have been around a long time and they just wouldn't . . ."

"Fire you?" Su laughed. "I'd been there twenty years when they fired me."

"That was different."

"How?"

"Besides, Mr. Flack promised that even if they use their own wire service, he'd personally see that we all got placed in some equivalent position on the paper—that it would be expanding and there would be jobs for everybody or almost . . ."

"You're going to be wanting to borrow my daughter?"

"Goddammit, Su, it's the best job I ever had, it's the only job I ever had where I felt I was really somebody, it was . . ." Bettina was crying.

Su reached out for her diminished shoulders and held her. "Listen, if I ever get my house sold you can have some of that money to live on."

"I was forty-seven last week. I'll never get another job. A decent job. I'm too old."

"I know," Su said, hugging her until the sobs stopped. "I know how you feel."

"What am I going to do?"

Facing Bettina in the June sun, Su saw that the lines had deepened around her mouth, above her eyes—as if released from the excess fat which had held her face stretched and plump, Bettina's skin now dipped into the valleys and rivers of her experience. "Happy birthday." Su reached out to touch her cheek, prove its age with her fingers. "Have you started flashing yet?" Bettina shook her head. "You will soon," Su said, kissing the crest of her cheek. "You'll be all right soon, Piglet. Age took away the child and only age can give her back. Have some more gin." Su fixed it for her this time.

Bettina did not go home until the bottle was empty, until her mind was so loose from dead-cell space that she gripped the wheel of her car like the arm of her enemy, squeezing through to the bone.

Su rinsed out the bottle, ran hot water over it until the labels came loose, dried it, and filled it with cornflowers from the garage-owner's garden, rose and blue and white. She pulled out her play, Act I, retitled it *Sister Gin*, and wrote a dedication to Mamie Carter:

> To her and to my mother and to my mother's mother, Fanny, and to my father's mother, Mary, and to their mothers whose names I don't even know although I know their husbands' fathers' names, both first and last, and to all my daughters named anger, nothing for short.
>
> Act I. Enter Mamie Carter, a seventy-seven-year-old member of old Wilmington, combining the beauty of age with the strength of woman, and, behind her, a timid hesitant woman of indeterminate age, about fifty, who is trying to tell her something.
>
> Mamie Carter: You know I can't hear you when you whisper behind my back, Su.
>
> Su, afraid of losing her job, is silent for a moment: It was nothing.
>
> M.C.: I know you said something.

Su: Nothing, really. It was only . . .

M.C.: Speak up, child.

Su sucked her pencil and read through what she had
already written for Act I, about the poor character who
wanted fame.

> Act II. Election night. The living room of an old
> moss-hung house overlooking Masonboro Inlet.
> Many people are there, including a number of
> women in their seventies.

> Puddin, a smallboned, very short woman whose
> house this is, to a little girl: Look around all you
> want to. If anyone asks you what you're doing, just
> tell him you'll tell him later. That's what I always
> say: I'll tell you later.

> Su, to the child: Run on and play, Anger. I'll join
> you after while. (To Mamie Carter) Well, you lost.

> Mamie Carter, snorting: Lost what? Didn't I make
> their ears prick up? What was lost? They'll never
> hear the same again. (Leans closer to Su) Of course
> you helped some. I'll give you that.

There were no camellias election night but the moss still
dripped to the ground. Su and Mamie Carter leaned against
the triplet tree claiming the whole lower yard by Masonboro Inlet.

"I'm sorry you lost."

"Lost?" Mamie Carter snorted. "We didn't lose anything. We made the whole town sit up and take notice.
You and I together did. Why, if you weren't going to be
so busy writing a play, I'd say we could . . ."

"I don't think I want to write a play now." The water

of Masonboro Inlet was darker than the night sky. Nestled into its ink were thousands and thousands of oysters, not yet polluted by industrial waste but pale and watery from the year's excessive rains. It tickled Su to think of them lying in their beds; not hiding, just slowly growing plump and making pearls. It made her laugh. She wanted them to be hiding; she wanted to be It. "Not exactly a play." She nuzzled Mamie Carter's ear and bit with her lips the wrinkled flap of her lobe. She wanted to dive into the water and find some of the oysters. She wanted to come back to the tree then and call: All out come in free! She wanted to climb to the top of the tree and hang from its five-hundred-year-old branches and shout so that all the women could hear, even those who didn't listen any more: *All out come in free!* That would be her play. Or book. Or . . .

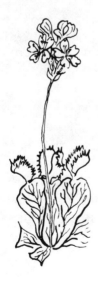

20

ISS SU, you haven't forgotten *May*. Oh, I know I'm in there, moving around the table, going through the door, but I'm not there. Now you know how you were feeling when those books put you in them. They let you move around a little while and then go on out the door. You didn't *say* anything but pretty soon you got you a Sister Gin to say it for you. Haven't I got as good a claim to that sister as you? I been drinking gin long as I can remember. The young ones they switched to bourbon now if they can afford it. If they can't afford nothing they switching to Scotch. But old May been faithful to gin. I don't care if they *do* say we like it, like we're supposed to like pink. If there're any messages in that bottle they surely are for me. Now *you* know, Miss Su. You ain't like those white folks that come down here from the North and treat us just like they do they own folks—they act like we aren't any different . . .

A hunger-pain tapped Su's stomach as the room suddenly darkened. Fear made her start—the fear that makes one's eyes look at the clock, check the calendar. She got up and opened the refrigerator on the comfort of a carton of raspberry yogurt. She picked up the telephone and dialed four digits of the number written so many times it now covered every inch of a torn envelope—and hung up.

She discarded the pencil for a ball point's greater authority.

. . . different. (Different?) Mrs. Davis. That's what they call me. There that Mrs. Davis is, right on the envelope. Mrs. Robert Davis. I wonder how it got delivered. I *know* I'm not going to get no envelope that says *Ms.* Davis. You sitting over there. You thinking, now how must I back this envelope? You thinking. Mrs. Davis. Ms. Davis. You got the pencil. You got to make up your mind . . .

Su looked at the telephone with an overwhelming longing.

"I never saw an eye could dial."

"Sister G.! Where've you been?"

Sister Gin crossed her toes, sat on her hands. "You know what shyness is? Feeling lowdown on the hit parade. That's all. The politics are so clear it's going to be hard to construct silly enough examples to illustrate them. You'd better just call her."

Miss May?

I'm right here in the same place you left me. Come on over, Miss Su. And bring your friend. That's a sister after

207

my own heart. You all are welcome to a drink of gin. This is House of Lords. Robert bought it for your visit. I say, House of Lords? Who you think you are, old man? I say, if you buy it, I'll drink it. Names don't taste, nor know who puts them in the glass. Miss Su, there's ice right there in the drawer of the refrigerator. That's my new refrigerator. Makes ice while you sleep. But do it make ice while you dance? I asked the man. I don't need all that much ice while I'm sleeping . . .

"Why don't you call her up?"

"You call her up."

Sister Gin's eyebrows arched high. "Too poor to paint and too proud to whitewash?"

"Listen to this, Gin."

And am I a Davis? Am I kin to that man standing up there on Market and Third? You know what that Davis say to me every time I hear it. Why I want to be *Ms.* Davis? My name's May Frances, and Frances was my dear mother's name. My little sister is Almeta Rose because that was my mother's mother's name. Like I say, it was different for Almeta. She hasn't slept since. Every night she hear someone cutting the kitchen screen and know they're coming after her because she *said.* What that man want with a woman her age? Well, *I* know—he want to make fun of us. He was looking at Clarita all last summer, Almeta know it, everybody know it. He think she owe it to him cause she don't want no job working in a white lady's house. She thinks she's freer working in the laundry and he thinks she's freer too. Robert usually picks her up after work but Almeta said she was going right by there that Friday night. And just as Almeta drove in, she seen *him* there where he had no business being and she knew what he was after. Everybody had gone home and she was—oh, Miss Su, when she didn't

see Clarita waiting outside like she usually was she jumped
out of the car and ran and tried the door. It was locked.
And she shook it. That was when he grabbed her. She
wasn't even studying him she was so set on getting to Clarita. "Where's that gal, Auntie?" he hissed in her ear and
then she knew he hadn't got Clarita. She felt delivered and
she said real quiet but like the Lord was talking through
her, "Now I'm going to ask you to take your hands off me,
please sir." And he said, "I ain't gonna touch you where
you want me to, Auntie, I just want to smell you and see
how you stink." And he threw her down. Hooked his leg
around hers and pushed and she fell flat on her hip. Now
Almeta's strong and she kicked and gouged at his throat
but he was twict her size and he grabbed her dress and
covered her face with it and bent his elbow onto her throat
till she was barely breathing and he said, "Now you just
lay still . . ." and he called her one ". . . and you're gonna
get something you really want and then you're gonna tell
me how much you like it." And then he said that if she
was too stretched out in there from all them—and he said
something—that he didn't like it then he was going to cut
her throat. He said she better get them muscles tight—and
he called her one—and squeeze. Then when he was through
he pulled her dress loose from her face and slapped her in
the mouth and hit her with his fist. Then he spit in her
face. Pulled back his foot and kicked her in between her
legs. She grabbed his foot with her thighs and he like to
fell sprawling. He was so mad he kicked her in the belly
and then he took out his knife and made a pass at her face
and she grabbed his arm and then he heard someone coming. He said, "You tell em and I'll kill you." He ran. It was
Clarita. She'd left work early to go to the dentist and was
coming back to meet her mother. Clarita come running

and hollering. The police had just turned the corner seeing as the white man was running as if he'd just robbed something. Then when they saw Clarita hollering they turned in to see what was it she'd done. She made Almeta tell the police and then she told them her own self. Almeta knew it wouldn't be any use but Clarita, she never would understand there are some things you're better off leaving alone. I guess we all spoiled her. She was such a little thing when her mama passed. Clarita never would believe it wasn't going to be like that when she was grown up. That's just the way her mind runs. The police almost ran Clarita in she was acting so loud.

And when Almeta's Tom, he come down to the station to take her home, the police told him he better stick that thing in his wife more'n every Saturday night cause she was having hallucinations. And the other police said, "Ain't you going to defend your woman's honor, boy? Ain't you going after that man?" And they all laughed and the first police said, "I hear of any white man getting cut up I know just where to come, you remember that, you hear, uncle?" And Almeta had to get her Tom outa there. She had to take care of him like she wasn't the one that needed taking care of. And she had to comfort Clarita who was too scared to go to work and wanted to get a lawyer at the same time.

"Well?"

Sister Gin shook her head. "It's not right. The story is probably right all right but the voice is wrong. Besides, Miss May wouldn't tell you all that. It's too consecutive. You think she doesn't have feelings?"

"I don't have to listen to you."

Sister Gin got up and opened all the cupboard doors.

"You don't have any gin? Listen, pal. You can't fool an old fooler."

"I'm not hiding the gin from you."

"You're hiding the sister. Su, even the village hussy is forgiven her sexy pleasures if she marries and bears the child, that being considered payment enough for any pleasure. Your story is too sticky with tears. There are tears gluing air to air in every line."

"You think I'm using Miss May as a fix?"

"Like those male poets who rush to the scene of a tragedy. Or like those old-fashioned women who search through the streets, hoping to call forth the ghost of someone dead. I *think* they want someone alive. Doesn't that hurt the ghost's feelings?"

"I *want* her to say it. *Her.*"

Sister Gin picked her nose, pulled her pants out from between her buttocks, rolled dirt out from between her toes. "She'll say, all right—if you ask her. But not *it.*"

"Okay, I'll call her." Su sat still. "I've gotten myself in a box. I feel like I'm ready to break out with measles but just can't do it, as Bettina would say."

Sister Gin picked up the telephone. "If it's the only way, we'll knock the sides out." She dialed. "Miss May? It's Sister Gin. Can we come over?"

"You're a brave woman," Su said.

"I want a drink."

"You want to ask me a question?" May sipped her gin and laughed. "You come all the way over here to ask me a question? Must be some question, you couldn't ask it on the telephone. Have a drink of gin, Miss Su? Miss Sister? I know you like gin. This is House of Lords. Robert bought it for your visit. House of Lords? I say. They name it that to make like a man invented it? I know it was a woman. Gathering berries in the sun one day and fell asleep. It was probably in June. Called it June-nip. Ask any old woman what she likes to drink and she'll answer, gin. If she wants to tell you the truth. Sometimes that's the last thing she wants to tell you." May laughed, rocking with her laughing.

"You want to know what I don't like about getting old? Ask me what do I like. Well, the worst thing is my knees. I don't understand it. Why do they give out so long before the rest of me? Last week after the company left my knees were both swoll up the size of footballs. And hurt? Miss Su, taste some of that shrimp there. Clarita brought it to me fresh this morning. It's not too hot? Clarita say, 'Grandmama, why you want to ruin good shrimp with all that red pepper?' 'Well, you want to taste it, don't you? Cayenne open up your nose so you can taste. You don't want to taste it, why you eat it? I see you eating it, you must want to taste it.'

"I ask Clarita why she don't want to be a doctor. She could find out how to cure my knees. Somebody's got to. And old men's knees don't act up on them like that. So it's got to be one of us. But Clarita wants to study politics. I say, 'Politics? Is that where the man says he's going to do this for me and that for me? I say, excuse me, are we acquainted? Oh I beg your pardon, I thought we must be acquainted. You was talking like you knew me. You were saying you was going to do this for me and that for me. I thought we must be acquainted. But you go on talking. It's a free country.' They tell me you can get a one-way ticket North just by talking. And you don't owe a dime for it.

"I try to tell Clarita that. I say, 'Miss Mamie Carter know what she's doing. If she and Miss Luz had done anything more'n tie that man up, if they'd hurt him in any way . . .' I told Clarita they'd of put Tom underneath the jail. As it was Almeta had to take care of him like he was the one. It didn't happen to him but who would have knowed it—the way he carried on. I say, if Miss Mamie Carter and Miss Luz had hurt that man . . . it was a good thing that the old folks were the ones to find him. Every one of them wanted to talk to the reporters. Every one of them had a different idea how he come to be in their bushes. By the time the police came, they were laughing. It was all for the best. It wasn't funny but it was for the best. I tried to tell Clarita. 'But supposing they hadn't done anything?' She say, 'Supposing they had messed up?' 'Just keep on,' I say. 'Just keep on asking questions and you're bound to get some answers that'll make you sorry.'

"Miss Luz, bless her heart. She's a fine white lady. She give me most of the things you see here. I keep them all out where I can look at them. And old Miz Swann, she left me a few little things when she passed. I'm not complaining. Miss Luz, she's not well, poor thing. I understand why sometimes she doesn't think about what she's asking me to do. I can't complain. I raised my children, and my grandchildren after my Florence passed. And Miss Luz's three too. And that was something. If you know Mr. Furious, you know he's not wrapped too tight. I'm not beholden to anyone for my gin. Have another little glass, Miss Sister. Don't be scared by that title. Thank you, I believe I will. I'm obliged to you for getting it. I told Robert one night, I said, 'Robert, sometimes it don't seem right that I'm a member of the family and still working for a salary.' He said, 'That's the gin talking, baby. You watch out saying that.' I say, 'What do you suppose would happen if I say, Miss Luz, you got to do something about thus and so?'

213

Cause it ain't right. I'm a member of the family and all we're sharing is the gin. He say, 'You watch out saying that, baby. That doesn't concern you.' Old man." May laughed. " 'What do you say, old man?' Yes. Old man. 'You tell me now.' It was real chilly that day. I say, 'What in the world you doing?' He was sitting on the front stoop. 'Studying.' I say, 'What you doing there?' 'Studying.' That's what he was doing. Studying." May's laughing brought Su and Sister Gin into the room of female laughter.

"What about Bettina?" Su said.

"A'nt Hannah? She just like her mama. I can't help but laugh. She used tó set in the kitchen with me every afternoon. I'd say, 'A'nt Hannah, you want to go on outside and play.' She'd say, 'I come to help you, May.' 'You want to help me, you get you a needle.' And she'd pick up a needle that was used to get splinters out, burned at the point. And she'd push that needle through her cloth. And she'd push. And push. I say, 'Why you don't get you a needle that has a sharp point on it?' She say, 'This one is just fine.' She don't want to get up. 'Lazy folk work the hardest,' I say. 'What do that mean?' she ask. She always asking questions then, just like Clarita. 'Layro ketch meddling,' I say. 'What do *that* mean?' she ask. 'That really do mean layro ketch meddling sure as your name is A'nt Hannah Blunt Susan Jane.'

"Miss Luz told her grandchildren to call me Miss May. Now everybody does so I know I'm getting old. Might as well say my piece while I've got the chance. It's a mighty funny use of the word family when we don't share nothing but the bottle. I hope we're not fixing to use sister that way. I'll just stick to plain old gin if that's the way it's going to be. Least then I know I'll get some relief for my knees. Layro ketch meddling." May laughed a long, deep, gold-toothed laugh.

Sister Gin put her brown bag on the table and shook her head. "No. Better, but no, Su, still no."

Su burst into tears.

"I know those leaks of menopause masquerading as tears of profoundity." Sister Gin twisted off the red cap, poured Su a drink. "Have some gin, Su. You just can't speak for Miss May, that's all. Let her go on out the door. And she doesn't need you to hold it for her, either."

Afterword

Under Review: How to Read a Hot Flash

SISTER GIN, like Beloved in Toni Morrison's novel of
the same name, is neither real nor not-real, or, rather,
she is both at the same time: the impossible-to-kill
woman-spirit, the genie in a bottle who magically
loosens women's ties to patriarchal patterns of living,
and a vibrant "living presence," as Virginia Woolf
called the ghost of her mother. A translation of the
physiology of the menopausal hot flash into the
language of the intellect, Sister Gin is a metaphor for
female subjectivity, for lesbianism, for coming-into-
writing, for political action, and for coming to terms
with white racism. Childbirth has a long literary history

of appropriation and reappropriation as a metaphor for creativity,[1] but June Arnold's bold experimental novel of 1975 seems to be the first feminist fiction to browbeat the beast, biology, into bearing another rich and enabling figure for women writers, more universally experienced than motherhood: menopause as the rebirth of the female self.

Menopause as rebirth might have been an exclusively female figure until researchers began to name a midlife malaise of men by the same name. In June Arnold's vivid and intense descriptions there is no mistaking the gender of the body undergoing such exciting changes. Each hot flash is different, as every birthing experience or beginning of menstruation is different. Su McCulvey's first hot flash, on a hot June day, "could easily pass," she thinks, as a normal response to the weather. The use of the word "pass" is the reader's clue to the political wit of Arnold's language. Menopause is one of the major "passages" of a woman's life, a crossing-over into age and an un/reproduction. This passage is generally unremarked in the literatures of our culture despite its commonality in women's experience. Something shameful still clings to the public exposure of its physical signs, and jokes testify to cultural fear of "the change." This major biological and emotional change is supposed to take place in the closet; menopausal women, like lesbians, are not supposed to present their disturbingly "aberrant" bodies in public. The natural is made to appear unnatural. The word "pass" calls into question the cultural assumptions of a white male norm, against which aging women, lesbians, and Blacks are to be defined. Passing as young, passing as white, and passing as heterosexual are all connected in *Sister Gin*.

When I first read *Sister Gin* I had never had a hot flash, but now that I am the age of her heroine, I can testify to the accuracy of Arnold's descriptions—the flushed face, the beads of sweat on the scalp, hair wringing wet, neck and back soaking your clothes, blanking out, cramping, sinking into the pain and coming out again—the odd experiencing of the way the body resists going gently beyond reproduction. But Arnold's sense of humor is irrepressible. When Su is sleepy, irritable, and "hysterical" (as she tells Bettina) during a business lunch with the visiting feminist publisher, Barbara Barbarachild, she and the text's boundaries become fluid and funny: "She must have talked straight through lunch, with sips of Bloody Mary for periods. 'I mean, *commas*,' she said quickly, 'What?' "[2] It is this "What?" that unsettles the reader. Who is talking back to whom?

I first read *Sister Gin* at the same time that I read Carolyn Heilbrun's moving and inspiring essay on Virginia Woolf in her fifties.[3] The novel and Heilbrun's essay remain inextricably intertwined in my mind along with a vision of the two witty authors as the angels of menopause—Gabriel/las—assisting at a new form of Annunciation, trumpeting a message about menopause as rebirth and empowerment, saying "Behold, handmaiden no more!" Surely some such ceremony should accompany the "change of life."

Although *Sister Gin* is steeped in salty Southeastern local color, like the Tidewater Basin and beaches of its Wilmington, North Carolina setting, reading the novel again reminds me of Texas. *Sister Gin* is hot and sweet, like jalapeño jelly, an outrageous and delicious Tex-Mex confection. Daughters, Inc., the remarkable feminist press that published Arnold's *The Cook and the Carpenter* in 1973, *Sister Gin* in 1975, and reprinted *Applesauce* (1966) in 1977, had disappeared by the time I read *Sister Gin* in the early eighties.[4] We had to photocopy it for my classes in Experimental Women

Writers at the University of Texas at Austin, and student fans joined other readers of an "underground classic," shoring up June Arnold's status as a writer's writer, and a lesbian writer of technical brilliance. She is also claimed as a Southern writer. And, of course, *Sister Gin* is so steeped in these traditions that we may want to read it as a study of how women break out of the genteel cedar closet, the scented world of white privilege, old money, and the romantic ideology of bliss and protection for the monogamous couple in their perfect house.[5]

Coming out of the cedar closet is celebrated in quite specific historical and geographical detail. *Sister Gin* is about metamorphosis, about change as the essence of femaleness, about the distillation of sweat and blood and gin that "sacralize" women's common experiences. Su McCulvey is "born again" at fifty, saved by the blood of menopause, and Sister Gin, her savior-self, is a delightfully Southern lesbian form of Amazing Grace. The Tidewater Basin, where fresh water and sea water meet and form a breeding ground for shrimp and oysters, is a good place to watch the menopausal flux, the change in the female body against the backdrop of another natural and transformative confluence of changes. The Tidewater is that magical, liminal borderline meeting between two elements, like the woman's body in its period of change, which anthropologists like to study when they analyze a culture. There are no Northern mothballs here, no whiff of camphor in the comic carnivalesque of Arnold's imagination. (Cedar, of course, has its own natural complications—it is so potent when pollinating that the allergies it causes are called "cedar fever.") Arnold's picaresque comedy is a natural daughter of the American Southern tradition. Her fantastic realism is neither South American nor Kafkaesque. It retains the orality of its traditions in gender and race, the jokes and stories of Black and white women in the patriarchal South.

So it seemed natural to me to speak about *Sister Gin* at the Texas Women Writers Conference held in Austin in 1984. Beverly Stoeltje had organized the conference as an antidote to the previous year's conference on Texas Writers, which hadn't included any women. We were resisting the move to canonize Katherine Ann Porter as *the* Texas woman writer to the possible exclusion of the Chicana tradition and all the other Others. I spoke about Lucy Parsons, the part Black and part Mexican anarchist whose husband was hanged in the Chicago Haymarket Trial, and I wished that the plaque on the main building at the University of Texas, which reads "Center for Creative Capitalism," honored the radical Texas tradition as well. June Arnold was a Texan. She was born in South Carolina and died (at age fifty-five) in Houston in 1982. Texas Monthly Press published her hilariously funny novel, *Baby Houston*, posthumously in 1987.[6] It seemed to be the right moment (though Karla Jay points out that Texas has never decriminalized homosexuality) to claim a lesbian feminist as a Texas writer. I was unprepared for the response—people walked out. Arnold had all the right credentials. Her maiden name was Davis and her mother's name was Wortham. She had been reared by people who showed horses; she went to Vassar College and Rice University, and "came out" as a debutante. She married, had four children, then divorced, and came east to set up Daughters, Inc. with her partner, Parke Bowman. I suppose I was violating the Southern tradition of good manners in mentioning the unmentionable, just as Su's mother in *Sister Gin* chides her for naming herself a lesbian, not for being one.[7] A coming-out story in that culture is about how many proposals of marriage a debutante receives.

If we read the plot of *Sister Gin* as an escape from the cedar closet of gentility and good manners, we may also note that it ends trying to set the Black woman's voice free, after having tried to write her story for her, and failed. It is a narrative of self-decolonization in which the heroine learns that it is ethically impossible to be free alone. The agent of Su's self-decolonization is anger. Expressing her anger, even nurturing it, is breaking a very serious taboo in this culture. Women's self-hating jokes, their drinking and their eating, are acceptable forms for the suppression of rage. Su embodies her rage as a child she is carrying in menopausal rebirth:

"I have to make up for so many years of letting things go by. . . . Every time I speak up I hear a pair of tiny hands clapping inside my head. They belong to a woman who doesn't dare say anything, who can't yet. But she claps like the devil. . . . And each time, if I think, no, I won't say anything, she pokes me. In my head. I imagine her as a little femina, two centimeters tall" (199–200).

The narrator goes on: "Her unemployment was about to run out. She had no car. She bicycled everywhere and claimed she would not work again until her anger was twenty-one" (200). Then Su waxes lyrical as the expectant mother of Baby Anger:

"I'm dedicating my life to her, whatever the trends of the times. No more anger-sitters. No more camps or schools. No more lollipops. She's going to get all the advantages my expanse of years can provide, every opportunity to become whatever she wants to become, even if she just wants to get married and have lots of little angers" (200).

Rebelling against the tidal pull of the reproduction of mothering, Su does not imagine in a child the reproduction of herself and her own values. One of the reasons *Sister Gin* is so important is that the plot of self-decolonization enacts the heroine's move from couple to family, to community, to political action, to recognition of her own complicity in the colonization of others. The lesbian text in this case does not wish to reproduce itself, but to act as midwife to the Black woman's text. *Sister Gin* understands that sixties slogan of the

Redstockings, "the personal is political," in a far more serious way than many white bourgeois feminisms of that decade. It was during the seventies that many brilliant lesbian fictions emerged, as the eighties have produced Black women writers coming into their own. Though homophobia was (and still is) a major social problem in the United States, for certain elite educated women, the lesbian was Everywoman, fetishized into representation of feminism, as now the woman of color is invested with the movement's aspirations, or, for other, often "French" forms of feminism, motherhood and mother-daughter relationships focus, fixate, and fetishize forms of femaleness. June Arnold's genius lay in the fact that she saw that one thing leads to another, and she participated in seeing that one movement was led into the arms of the other, even if unwillingly.

Arnold's critique of lesbian life-styles is more powerful than her celebration. Bettina's overeating and alcoholism are just a little more acute than her heterosexual sister's, though both are wives at home. The house Su has designed is the haven of lesbian separatism, mimicking the female body with stairs like "stepped fallopian tubes," but it proves to be less of a protection from outside aggression than a smothering womb. Su has "corrected" everything about herself to fit the slim well-groomed image required of a lady newspaper columnist. But when Bettina sheds her pounds and curtails her drinking as soon as she has to work, she begins to develop the same conservative fearful ideology that had earlier enraged her in Su. Su's competitive hostility toward her young assistant turns into sisterhood when they are both out of a job. The scene in which they ask a newsagent for a glass of water to relieve Su's hot flash, and then make off with all his copies of *Playboy* in their antipornography campaign, is one of the most telling in the novel—using woman's "weakness" to outwit a man, as Blacks have used white expectations of ignorance to trick the boss.

Oppression is always grounded in the social structure, not in people's characters.[8]

The idea of political change is then naturalized by analogy to women's bodies. The white women's bridge club, the Shirley Temples Emeritae, carries out revenge against the town rapists, overcoming their own racism in outrage at the offense to the dignity of age when a sixty-five-year-old Black woman is raped. They humiliate the man who has divorced one of their daughters and won all her property in the settlement, easily connecting rape and the theft of property as "the same thing." When they realize that the Southern tradition of vigilante justice does not extend to women and that their kooky Klan act is not appreciated, they run for public office, learning how fragile their (white female) privilege is. In "Exiting from Patriarchy," Bonnie Zimmerman has argued that *Sister Gin* reverses the female *bildungsroman* by developing the heroine's character "backward"—"from a fifty-year-old closeted middle-class lady to a ten-year-old activist."[9] She also points out Arnold's use of the old hide-and-seek cry "All out come in free" as an expression of political solidarity and active struggle against all the interconnected oppressions explored in the novel. Lesbianism in this novel is lost (utopian?) childhood freedom, and the reader engages in its recovery. Zimmerman titles her book on contemporary lesbian-feminist fiction *The Safe Sea of Women* from a visionary passage in *Sister Gin*. Zimmerman is developing an argument about the relations between the lesbian mythology expressed in fiction from the late sixties onward and its relation to the reality of lesbian lives.[10]

I am a little more suspicious about the "truth value" of any mythology, fiction, or history, and I would wholeheartedly resist all notions of the relation of fiction to "reality" that define or universalize. We might here begin to interrogate the meaning of the word "lesbian," as Denise Riley has called into question the meaning of "woman" and "women" in her brilliant and provocative *"Am I That Name?": Feminism and the Category of "Women" in History.*[11] Riley is especially suspicious of our historical attempts as feminists to get at the lives of "women themselves," when this category itself is unstable, socially constructed, historically different in each specific case, and troubling, often from hour to hour, for "women themselves." Riley points out that "there are no completely naive or completely knowing linguistic subjects."[12] *Sister Gin* and its author do not claim to know what a lesbian is, only how difficult it is to be continually represented by the word in one's own mind and the minds of others. How are we going to call this a lesbian text? Does the meaning of lesbian lie in the author's self-naming? the narrator's? the characters? in their sexuality? in their politics or lifestyles? in the reader? in the language of the text? Is good girl Su McCulvey a woman writer and Sister Gin a lesbian writer? It seems to me that the novel questions these categories and enacts the problematics of knowing where the meanings are because there are never words for the feelings of struggling against dominant ideologies while half-consciously accepting them and speaking their language.

Sister Gin exists only in language—she reviews the reviewer. If she is what lesbian means she also carries the freight of the representation of "lesbian" in our culture for the reader. She is the deconstructor or unraveller of ideologies, including the romantic lesbian myth of perfect love and community among women. Under Sister Gin's influence Su "reviews" the myths of her own life. She is shocked into recognizing that her ten-year relationship with Kip was a retreat from her earlier feminism. Kip was an alcoholic who committed suicide and Su had been her "pet," socialized into being a "wife" at home raising Kip's daughter. Kip laughed at her feminist play, her attempt to write like a female Aristophanes, the comic dialogue that is her natural gift. Kip is the agent of the patriarchy, constantly "correcting" her, and, gradually, Su's illegible and

225

scrawling handwriting (Kip mockingly reads her signature as "Sece," a signature the reader may read as "see, see" or as short for *secede*, a Southern feminist's gesture toward the patriarchal Union) grows "smaller and neater" (54). Kip gets her a job on the Wilmington *Commercial-Appeal*, once Su's own "commercial appeal" has been developed into dressing like a lady and writing mild, ladylike book reviews that keep the force of seventies feminism from being disseminated in her hometown. She becomes the agent of her own oppression. In a mental "hot flash" Su remembers what it was she had suppressed. While she and Kip were making love on a rainy afternoon, Kip's rejected daughter Sherry cried herself to sleep, dreaming that she was being chased by a cow. When Su is startled into recognition of her own change from wild colt to "palliator" by a man who praises her moderation, Su deromanticizes the dead Kip as a bull whale. But, the reader asks, what ever happened to Sherry? Did Su abandon the "daughter" she raised? Sherry, the daughter of the lesbian couple, is the marginalized other of this text, like Jerry, Su's cover boyfriend, whom she parades in public places over dinner whenever panic about her lesbian life seizes her. Sherry (what is her relation to Gin?) and Jerry are part of the family structure in which lesbian couples live. Their feelings and subjectivity are not explored in this narrative, a reminder of the stereotyping of lesbians in other fictions.

The couple, then, is not an island of safety in a hostile world. Bettina's mother, Luz, entertains Su and Bettina as a couple, but her own class coupling with her Black maid, Miss May, its oppression and dependencies based on race, remain beyond her powers of analysis. Su's mother, Shirley, the former hat saleswoman, runs away to see her best friend, Marietta, after Su's insistence on recognition of the word lesbian. She has an orgasm in the dentist's chair under laughing gas when the assistant puts her finger in an empty socket in her gum. Her fantasy includes the words of the joking dentist and her confusion about whether "it was rape." She goes to the library to see if the joke comes from a recent magazine. This confusion about the relation of words to physical feelings, similar to Shirley's confusions about her daughter's confession, is Arnold's brilliant construction of the indeterminacy (as Riley points out) of one's consciousness about gender and sexuality. Shirley and Marietta had felt guilt and unease in their book club's discussion of sexuality in *Gone with the Wind* and Shirley relives under gas her love for Marietta from childhood on, concentrating on her "boldness," and her political support of Blacks, which resulted in a cross being burnt on her lawn. She dreams of being kissed by Marietta and confuses her feeling with the dentist's joke about a spotted dog and the "spot" of clitoral sexuality named by *Ms.* magazine (91). Frightened by the realization that her feeling for Marietta (and the dental assistant) is sexual, Shirley flies back to her husband. Even at age seventy-seven, she cannot come to terms with her desire. Just as she puts her finger on the telephone button when she thinks someone is listening to her conversation with Marietta, for Shirley, the clitoral spot/button is a place in her own body with which she must sever connection in order to remain safe. The narrator says she breaks the ties of friendship and love with "her memory finger" (84).

It is in the figure of Mamie Carter Wilkerson, who can say the word "lesbian," as well as accept her own lesbianism, that the novel and Su imagine a mother-daughter bonding rebirth. Some critics have complained that *Sister Gin* romanticizes age as a time of endlessly drawn out orgasms. Mamie Carter is deaf but otherwise she is "an old forty" at seventy-seven. Her papery skin is fetishized by Su and by the reader in an eroticism that the narrator calls "decadent" but still revels in: her "silk bones" and "dimpled flesh," "skin so old it had lost all abrasives, rid itself of everything that can shield the body against the world; skin vulnerable, nonresilient, soft forever" (128). Driving back from

227

Mamie Carter's to Bettina, Su fantasizes the
menopausal revolution:

"The menopausal armies mass on the brink of every city
and suburb; everything that was is over and there is nothing
left there to keep our sights lowered. See the rifles raised?
This army doesn't travel on its uterus any more . . . I can
still reach out to age itself, lust after a final different dry
silken life and so much grace and elegance from all that
knowledge of days. . . . There is no more beautiful word in
the language than withered" (133).

It is that last sentence, "There is no more beautiful
word in the language than withered," which I find the
most erotic in the novel. Mamie Carter's withered skin,
the surface on which Su finds herself and chooses an
old age different from her mother's, is that "blank
page" on which she will write the play she started to
write at twenty. It is Mamie Carter, "brain-marked" by
having gone to Radcliffe, who invents the abduction of
the rapists by the old ladies, a splendidly cinematic
scene. (Wouldn't *Sister Gin* make a wonderful film?) She
advocates drinking as a way of clearing out useless
brain cells, lecturing Su on the joys of post-menopausal
clear-headedness. She is also a writer, a book reviewer
who chooses to write only two reviews a year. Unlike
Su, she has not sold out. She reviews *The Brain
Changers*, but will not go to the party for the author
Maya Pines, because the only females in her books are
chimpanzees. Su finds Mamie Carter's style "stiff,
crochetty, trimmed and pared as if it were going into a
doll house, and brilliant" (17).

I have named this essay "Under Review" because it
seems to me that *Sister Gin* is about seeing and re-
seeing, re-view and re-vision, the search for the lost
signature of feminist politics, "Sece," Su's seceding
from passing in patriarchy as part of a debilitating
couple and moving on to grapple with all the social

problems of her community, especially race. The text makes clear by juxtaposing Su's reviews of the books of Joyce Carol Oates, Erica Jong, and the sex manuals, with those of Sister Gin, that reviewing books is not a harmless activity. The book reviewer is the producer of ideology. By not saying what she thinks, Su is doing to her readers what Kip did to her. She is "correcting" feminism for the sake of cultural peace, de-fanging it, domesticating and infantilizing her readers as she has domesticated and infantilized Bettina.

Bettina's behavior, especially the heartbreakingly funny scenes about the proper disposal of Nefertiti's dog dish in the dishwasher and her meditation on the difficulties of getting dressed when you are fat, is a result of her colonized role. Even after twenty years with Su, Bettina "collected omens against the day their love would end" (6). Kip also lived in a state of disbelief in a permanent lesbian love, a time when the present was already a memory: "each moment contain[ed] its own memory" (44). This dislocation of linear time and its enactment in the narrative voice of *Sister Gin* might be read as the lesbian signature of this text. As Victoria Smith writes:

The anticipation of the present's future status as a memory, gives the present moment a quality of pastness. That same anticipation posits a relationship between a series of present moments, each of which contains its own pastness. This experience of time then is a way of living historically, or inscribing one's present into history and assuring a future. By experiencing existence as history, as a moment of being which is not identical with itself [the lesbian characters and the author are writing a] double materialization of self.[13]

Smith argues that the textualization of the past in the present is a specific characteristic of lesbian narrative, that

Bettina lives in the present as if each moment constructs a past. This past that the present makes only occurs in the future . . . Bettina experiences her lesbian present as history, definite artifacts ("predated shards," 6) that can be read and interpreted in the future. The way Bettina lives her present is non-linear because it is a lesbian present. She is outside the framework that reinforces heterosexual relationships in patriarchal society . . . The lesbian must create her own system of time in order to free herself from a patriarchal non-existence.[14]

Smith's formulation can be extended to other lesbian texts and fruitfully examined in relation to Gertrude Stein's "continuous present."

The relation between "lesbian time" and what theorists have called "women's time" in narrative is another provocative question, and one that depends on establishing some notion of the meaning of the word lesbian and where it is situated. One mark by which the dominant announce their difference from the other is the claim by men that women are always late, by whites that Blacks or Mexicans don't share the same notions of the "importance" of time. When I was a child in Boston, WASPS claimed that the Irish had no sense of time. Now travel agents advertise the pleasures of irresponsibility and relaxation in "Miami time" or "Hawaiian time," a division of play time and work time. Gay time is another "irrational" claim on the temporal. When you have to live by other people's schedules, the need to rebel is often expressed in choosing another rhythm, speeding-up or slowing-down or reversing day and night. In my work on women's writing in World War I, I have seen that the state controlled women workers with an ideological call for extra work, "for the duration" of the war. Virginia Woolf's character Ginny in *The Waves* dreams continually of an unbroken time without the arbitrary divisions of days and weeks.

One site of the meaning of the word lesbian is in the reader's experience of pleasure in the text, and this does not prescribe that either the writer, narrator, or reader is a lesbian in the sense of sexual practice, or even that either is a woman. These questions are being debated at the moment around two different sets of ideas, Adrienne Rich's analysis of "compulsory heterosexuality" and Monique Wittig's argument that "lesbians are not women," that "woman," "man," and "lesbian" are all linguistic and social constructs. In "Toward a Definition of the Lesbian Literary Imagination," Marilyn Farwell summarizes the issues, provides a useful history of these debates, and argues for the use of the word lesbian as a metaphor for creativity.[15]

Equally suggestive is Biddy Martin's "Lesbian Identity and Autobiographical Difference(s)."[16] Martin is sympathetic to Bertha Harris's 1978 definition of lesbian writing as that which engages desire in excess of categories, but she cautions against the privilege of those who can see themselves as outside the limits of "identity politics." Essentialism and "difference" by race and class inside certain feminisms marginalize the lesbian as a separate category. As Biddy Martin points out, Foucault's questioning of contemporary Western grounding of identity in sexuality reveals "the repressive hypothesis" as a mask for maintenance of power in the family and racist eugenics. She argues that Teresa de Lauretis's *Technologies of Gender* critiques Foucault and discourse theory because it suppresses questions of subjective agency and self-representation and agrees when de Lauretis asks for the kind of specific historical grounding of intersections of relations between sexuality, gender, race, and ethnicity found in Cherríe Moraga's work and that of the other contributors to *This Bridge Called My Back*.[17]

What do these philosophical questions have to do with reading *Sister Gin*? It seems to me that June Arnold's novel engages in these issues aesthetically, and reading it may help to focus arguments in a constructive way. There is a rich description of a particular group of lesbians in a particular time and place. Monique Wittig's claim that language constructs identity may be examined in Arnold's brilliant earlier novel, *The Cook and the Carpenter*, where she uses "na" and "nan" as pronouns, interchangeable for male or female, as well as in *Sister Gin*, where race, class, and gender identities overlap and conflict.

Su's work as a book reviewer is a form of reproduction—reviewing is the reproduction of culture when it either validates the status quo or acts as "gatekeeper," preventing new ideas from seeping through to the public. In her struggle with Sister Gin out of "the loneliness of being right," Su learns to reject openly the biological and cultural imperative to "reproduce mothering," even if only in the shape of her house and her manner of dress and behavior. She takes birth control pills only after the "need" for them is gone. Sister Gin's review of *Combat in the Erogenous Zone* points out that the author claims that there is little sex for women after middle age. Sister Gin then forces Su to review her relationship with Bettina, its pretense at mutual mothering.

She taunts Su in her review of May Sarton's *As We Are Now* with her own feelings of disgust with old women, despite her love for Mamie Carter. Su answers her, "Don't you know the difference between an author reporting her character's feelings and her own? *Lesbianism*. I hope I never *hear* that word again." The narrator tells us, "Su crumpled the page and threw it in her wastebasket, then retrieved it, spread it out and drew a heavy felt-pen black line through lesbianism until it was dead. Then she folded the paper several times and put it in her purse to throw it away safely at home" (102–103). This scene recalls Virginia Woolf's bonfire for the word "feminist" in *Three Guineas*. Su's retort to Sister Gin is a real joke when the text we are reading blurs all those "normal" narrative boundaries and crosses over from realism to fantasy and back again. Su's play (or the novel we are reading), the result of her re-viewing her life and her career, is an *un/reproduction* or dismantling of the culture whose ideology she had worked so hard to secure (menopausal labor?).

The narrative reaches beyond the borders when Su and Sister Gin review the novel we have just read and together try to write what has been left out—the Black woman's story. Each time she tries, Su fails and Sister Gin tells her she has failed. Miss May will write her own story. But the reader has read the two "views," the white woman's versions of the Black woman's story, along with the acknowledgment in the beginning of the book in which June Arnold thanks Roberta Arnold and "Miss May" "for their loving assistance with the final chapter." In the process of writing and failing to write and exposing that failure to her readers (Dare one call this writing practice, which exposes its own processes and limitations, its commitment to change, not permanent "art," menopausal *writing*?), June Arnold/Su McCulvey/Sister Gin has decolonized herself and admitted that she cannot effect the decolonization of the Black woman but must concentrate on straightening out the story of her own racism. She sees that the "story is probably right all right but the voice is wrong." What reviewing has taught her is that she had repressed and silenced her own voice and is in no position to speak for the Other.

Bonnie Zimmerman argues that Arnold has not solved the problem of white racism in the lesbian community in what she calls an evasive ending, using "a literary trick, a postmodernist disruption of the text through which the author poses the problem and comments on her inability to solve it."[18] To me, this self-decolonization, minus the romantic delusion that she could cross the racial borders so easily, makes *Sister Gin* survive. *Sister Gin* says that it is a *white* novel, that it has its limits, is not "universal." That's a pretty radical thing to say. *Sister Gin* announces that racism is a white person's problem. It is an explicitly anti-racist novel and sends the reader on to read Black fiction. It does not end with a plea to the white lesbian reader to reproduce this text, another coming-out story. Miraculously, "the change of life" has become a metaphor for political change. It ends pregnant with the Black woman reader's text, a prophecy of the extraordinary rebirth of American fiction in Black women's writing. And the prophecy came true.

Jane Marcus

Notes

My thanks to Angela Ingram, Blanche Wiesen Cook, Bonnie Zimmerman, and Karla Jay for their helpful comments on a draft of this essay.

1. See Susan Stanford Friedman, "Creativity and the Childbirth Metaphor: Gender Difference in Literary Discourse," in *Feminist Studies* 13, no. 1, 1987, 49–82. I use the word un/reproduction after Angela Ingram's "Un/Reproductions: Estates of Banishment in English Fiction after the Great War," which studies censorship and the interconnections between several outlaw ideologies, in *Women Writers in Exile,* ed. Mary Lynn Broe and Angela Ingram (Chapel Hill: University of North Carolina Press, 1989).

2. June Arnold, *Sister Gin* (Plainfield, Vt.: Daughters, Inc., 1975). All subsequent references will be cited parenthetically in the text. For a possible precursor to *Sister Gin*, see Sylvia Townsend Warner's *Opus 7*, a narrative poem about the hard-drinking Rebecca Random, in her *Selected Poems* (New York: Viking, 1982).

3. Carolyn Heilbrun, "Virginia Woolf in Her Fifties," in *Virginia Woolf: A Feminist Slant,* ed. Jane Marcus (Lincoln: University of Nebraska Press, 1983).

4. Daughters, Inc. published important lesbian fiction in the 1970s—Bertha Harris's *Lover*, Rita Mae Brown's *Rubyfruit Jungle*, Elana Nachman's *Riverfinger Women*, and Monique Wittig's *The Opoponax*, among others.

5. I use the term "cedar closet" to suggest the gentility of the white Southern lesbians in this novel, but it also resonates with gin. In the South the juniper, from whose berries gin is made, is called cedar. For a discussion of Southern lesbianism, in particular autobiography as a "decolonization of self" that leads to antiracism, such as *Sister Gin* enacts, see Mab Segrest, *My Mama's Dead Squirrel: Lesbian Essays on Southern Culture* (Ithaca, N.Y.: Firebrand Books, 1985).

6. I reviewed *Baby Houston* in the *Women's Review of Books*, October 1987.

7. On the stigma of naming, see Catharine R. Stimpson, "Zero Degree Deviancy: The Lesbian Novel in English" (1981), reprinted in her *Where the Meanings Are: Feminism and Cultural Spaces* (New York: Methuen, 1988) 97–110. Stimpson writes: "Lesbian novels in English have responded judgmentally to the perversion that has made homosexuality perverse by developing two repetitive patterns: the dying fall, a narrative of damnation, of the lesbian's suffering as a lonely outcast attracted to a psychological lower caste; and the enabling escape, a narrative of the reversal of such descending trajectories, of the lesbian's rebellion against social stigma and self-contempt." *Sister Gin* is, arguably, one of Stimpson's escape narratives, but it is also a self-decolonization narrative that breaks the pattern by attempting to deal with racism.

8. I suggest that an interesting study of the connection between the lesbian as tragic invert (see Stimpson's "Narrative of Damnation," reprinted in *Where the Meanings Are*) and the tragic mulatta might be begun by looking at Hortense Spillers's "Notes on an Alternative Model," in *The Difference Within: Feminism and Critical Theory*, ed. Elizabeth Meese and Alice Parker (Amsterdam and Philadelphia: John Benjamins, 1989) 165–187; Teresa de Lauretis, "Sexual Indifference and Lesbian Representation," *Theatre Journal* 4, no. 2, May 1988, 155–177.

9. Bonnie Zimmerman, "Exiting from Patriarchy," in *The Voyage In: Fictions of Female Development*, ed. Elizabeth Abel, Marianne Hirsh, and Elizabeth Langland (Hanover, N.H.: University Press of New England, 1983) 244–257.

10. Bonnie Zimmerman, *The Safe Sea of Women: Contemporary Lesbian Feminist Fiction* (Boston: Beacon Press, forthcoming 1989). Bonnie Zimmerman kindly supplied these and the following quotations from her draft manuscript in progress, for which I am very grateful.

11. Denise Riley, *"Am I That Name?": Feminism and the Category of "Women" in History* (Minneapolis: University of Minnesota Press, 1988).

12. Denise Riley, "Some Peculiarities of Social Policy Concerning Women in Wartime and Postwar Britain," in *Behind the Lines: Gender and the Two World Wars,* ed. Margaret Higonnet, Jane Jenson, Sonya Michel, and Margaret Weitz (New Haven: Yale University Press, 1987) 260–271.

13. Victoria Smith, "The Text of Her Self: Be-ing in *Sister Gin,"* unpublished essay written for my seminar in Experimental Women Writers at the University of Texas, 1985.

14. Ibid.

15. Marilyn R. Farwell, "Toward a Definition of the Lesbian Literary Imagination," *Signs* 14, no. 1, Autumn 1988, 100–118. See also Adrienne Rich, "It Is the Lesbian in Us . . . " in *On Lies, Secrets and Silence* (New York: Norton, 1979); Monique Wittig, "The Straight Mind," *Feminist Issues,* Summer 1980, 102–110. For arguments on identification of lesbians in historical research see Blanche Wiesen Cook, "'Women Alone Stir My Imagination': Lesbians and the Cultural Tradition," *Signs* Summer 1979, 718–739, and "Support Networks and Political Activism: Lillian Wald, Crystal Eastman, Emma Goldman," *Chrysalis* 3, Spring 1977, 43–60.

16. Biddy Martin, "Lesbian Identity and Autobiographical Difference(s)," *Life/Lines: Theorizing Women's Autobiography,* ed. Bella Brodski and Celeste Schenck (Ithaca, N.Y.: Cornell University Press, 1988) 77–103.

17. Ibid., 94, and Cherríe Moraga and Gloria Anzaldúa, *This Bridge Called My Back: Writings by Radical Women of Color* (Watertown, Mass.: Persephone Press, 1981); Teresa de Lauretis, *Technologies of Gender: Feminism and Film* (Bloomington: Indiana University Press, 1987).

18. Bonnie Zimmerman, *The Safe Sea of Women.*

The Feminist Press at The City University of New York offers alternatives in education and literature. Founded in 1970, this nonprofit, tax-exempt educational and publishing organization works to eliminate sexual stereotypes in books and schools and to provide literature with a broad vision of human potential. The publishing program includes reprints of important works by women, feminist biographies of women, and nonsexist children's books. Curricular materials, bibliographies, directories, and a quarterly journal provide information and support for students and teachers of women's studies. Through publications and projects, The Feminist Press contributes to the rediscovery of the history of women and the emergence of a more humane society.

New and Forthcoming Books

Always a Sister: The Feminism of Lillian D. Wald, a biography by Doris Groshen Daniels. $24.95 cloth.

Bamboo Shoots after the Rain: Contemporary Stories by Women Writers of Taiwan, 1945–1985, edited by Ann C. Carver and Sung-sheng Yvonne Chang. $29.95 cloth, $12.95 paper.

A Brighter Coming Day: A Frances Ellen Watkins Harper Reader, edited by Frances Smith Foster. $29.95 cloth, $13.95 paper.

The Daughters of Danaus, a novel by Mona Caird. Afterword by Margaret Morganroth Gullette. $29.95 cloth, $11.95 paper.

The End of This Day's Business, a novel by Katharine Burdekin. Afterword by Daphne Patai. $24.95 cloth, $11.95 paper.

Families in Flux, (formerly *Household and Kin*), by Amy Swerdlow, Renate Bridenthal, Joan Kelly, and Phyllis Vine. $9.95 paper.

How I Wrote Jubilee *and Other Essays on Life and Literature*, by Margaret Walker. Edited by Maryemma Graham. $29.95 cloth, $9.95 paper.

Lillian D. Wald: Progressive Activist, a sourcebook edited by Clare Coss. $7.95 paper.

Lone Voyagers: Academic Women in Coeducational Institutions, 1870–1937, edited by Geraldine J. Clifford. $29.95 cloth, $12.95 paper.

Not So Quiet: Stepdaughters of War, a novel by Helen Zenna Smith. Afterword by Jane Marcus. $26.95 cloth, $9.95 paper.

Seeds: Supporting Women's Work in the Third World, edited by Ann Leonard. Introduction by Adrienne Germain. Afterwords by Marguerite Berger, Vina Mazumdar, Kathleen Staudt, and Aminata Traore. $29.95 cloth, $12.95 paper.

Sister Gin, a novel by June Arnold. Afterword by Jane Marcus. $8.95 paper.

These Modern Women: Autobiographical Essays from the Twenties, edited and with a revised introduction by Elaine Showalter. $8.95 paper.

Truth Tales: Contemporary Stories by Women Writers of India, selected by Kali for Women. Introduction by Meena Alexander. $22.95 cloth, $8.95 paper.

We That Were Young, a novel by Irene Rathbone. Introduction by Lynn Knight. Afterword by Jane Marcus. $29.95 cloth, $10.95 paper.

Women Composers: The Lost Tradition Found, by Diane Peacock Jezic. $29.95 cloth, $12.95 paper.

Between Mothers and Daughters: Stories across a Generation, edited by
Susan Koppelman. $9.95 paper

Brown Girl, Brownstones, a novel by Paule Marshall. Afterword by Mary
Helen Washington. $8.95 paper.

Call Home the Heart, a novel of the thirties, by Fielding Burke. Introduction
by Alice Kessler-Harris and Paul Lauter and afterwords by Sylvia J. Cook
and Anna W. Johnson. $9.95 paper.

The Changelings, a novel by Jo Sinclair. Afterwords by Nellie McKay, and
Johnnetta B. Cole and Elizabeth H. Oakes; biographical note by Elisabeth
Sandberg. $8.95 paper.

The Convert, a novel by Elizabeth Robins. Introduction by Jane Marcus.
$8.95 paper.

Daddy Was a Number Runner, a novel by Louise Meriwether. Foreword by
James Baldwin and afterword by Nellie McKay. $8.95 paper.

Daughter of Earth, a novel by Agnes Smedley. Foreword by Alice Walker.
Afterword by Nancy Hoffman. $8.95 paper.

Daughter of the Hills: A Woman's Part in the Coal Miners' Struggle, a novel
of the thirties, by Myra Page. Introduction by Alice Kesssler-Harris and
Paul Lauter and afterword by Deborah S. Rosenfelt. $8.95 paper.

Doctor Zay, a novel by Elizabeth Stuart Phelps. Afterword by Michael Sar-
tisky. $8.95 paper.

An Estate of Memory, a novel by Ilona Karmel. Afterword by Ruth K.
Angress. $11.95 paper.

Guardian Angel and Other Stories, by Margery Latimer. Afterwords by
Nancy Loughridge, Meridel Le Sueur, and Louis Kampf. $8.95 paper.

*I Love Myself When I Am Laughing . . . And Then Again When I Am Look-
ing Mean and Impressive: A Zora Neale Hurston Reader,* edited by Alice
Walker. Introduction by Mary Helen Washington. $9.95 paper.

Leaving Home, a novel by Elizabeth Janeway. New foreword by the
author. Afterword by Rachel M. Brownstein. $8.95 paper.

Life in the Iron Mills and Other Stories, by Rebecca Harding Davis.
Biographical interpretation by Tillie Olsen. $7.95 paper.

The Living Is Easy, a novel by Dorothy West. Afterword by Adelaide M.
Cromwell. $9.95 paper.

My Mother Gets Married, a novel by Moa Martinson. Translated and intro-
duced by Margaret S. Lacy. $8.95 paper.

The Other Woman: Stories of Two Women and a Man, edited by Susan
Koppelman. $9.95 paper.

The Parish and the Hill, a novel by Mary Doyle Curran. Afterword by Ann
Halley. $8.95 paper.

Reena and Other Stories, selected short stories by Paule Marshall. $8.95
paper.

Ripening: Selected Work, 1927-1980, by Meridel Le Sueur. Edited and with
an introduction by Elaine Hedges. $9.95 paper.

Rope of Gold, a novel of the thirties, by Josephine Herbst. Introduction by
Alice Kessler-Harris and Paul Lauter and afterword by Elinor Langer.
$9.95 paper.

The Silent Partner, a novel by Elizabeth Stuart Phelps. Afterword by Mari Jo Buhle and Florence Howe. $8.95 paper.

Swastika Night, a novel by Katharine Burdekin. Introduction by Daphne Patai. $8.95 paper.

This Child's Gonna Live, a novel by Sarah E. Wright. Appreciation by John Oliver Killens. $9.95 paper.

The Unpossessed, a novel of the thirties, by Tess Slesinger. Introduction by Alice Kessler-Harris and Paul Lauter and afterword by Janet Sharistanian. $9.95 paper.

Weeds, a novel by Edith Summers Kelley. Afterword by Charlotte Goodman. $8.95 paper.

The Wide, Wide World, a novel by Susan Warner. Afterword by Jane Tompkins. $29.95 cloth, $11.95 paper.

A Woman of Genius, a novel by Mary Austin. Afterword by Nancy Porter. $9.95 paper.

Women and Appletrees, a novel by Moa Martinson. Translated from the Swedish and with an afterword by Margaret S. Lacy. $8.95 paper.

Women Working: An Anthology of Stories and Poems, edited and with an introduction by Nancy Hoffman and Florence Howe. $9.95 paper.

The Yellow Wallpaper, by Charlotte Perkins Gilman. Afterword by Elaine Hedges. $4.50 paper.

Other Titles

Antoinette Brown Blackwell: A Biography, by Elizabeth Cazden. $24.95 cloth, $12.95 paper.

All the Women Are White, All the Blacks Are Men, but Some of Us Are Brave: Black Women's Studies, edited by Gloria T. Hull, Patricia Bell Scott, and Barbara Smith. $12.95 paper.

Black Foremothers: Three Lives, 2nd edition, by Dorothy Sterling. $9.95 paper.

Carrie Chapman Catt: A Public Life, by Jacqueline Van Voris. $24.95 cloth.

Cassandra, by Florence Nightingale. Introduction by Myra Stark. Epilogue by Cynthia McDonald. $4.50 paper.

Competition: A Feminist Taboo? edited by Valerie Miner and Helen E. Longino. Foreword by Nell Irvin Painter. $29.95 cloth, $12.95 paper.

Complaints and Disorders: The Sexual Politics of Illness, by Barbara Ehrenreich and Deirdre English. $3.95 paper.

The Cross-Cultural Study of Women, edited by Margot I. Duley and Mary I. Edwards. $29.95 cloth, $12.95 paper.

A Day at a Time: The Diary Literature of American Women from 1764 to the Present, edited and with an introduction by Margo Culley. $29.95 cloth, $12.95 paper.

The Defiant Muse: French Feminist Poems from the Middle Ages to the Present, a bilingual anthology edited and with an introduction by Domna C. Stanton. $29.95 cloth, $11.95 paper.

The Defiant Muse: German Feminist Poems from the Middle Ages to the Present, a bilingual anthology edited and with an introduction by Susan L. Cocalis. $29.95 cloth, $11.95 paper.

The Defiant Muse: Hispanic Feminist Poems from the Middle Ages to the Present, edited and with an introduction by Angel Flores and Kate Flores. $29.95 cloth, $11.95 paper.

The Defiant Muse: Italian Feminist Poems from the Middle Ages to the Present, a bilingual anthology edited by Beverly Allen, Muriel Kittel, and Keala Jane Jewell, and with an introduction by Beverly Allen. $29.95 cloth, $11.95 paper.

Feminist Resources for Schools and Colleges: A Guide to Curricular Materials, 3rd edition, compiled and edited by Anne Chapman. $12.95 paper.

Get Smart: A Woman's Guide to Equality on Campus, by Montana Katz and Veronica Vieland. $29.95 cloth, $9.95 paper.

Harem Years: The Memoirs of an Egyptian Feminist, 1879–1924, by Huda Shaarawi. Translated and edited by Margot Badran. $29.95 cloth, $9.95 paper.

How to Get Money for Research, by Mary Rubin and the Business and Professional Women's Foundation. Foreword by Mariam Chamberlain. $6.95 paper.

In Her Own Image: Women Working in the Arts, edited and with an introduction by Elaine Hedges and Ingrid Wendt. $9.95 paper.

Integrating Women's Studies into the Curriculum: A Guide and Bibliography, by Betty Schmitz. $9.95 paper.

Kathe Kollwitz: Woman and Artist, by Martha Kearns, $9.95 paper.

Las Mujeres: Conversations from a Hispanic Community, by Nan Elsasser, Kyle MacKenzie, and Yvonne Tixier y Vigil. $9.95 paper.

Lesbian Studies: Present and Future, edited by Margaret Cruikshank. $9.95 paper.

Library and Information Sources on Women: A Guide to the Collections in the Greater New York Area, compiled by the Women's Resource Group of the Greater New York Metropolitan Area Chapter of the Association of College and Research Libraries and the Center for the Study of Women and Society of the Graduate School and University Center of The City University of New York. $12.95 paper.

The Maimie Papers, edited by Ruth Rosen and Sue Davidson. Introduction by Ruth Rosen. $10.95 paper. *Special price for limited time: $6.00.*

Mother to Daughter, Daughter to Mother: A Daybook and Reader, selected and shaped by Tillie Olsen. $9.95 paper.

Moving the Mountain: Women Working for Social Change, by Ellen Cantarow with Susan Gushee O'Malley and Sharon Hartman Strom. $9.95 paper.

Portraits of Chinese Women in Revolution, by Agnes Smedley. Edited and with an introduction by Jan MacKinnon and Steve MacKinnon and an afterword by Florence Howe. $10.95 paper.

Reconstructing American Literature: Courses, Syllabi, Issues, edited by Paul Lauter. $10.95 paper.

Rights and Wrongs: Women's Struggle for Legal Equality, 2nd edition, by Susan Cary Nichols, Alice M. Price, and Rachel Rubin. $7.95 paper.

Salt of the Earth, screenplay by Michael Wilson with historical commentary by Deborah Silverton Rosenfelt. $10.95 paper.

Sultana's Dream and Selections from the Secluded Ones, by Rokeya Sakhawat Hossain. Edited and translated by Roushan Jahan. Afterword by Hanna Papanek. $16.95 cloth, $6.95 paper.

Turning the World Upside Down: The Anti-Slavery Convention of American Women Held in New York City, May 9–12, 1837. Introduction by Dorothy Sterling. $2.95 paper.

Witches, Midwives, and Nurses: A History of Women Healers, by Barbara Ehrenreich and Deirdre English. $3.95 paper.

With These Hands: Women Working on the Land, edited and with an introduction by Joan M. Jensen. $9.95 paper.

With Wings: An Anthology of Literature by and about Women with Disabilities, edited by Marsha Saxton and Florence Howe. $29.95 cloth, $12.95 paper.

The Woman and the Myth: Margaret Fuller's Life and Writings, by Belle Gale Chevigny. $8.95 paper.

Woman's "True" Profession: Voices from the History of Teaching, edited and with an introduction by Nancy Hoffman. $9.95 paper.

Women Activists: Challenging the Abuse of Power, by Anne Witte Garland. Introduction by Frances T. Farenthold. Foreword by Ralph Nader. $29.95 cloth, $9.95 paper.

Women Have Always Worked: A Historical Overview, by Alice Kessler-Harris. $9.95 paper.

Writing Red: An Anthology of American Women Writers, 1930–1940, edited by Charlotte Nekola and Paula Rabinowitz. Foreword by Toni Morrison. $29.95 cloth, $12.95 paper.

For a free catalog, write to The Feminist Press at The City University of New York, 311 East 94 Street, New York, NY 10128. Send individual book orders to The Talman Company, Inc., 150 Fifth Avenue, New York, NY, 10011. Please include $1.75 for postage and handling for one book, $.75 for each additional.